Yasser Abdel Hafez is a journalist an
the literary magazine *Akhbar al-Adab*. Hi
Life was longlisted for the International
lives in Cairo, Egypt.

Robin Moger is the translator of *Otared* by Mohammad Rabie and *Women of Karantina* by Nael Eltoukhy, among other books. His translation for *Writing Revolution* won the 2013 English PEN Award for outstanding writing in translation. He lives in Cape Town, South Africa.

The Book of Safety

Yasser Abdel Hafez

Translated by
Robin Moger

hoopoe

AN IMPRINT OF AUC PRESS

First published in 2017 by
Hoopoe
113 Sharia Kasr el Aini, Cairo, Egypt
420 Fifth Avenue, New York, 10018
www.hoopoefiction.com

Hoopoe is an imprint of the American University in Cairo Press
www.aucpress.com

Exclusive distribution outside Egypt and North America by I.B.Tauris & Co Ltd.,
6 Salem Road, London, W4 2BU

Dar el Kutub No. 14205/16
ISBN 978 977 416 821 5

Dar el Kutub Cataloging-in-Publication Data

Abdel Hafez, Yasser
        The Book of Safety / Yasser Abdel Hafez.—Cairo: The American
    University in Cairo Press, 2017.
            p.   cm.
            ISBN 978 977 416 821 5
            Arabic Fiction — Translation into English
            892.73

1 2 3 4 5   21 20 19 18 17

Designed by Adam el-Sehemy
Printed in the United States of America

To every battle its weapons, and should you shrink from using any of them on ethical grounds then that shall be to your credit, but expect no tributes when you are defeated simply because you were honorable.

Mustafa Ismail
The Book of Safety (original version)

The Book of Safety

By Khaled Mamoun

Would you like to know your end, then arrange your life accordingly?

"SELECT WHAT YOU CONSIDER TO be the correct answer, making sure to dictate your response to the clerk. Please do not write anything yourself. There's no need. The pen and paper in front of you are for jotting down anything not immediately relevant to the subject at hand but which you consider crucial and would like to return to later.

"Here, you may enjoy your confession. You might care to take a stroll around the room to let your thoughts flow calmly out—that's right, like those clichéd scenes that doubtless find an echo in your memory: one man muses, another writes. Between friends, let me assure you that this one is a quite excellent machine, his handwriting neat and more than capable of keeping up with you, no matter how pushed for pace. He doesn't stall. Try him out, you won't regret it. Don't be shy. It's no fault of yours that this is his job. My dear fellow, doing what we were made for comes easy to us all. I mean, do you despise the miner for coming out of the ground all caked in black?"

No answer.

"Ah well, fair enough. You've never seen a miner. Nor have I. My apologies, the image is a little too 'of-the-West.' Are there no mines in the East? Just imagine, it had never occurred to me before now! But surely you get the point. Come, let's not waste time with any more metaphors; what I'm saying is that my assistant here is at your service and will remain so until mankind invents a reliable automated transcriber. They're almost there, I believe, but—and let me be frank with you, even at the risk of you thinking me a traditionalist—what a hateful innovation that would be! Wouldn't you agree with me that the further science progresses the further we move from a human communion? Do you not sense, even in your current situation (and I sincerely hope you feel in no way constrained), the human warmth that binds we three together in this room? Now, imagine if that third fellow were nothing more than a machine—a machine that never erred, that carried out its instructions with matchless fidelity. We would feel reassured, certainly, because neither my questions nor your answers would be meddled with. No worries there. But how did fellow feeling become civilization other than through a muddle of error and coincidence?"

1

Usually, nobody noticed me. I banked on it, and it was what I wanted: for the victim's gaze to stay fixed on the man sat handsomely at the massive desk. Which was how all the accused brought in to us behaved, however alert they were—only seeing me when my superior, Nabil al-Adl, would point me out, at which juncture I would be forced to emerge from the shadows.

"Stay as you are, handmaiden to the truth."

My preferred designation. He thought and I wrote. They wished me to be his hand and his pen. I was not to sit level with him, and when he walked I would be a step behind: a countrywoman trailing a husband as yet untouched by urban mores. And those who came here understood in advance, which was why they gave me not a single glance, their eyes fixed on the man who decided their fate and not the one who transcribed it. Transcription is merely the documentation of the final verdict, a cosmetic enactment. Yet Mustafa Ismail, former law professor and the man dubbed the most skilled thief of the 1990s, was aware of my presence from the very first. He gave a fleeting turn behind him to where I sat. Later, after I'd become captivated by his ideas, I would remain haunted by that turn, searching for its explanation.

Truthfully, though, neither I nor my profession were quite so inconsequential. What can I call it? False modesty? A deep-seated desire to draw back from the limelight? Some blend of the two blinded me to the potential of a unique position which I never made use of as I should. Another sufficiently rebellious character might have published secrets the likes of which you've never dreamed. Mustafa, looking to immortalize his tale, realized this, and in me he found his messenger.

Maybe it was for this reason that I had responded to the strange advertisement stuck up on the wall of the café and had set out to claim the role that seemed written with me in mind. During my time in the job, a limitless sensation of power mounted inside me. I would overhear regular citizens discussing the big issues of the moment, each taking a stand and staunchly defending it as they advanced their conclusions and proofs; yet the truth is always different from the way things seem, and I was one of the few allowed to know it—though I couldn't let them in on what I knew, bound to silence without being ordered, in keeping with the customs of all those who came to the Palace of Confessions. Yet it suited me; secrecy did not vex me. The power was quite enough: the growing self-confidence that compelled those around me to approach with caution, as though I were a modest godling come down to walk among them.

My initial assumptions about Mustafa's intentions were blown away by his confessions. He didn't want me to immortalize his story, as I'd imagined. He didn't care. This much seemed clear from what he said:

They lie who say that a man's life story is all he leaves behind. They set us in motion with profound utterances that fix themselves in our thoughts, and we move accordingly, like machines with no minds of their own. You are the totality of the actions you undertake now, in the moment, and when you pass on that space you filled is taken by the breeze. Actions are fated to be forgotten, and the history books never pay attention to what you had intended they should. They see what they want to see: a beautiful woman who gazes your way, but her heart and mind don't see you. Don't act the fool by troubling yourself with immortality.

✱

He was doing as he pleased, as though he were still free as a bird, one more soldier enlisted, just as he'd picked out his chosen men before: a nod of the head to make them instruments of his will, awaiting orders and a time to carry them out. I was one of the chosen. He saved me from research in the bookstacks, from concocting patchwork theories snipped from dozens of different books—criminal motive, the behavior of the masses in the absence of a unifying objective, the resentment of the poor as a driver for human history. He saved me from playing an unsatisfactory role.

"Not useful."

Thus Nabil al-Adl, my terror of whom—or of what he represented—I had spent the first part of my training battling to master. The softest manifestation of the state's power, the sort whose thoughts and plans lie beyond your power to guess at.

"Well, maybe useful, but you have to hitch it to reality. We're not a research center—in part perhaps, but we have other facets you will have to experience for yourself."

Mustafa helped me discover these facets. He vouchsafed me passage to the other shore, from enemy to ally, and all I had to do was wait to be told the details of my mission.

We knew about him before he arrived, from old files in the archive, but ordinarily we wouldn't place much faith in them. We knew how they were written. As al-Adl sighed:

"Torture, fabrication, and filth."

But nor was he much impressed with what I gave him, selecting from my report only the most obvious passages, those whose meaning was plain. I had written:

What Mustafa Ismail and his associates achieved evokes both a legend and a scientific fact. The legend is that of the Merry Men who banded around Robin Hood, and associated with this legend is a scientific fact, to wit: psychologically and physically, men require an activity that might theoretically be beyond their capabilities. This 'merry' part of man, this

7

ribaldry, must be sated, which explains why, for instance, the male prefers war over dialogue. Castrated by civilization, this aspect of his nature may find its outlet in addiction—to sex, to sport, to drink—but others can only fill the void by engaging in a rebellion that liberates them from authority.

My superior described what I presented to him as 'a sentimental report.'

And although in a professional context the phrase was meant harshly, it pleased me. Perfect as a cryptic title for a book. Perhaps I'd use it, would agree to the terms offered by Anwar al-Waraqi, owner of a printing press who was seeking to rise a rung on the ladder of his trade and take on the title of publisher. He thought the stories I told him about what went on in the Palace of Confessions would make a good book, showing how things really got done in this country.

"And anyway, brother," he'd said, "it's a chance for us to get out of here! See the world a bit before we die."

I would make al-Adl a character, would overstep the bounds and write his name. Who would ever believe that Nabil al-Adl was flesh and blood, and genuinely occupied a position of such sensitivity? Who would ever know but members of the club, the cream of the crop? Who would ever credit that these things were real? Regardless of risk, there was no way such an artistically satisfying character could be allowed to slip through my hands. He had all the qualities to ensure the book's success: his blind devotion to traditional values, his passion for (enslavement to) the ringing lines whose phrases, no sooner uttered, burrowed themselves inside my mind as though I was being mesmerized. Could he ever have allowed himself to sacrifice his fine-sounding 'torture, fabrication, and filth,' and cast around for something more in keeping with my sentimental report?

I may say that I knew him; I worked with him for five years. It was he who chose me. An official in his position has the right to choose his assistant.

8

∗

The wording of the advertisement, torn from a newspaper, had forced me to stop and read it through:

> In your own hand, write the story of your life as you see it in 300 words. You may use any literary style or approach to convey your message. Send the document in a sealed envelope to the address provided, writing below the address: c/o THE OFFICIAL RESPON-SIBLE FOR THE 'TO WHOEVER WISHES TO KNOW ME' COMPETITION. We will be in touch.

And with that, I sent off the necessary, without the faintest idea who was behind the advertisement or what they might want with the applicants. Subsequently, I would learn to my astonishment that thirty letters had been chosen from thousands upon thousands of submissions. Let's think clearly here: do you, as I did, send your life story to an unknown address for an unknown purpose unless you are ready and waiting to entertain a mystery? The days go by, but your enthusiasm remains undimmed. You keep your senses sharp lest the call go unheeded. And when it comes, it's to reveal this farce: I'd always thought myself different from other people, and had made sure to keep clear of them, but I was now to find that thousands of them had had the same idea, and had been waiting to be summoned as I was!

The thirty were soon whittled down to five. Someone came along to look over the queue standing outside the door. Three years later, this person would be me. I came straight from home and joined a crowd of about forty souls all hoping to get their hands on the prize, pretending to be one of them. For exactly two hours, instinct guiding my judgment, I struck up conversation. I provoked, played on nerves: one of many tests to determine the five who would be chosen.

The final test, briefly stated, was that each of us rewrite his life story from the beginning, not necessarily with the selfsame words and sentiments we'd sent off in our letters, but any way that took our fancy—just for purposes of comparison and to make sure that our first efforts hadn't been plagiarized or written for us by others. One of us withdrew for a reason we never had explained to us, though it was clear enough: he had no story to call his own.

I wrote:

The first time I mourned anyone was at the death of Fahmi, son of al-Sayyid Ahmed Abdel-Jawwad, and the first time I felt fear was when I read about Gregor Samsa's metamorphosis. Awaking to find that you're an insect, and must now deal with the world on that basis, and because you know the world has no logic, and that stories are truer than reality. Then all things are possible, even things as nightmarish as this. Then The New York Trilogy showed me that meanings are tangled together and confused to an extraordinary degree, and that most likely nothing has any value. That is how I might describe my life: from one book to another, from one story to the next. I could list dozens—no, hundreds—of works, but this is not what you're after. You want to know what happened to me in real life. Only, unfortunately, I have done nothing worth mentioning to date. Of course, I engage in the quotidian activities that keep me alive; it's just that now, approaching thirty, I cannot think of anything worth telling. The dilemma may have its root in my attitude. There are those who can turn the simplest incident into a dramatic happening worthy of the world stage, but it is my belief that certain conditions need to be met before adventure can claim the name, that there are conditions that make a life fit to be written down. The power to breathe, and speak, and mate is not enough to make your tale worth telling.

This, in short, is my story, which you asked for; and, as you can see, it is finished inside your limit of three hundred words. And because I believe this limit has to matter to you—it was the only condition you mentioned, after all—I shall add the following: my way of thinking is liable to lead to nervous collapse, but what spares me is that Florentino Ariza is my favorite protagonist. Like me, he spends his time engaged in trivial things, waiting for his one ambition to be realized: to be reunited with his sweetheart. A lucky man, who gets what he wants.

After we had passed through a battery of tests, they gathered us together in a large room. We'd no idea what to expect and hadn't dared ask. Not a sound. None of the usual chatter between office workers. No doors opening and closing. The person who'd escorted us to the room hadn't uttered a single syllable. We had climbed from the ground floor to the third, then down a long corridor, and our guide had pointed to the far end of it and walked off. A room, empty but for five chairs.

I hadn't been able to get a precise fix on al-Adl's age; his features were so bland that it was difficult to form impressions. He inspected us, our files between his hands, then spoke two words, no more—"Khaled Mamoun"—before turning to exit the room, leaving the door open. I went out after him and shut the door behind me, making sure it did not slam. I fancied that there was a smile on his face. His guess had been on the money, his instinct true: he had picked out an obedient helper who required but few words to do what was asked of him.

The next day, I received a plastic card, blank but for my name. No logo, no phone number, no job description, just, in its center, engraved in black: Khaled Mamoun. The first of the avatars of a mystery which I must accept without question. No one ever brought it up. They acted as though everything were completely normal. I couldn't tell: was this deliberate disregard or was it stupidity? Was it, indeed, the long habituation that leaves the strange familiar? Would a time come when I would cease to be brought up short by the thought of my existence within an institution unlisted as part of the state establishment, headquartered on a patch of wasteland, and ringed by a wall shielding the mounds of sand we were forbidden to approach?

But perhaps I was overdoing the astonishment. What did I know of the world, anyway? Other eras have played host to dinosaurs the size of buildings, and seas that part to swallow kings. What's one more wonder? Why did I obsess over peripheral details and miss what my coworker Abdel-Qawi called 'the crucial point':

"Why can't you just accept that we're as high as it gets—the agency that only takes on the most critical and sensitive cases?"

Logically speaking, I agreed with him, but one thing stood between me and acceptance:

"But whose agency?"

An exasperated sigh, then he would pull himself together, invoking the patience of a father confronted with an offspring's mulishness, a father who believes such patience is the way to ensure that his son learns all there is to know:

"Just so you'll stop pestering me, then. We are an agency tasked with looking into and keeping tabs on *everything*—on whose behalf I couldn't say for sure, but what's certain is that we are on the side of good against evil. Not that I'm bothered myself, but I'm telling you to help you get past this silly muddle you're in. Why do you ask questions that can't help you? This place has been around forever, as far as I know. It's a miracle we were chosen. And quite honestly I reckon you're asking the wrong thing. Instead of 'What's our job?,' ask yourself 'How am I doing?'"

A pointed observation, and one I had heard on numerous occasions. He would repeat it robotically.

It was either that, in the instant he was made, air had out-weighed the other elements in his body, or that he was able to manipulate this balance for his own purposes. He moved just like it, light and quick. His presence took me unawares: I would hear neither door opening nor the sound of footsteps. He had a physical slightness at odds with his morbid craving for food. After he had departed my life, a caricature of the man lived on in my mind: using a chicken bone to write or comb his hair, out-fits accessorized with vegetables—a collection of contradictions called Abdel-Qawi. For all the settled calm with which he was endowed and which imbued his features, he was the most trying person I have ever met, flitting without warning from mood to mood. He would decide to speak and it would be impossible to interrupt him: loud tones to make his point, frequently lapsing into silence midway through his inexhaustible stock of stories for the air to fall still once more. Before we bonded, this behav-ior had incapacitated me. This reaction of mine astonished him, and he regarded it as evidence of an unhealthy absent-mindedness—or worse, a disregard for others. And, as always with him, what he believed was not up for discussion.

I couldn't make up my mind which position best suited him. Uncategorizable in a place whose function was to cat-egorize and judge. Which is why I left and he stayed on. His experience enabled him to sidestep the difficult ques-tion. Commenting on his behavior, I once told him, "We are obliged to be serious."

And he replied, with a simplicity that defeated my asser-tion, "Says who?"

Is this why everybody loved him?

We got caught up in a friendship, ignoring, like teenagers, our lack of anything in common. With the self-centeredness of someone on a voyage of discovery, I didn't care; I needed a guide through the initial stages, and for the duration of that period there was nothing I hid from him, with the exception of the fact that I was writing down everything that happened.

I was, as they say, swept away: bewitched by his regional dialect and the childlike laughter that vied with his constant chatter, and obsessed with the riddles he left dangling over my head.

"They called me today from Alexandria. Try and guess what's happened."

I had no way of knowing who 'they' might be, but I had learned not to ask, because he would manage to sidestep my inquiries by deploying one or other of his extraordinary stratagems. Family, I guessed, his relationship to them reduced to financial assistance. But as I grew closer to my other colleagues, the mystery surrounding Abdel-Qawi—his roots and family—only deepened. The way he spoke about Alexandria gave the impression he'd lived there as baby and boy, but the occasional southern phrase left the connection he sought to imply open to question. Everyone had a different story for him, which they'd swear to as if they'd know him since childhood—one of the entertainments of our Palace, built as it was on secrets and paradox. Stories from the world of hackneyed melodrama: on the run from a blood debt unavenged; no, his family had been killed in mysterious circumstances; no, they hadn't been killed and there was no blood debt, either. It was simpler than that: he dumped them in order to live as he pleased. A family of exaggerated indigence, vast in number. A father whose favored pursuit was screwing his wife, siring seven more besides our man. Should Abdel-Qawi shoulder another man's burden? Even nobility has its limits—and to describe him as cowardly just because he took a pragmatic view would hardly be fair. The long and short of it: he saves himself or they take him with them. And what good would that do?

People loved him, and they cared about him, and whenever he disappeared—on a mission or for personal reasons—our institution lost its soul. Even so, I found someone leaning in with a word of warning:

"Watch out for that one."

One sentence sufficient for fear of him to meld with my friendship; for everything he did to take on an aura of awe and respect. Yet I was not wary. I represented no threat to anyone, him least of all. I played the part of someone passing through, and placed myself outside the fight. What I genuinely feared was the terrifying emptiness that surrounded him and into which he dragged anyone who associated with him: no history, no present, and no future—just the moment in which he was. And when he withdrew, it was like he'd never been.

After the curtain had come down, and while the players were bowing to the audience, it seemed to me suddenly as though the five years in which I'd known him had been a mirage. I would walk for hours and suddenly come to, almost out of my mind, without a single fixed memory—each frame erased before it could be linked up to the next. And not just memories of him, but of everything he touched, everyone who'd shaken hands with him, everyone to whom I'd told his story. Had it happened, or was it just a flight of fancy drawn out longer than was proper?

Does prison guarantee that your sins will be paid off? When we step out-side the law, does this mean we have a debt toward society that we must pay? And why does the regime, too, not pay its debt toward society? Why is it not held to account as we are?

These are questions it is imperative to answer before undertaking any act of rebellion. Your conviction that you are in the right will grant you an incredible freedom of thought, such as you never dreamed you possessed, and will assist you in planning every detail—starting with selecting your victim, and by no means ending with how to emerge intact from various desperate situations and dead ends.

Mustafa Ismail
The Book of Safety

2

Do what you have to.

An almost meaningless line, one that belongs on paper, in the pages of some novel or movie: a thriller's hero addressing his sidekick in Delphic terms, an indirect order to kill, to burn all the files.

Nothing to be proud of that this fantastic sentence is my father's legacy to me. No money, no memories, nothing but five words bequeathed to my mother, a woman no less peculiar than him. She considered them a message to me, one that I had to memorize, and from childhood on she drilled them into me, enunciating in a classical Arabic appropriate to a man who had dedicated his life to the love of poetry and the Arabic language, yet ill-befitting a witless woman who apprehended life through instinct alone.

And yet, after a journey that has lasted long enough, I find that I am proud of what I inherited and, like my father before me, I shall, unless I find someone stronger, pass it on to my daughter Hasna. I shall not leave her to live her life with no wise words to light her way in times of need.

At the time, I paid no particular attention to this part of Mustafa's confession. As far as I was concerned, it had no bearing at all on the overall story. That people have children is only natural. That they have Hasna, whom I would come to know, is not. Had Mustafa spoken more about her, perhaps I would have had the information I needed to be able to deal with her; and perhaps if I'd sought her out back then, much would have changed in the approach I took to my book about her father. But I let the chance slip. After getting to know her, I went back to the case files, but in all I'd written I could find nothing about her save her name.

I was drawn to Mustafa and his grand style:

My father died when I was nine. Nothing of him remains except a single, terrible scene: I stand beside my mother, leaning against the wall that has been hastily thrown up across the entrance to the houses as part of the protection measures ordered by the army. He waves farewell to us, but the sun is glinting off the medals that adorn his uniform; it flashes into my eyes and I do not see him. Off he went to turn back the Tripartite Aggression, and nothing now remains of him save that glare and an open-topped truck that whisked the dust up in our faces. He left me in the care of the fool he had married to score the double: God's favor and a young body he could enjoy as he pleased without the domestic give-and-take that comes with an equal match. This was common knowledge in the neighborhood where I was raised, and as I grew older I learned of it, too. I would hear it alluded to at all manner of events and occasions. The first time I heard my circumstances so described was at the conclusion of a boyhood squabble over the result of a football match. We had disputed a goal with the opposition. They said that the ball had passed inside the post of piled bricks, and we insisted on our view, while the referee—because he was the least physically robust of us all—stated that the incident had taken place some distance from him and so he was unable to say one way or the other. As captain, I was obliged to stand fast and defy. A member of the opposition shouted in anger:

"Son of a retarded bitch, just shut up, you don't understand anything!"

When the time is right, the meaning of my father's counsel glitters like a jewel. The lot of the one who insulted my mother was a rock to the head. His blood flowed as he fled, screaming out the second truth:

"You really are a bastard!"

Would you care to know everything about my past, or just glimpses? Shall I tell it to you as an entertaining story, leaving you with nothing but the pleasure of its telling, or would you prefer it served up with what it betokens? If so, you will have to shoulder some of the pain that accompanied the tale's unfolding. What do you want? The burden of choice falls on you, and you alone must bear its consequences.

This question leads us to another. My apologies. Bear with me. One's life, if you weren't already aware, is a chain of question and exclamation marks all linked together; summon one and the rest snowball after. And so: would you like the story from the beginning or the end? I can tell it both ways, with my assurance that no errors will creep in. I ask, because there are those who only like to look at the end once events have unfolded. These individuals are blessed with a great deal of childlike naiveté, which leads them to resent the flashback—not just because it spoils the pleasure of surprise, but because it forces you to use your mind, to become an active participant, anticipating events according to the end that you have glimpsed. The flashback is the desire to intervene in the divine plan.

Would you like to know your end, then arrange your life accordingly?

This question was the true beginning of my relationship with Mustafa Ismail. I had heard dozens of confessions, and none had affected me as his did. One might reel me in with its romanticism, another with its violence, but neither would be more than a story—transcribed professionally and as tantalizingly as possible, yet dead. Soulless.

The records stated that he was over fifty, but his face and body paid no heed to the records. Powerfully built, he was possessed of a considerable charisma which stemmed from an unfeigned gravity of manner. Like the heroes of legend, something in his expression gave the impression of a deep-rooted grief, and in the very instant of our meeting I realized that the descriptions of facial features which are always attributed to these heroes were no laziness on the part of scribes, as I'd assumed, but rather that faces are shaped by the roles appointed them.

Nabil al-Adl treated the question as he did the majority of Mustafa's confidences: as blasphemous, and a cunning

19

attempt to divert us from the case by turning it into a debate over fundamentals.

"And anyway, what end?" al-Adl asked, reading through my transcript. "Death? The final reckoning? Eternal repose? Getting pensioned off, perhaps? Divorce? They're all ends. Which one does His Lordship mean?"

"You're right."

I whispered the words with a lack of conviction not lost on him. Ever since I had started looking through the case files in order to draw up the guidance report that would help us deal with him, a special bond had developed between Mustafa and myself. I have a talent for discovering other people's weaknesses. I could hand Nabil al-Adl the short-cut to the character of whoever was brought before him, so that he might extract what information he needed without effort—but confronted by Mustafa's personality, I found myself baffled. He seemed exemplary.

"It's good that you believe him, in any case. It adds some balance to the case. But I would like to draw your attention to something: you have to draw a line between yourself and those we deal with. Never forget whose side you're on."

Another stern warning from the chief. In recent times, I had heard more than one warning, and this had been the roughest. I was aware that I was on the verge of severing my links to the place and to its laws, but I had nothing to dissuade me from this course. Al-Adl would never understand that anyone capable of framing a question like Mustafa's has the strength to make it a reality. I understood; and I understood, too, that I would not be granted the opportunity to get Mus-tafa's response. We would not be friends or partners. I must be content with my role; and yet I set down his words ashamed that I was cast in the role of his enemy. It is the case that if we do not possess the courage to evaluate our selves and place them in the setting they long for, the world will toy with us and make itself a farce.

*

Behind the children's park was my place of work. A place unknown and unvisited by all but those fated to embark on a most unique experience.

The Palace of Confessions.

My private name for it, telling myself, as the microbus conveyed me from Shubra in the city's center to the furthest inhabited spot in the eastern suburb of Medinat Nasr, *Khaled's off to the Palace of Confessions to have some fun.*

The spacious park lay between the Palace of Confessions and a modest huddle of residential buildings, the greater part of it fringing a vast area ringed by a dull gray wall. No buildings could be seen behind the wall, only hillocks of sand, and it was topped by signs warning against approaching and taking pictures. From here, the park narrowed, terminating at a path wide enough for two to walk abreast and lined by cacti. When the employees all arrived at the same time, they were obliged to form a queue beside the cacti, one plant per employee. The door would only admit one person at a time— after the security device had checked their ID and allowed them in—but the throng I'm picturing never came to pass, not once, perhaps because there weren't that many employees to begin with, or perhaps because I would arrive late, choosing to linger in the park, to take time out amid the dazzling hues of its flowers and plants—so captivated, indeed, that I was increasingly convinced that Chagall himself had arranged them, the only person capable of playing with color thus, of combining it to bring such joy to the heart of those who saw it.

Yet, for some reason, this joy was absent in the children there, their numbers never rising or falling; they seemed distracted in a way quite at odds with my assumptions about childhood. I've no experience with children, but generally speaking, shouldn't they seem joyous and uninhibited? These ones weren't like that. They played with a busy discipline that made it appear as though they'd been drilled. One would come

down the high slide, then turn and pad back to its ladder, waiting his turn like an adult who has learned that the system is
the way to get what he wants. No shouting. No fighting over
toys. I memorized their faces. No names. I never got to know
them, because the mothers on the wooden benches never
called them. Not one ever shouted for her child to take care, or
dashed wildly toward their fallen offspring. They sat there contentedly, in their faces the placidity that comes from certainty.
Women in their thirties and forties, elegant in the beauty-free
way of wealthy women from Medinat Nasr, immersed in hobbies from their mothers' era: three or four crocheting, a similar
number flipping through fashion mags, while a lone blonde,
younger than the rest, sang outside the flock and read books
with old covers. Most likely their husbands worked behind the
dull gray wall, pursuing mysterious callings in nameless buildings, or else were colleagues of mine I hadn't met.

The ground floor of the Palace comprised a reception
room where an ancient functionary passed his time solv-
ing crossword puzzles. My relationship with him lasted the
seconds it took for my bag to pass through the scanner. I'd
greet him and he'd pay me no mind. He couldn't even see
those passing him by. He'd been programmed along with the
machine—and provided the row of lights on top didn't turn
red and its tiresome siren didn't sound, he had no cause to lift
his gaze. I was tempted to put a knife in the bag so his scanner
would scream and he'd be forced to notice me.

The old man was the lobby's center, surrounded by four
flights of stairs, each running up to a different department,
and behind his desk a flight down to the basement where the
guilty were housed: comfortable little cells, tidied and searched
each morning while their occupants took breakfast in the small
cafeteria next to the games room. They were free to move
between their cells, the games room, and the café. There was
no fixed schedule and no locked doors, but the basement was
their world until the interrogation was over.

*

Mustafa brought us a fearsome list of his victims: ministers, diplomats, artists, religious leaders, businessmen; people and crimes for which he provided the proof, the individuals concerned having preferred to make no report out of embarrassment or the desire to avoid scandal. Who would welcome detailed discussion of what went on in his bedroom? Who could ignore the many warnings designed to stop him telling? Documents vanished, and it was best not to bring it up. Private pictures of husband or wife, carefully concealed from the spouse, now laid out before sensitive eyes; the hidden revealed. Threats whose attendant instructions it was impossible not to obey. Nabil al-Adl himself had gone against his own creeds and convictions in order to keep hidden the photograph of his sister-in-law, Sawsan al-Kashef—near-naked and sprawled in her lover's arms—which had confronted him one day, and written beneath it in fiery red ink, a warning: *Don't squeal.*

What frightened the authorities, and got Mustafa's file referred to the highest levels, was not simply that his victims included names whose homes were fiercely guarded around the clock. More pertinently, one of these names, the major general whose apartment Mustafa had been robbing when apprehended, headed a team responsible for updating strategic plans for guarding the president himself—a fact itself outmatched by Mustafa's confession that he'd been planning to rob the president's residence, and that he'd intended it to be his final job in this country. If brought off successfully, he explained, it would have meant there were no challenges left for him here, and the time would have come to test his skills in other, more stimulating climes.

More surprisingly, however, his statements transcended mere confession to reach the level of theory:

The heavier the guard, the easier it is to get through. The higher the wall, the easier you feel on the other side of it, no matter how poor a climber you might be.

*

Why? If the question could be asked of any man and remain unanswered, it meant that he would be referred to us, for us to eradicate and remake it—innocent and free of question marks—as 'Because.' His coming to us was an admission that he was the best and most skillful in his field, a special breed of man who belonged with his ilk: unseemly geniuses, outcasts from the paradise of lawfulness.

The purpose of our research was to uncover the aims of Mustafa's organization and find any followers that he had not identified. There was concern that his ideas might spread and though his most senior assistants had been detained and had given detailed confessions, the suspicion that even one individual with the same mental powers might be lurking out there compelled our attention. Those who had been arrested were dangerous criminals. That was something we could accept. They were not particularly convinced by his views and credos, but had gone along with him in the pursuit of gain. It was quite possible, they said, that their criminal operations might have continued undiscovered, because the plans he laid adhered to a principle of absolute caution and were based on what he termed *The Book of Safety*, a volume containing hundreds of observations on the most propitious times to commit a crime, the risks that must be avoided, lists of addresses, the names of occupants and their professions, the phone numbers of state officials, escape routes and hideouts, instructions for issuing threats, and blackmail. It was a book he had fashioned with patience and love out of his experience and the experiences of others. He loathed error, seeking an ideal state in which he might attain absolute self-possession and control circumstances around him—a dream of perfection. En route to this state, he had managed to convert ordinary citizens into partners, some unwitting and others sympathetic to his ideas and dreams. What he hadn't realized was that error occurs precisely when we are taking care to avoid it.

Even so, he would never have allowed his ideas to disappear, hence the fundamental question: to whom had they been passed on?

"We concluded you were trying to revive the legend of Robin Hood."

"What do you mean by that? You've been unable to deal with us using the standard methods, so you're taking refuge in myth? Or is this an honor reserved for me?"

For all his intelligence, Mustafa didn't know what to make of the place in which he found himself. He attempted to conceal his nerves behind insouciance and grit, but there is no strength of will too tough for taming. The system grinds on, and has all the patience and all the time it needs to reach its goal—while Mustafa was a romantic who didn't understand that it wasn't the Sixties any more. He lived according to that era's vision of the world, trying to assume the guise of a god. And the upshot? He had fallen into an elementary mortal trap. And like they say, you only need to fall the once to go on falling forever thereafter. I observed his bafflement in sneaked glances; skillful forays slipped into the flow of his words to keep his secret burnished. One day, al-Adl had gone out of his office, leaving us together. Dropping his impersonal air, Mustafa asked me directly, "Where are we?"

I was flustered by his boldness. We had never exchanged words before. I attempted an answer, filled with pride that he had noticed me, but most likely he knew that I was no less confused than he. For his part, Nabil al-Adl was intent on intensifying the mystery surrounding our location—his way of meeting Mustafa's challenge to his authority:

"My job is not to condemn or exonerate. When it comes to our concerns, your guesses are wide of the mark. You cannot imagine the sheer number of unusual situations that we come up against and that oblige us to update our research techniques. Which is why, when I say that you are trying to revive the legend of Robin Hood, this isn't some whim of mine, but a statement based on a report on you which has been specially prepared by an educated and experienced operative."

I was the educated and experienced operative Nabil al-Adl referred to, and his kind words were not meant as a deft little summation of my person, but rather as the shot from the starting gun at which I must spring forward, must bite to inject the poison, the victim anesthetized so as not to cry out when he was skinned. Neither pain nor blood held any pleasure for us.

"We are the most refined and respectable level of sadism."

This would be my answer to the meaningless definitions of our trade bestowed on me by Abdel-Qawi.

With childish malevolence, al-Adl was trying to embroil me in an enmity with Mustafa, but I ignored it. I didn't enter into the conversation, hoping that Mustafa would be aware just what I was offering him. But he did not take the bait. Instead, he set about destroying my pet theory, giving al-Adl what he was after:

"I'm no reformer or political leader. I just rob rich people because they own what's worth stealing, and maybe because they don't miss what's gone missing. I don't mean whether or not they're psychologically affected, of course. That's not my point. It's just that with a little pressure they manage to turn a blind eye to what's been stolen—and they don't report it, which is how I manage to avoid situations like the one I'm in right now."

"But our investigations show you gave some of the money you stole to the poor. That proves you were attempting to turn yourself into a legend, to be whispered about by the people. . . ."

"Contrary to what you believe, I've no sympathy for the poor. In my view, they are largely responsible for their condition. There is something called the human will. If those who possess it don't use it to escape their predicament, then they've no one else to blame. I worked harder than you would believe

26

to plan and carry out each theft. Do you think I'd do all that for the sake of some pauper who just sits there whining day and night? Plus, I don't consider what I've done as something wrong that I must atone for, nor am I so dead to the wellsprings of satisfaction that I have to get it from making others happy."

The interview would come to an end, and his words would echo in my mind, so that it was no hardship to rewrite them when I returned home, adding to them my own interpretation of how the interrogation was proceeding, the questions that Nabil al-Adl should have asked or that he'd asked at the wrong time.

How did you come to take up thievery?

How did you come to justify it?

The truth is that it becomes easier when you define your options quickly. Abandon whatever resists you and take what comes to you. To turn failure into success—to transform from one thing to its polar opposite if need be—is a power you gain by looking hard at your disappointments. Where does it come from, this power of transformation? From university professor to thief. From lawful to illicit. This is our nature; if you are not aware of it, you will be lost—an astonishing mix of earth, and water, and fire. I am testing myself, nothing more. Later, perhaps, I shall become something quite different.

Can this be mine? Can I transform? I appreciated how difficult it would be, the transformation that Mustafa—who, for all his symbolic violence, was a traditionalist—had made from good to evil. A human story repeated a million times over, his own personal contribution a reversal of mankind's general law: the evildoer who gropes his way toward good. He had his own private concepts, and there were no ethical concerns to hamper his transition from one code of conduct to the next.

I proceeded in a daze: no signpost to teach me good from evil. Over and over, I reread the thoughts of the philosophers and thinkers, yet the distinction remained elusive. And I came to believe that they, like me, had not been able to separate the two principles. Then I understood that to rise above this system one must first pass through it, one must experience good and evil for oneself, and that I'd been nothing but a fool to believe that observation and reading could be fit substitutes for getting involved. Such lies. Writers are liars. Fools like me. They stick to the shore and write down their fantasies—and those fantasies took me in. I thought them the product of experience, when they were just the product of impotence and fear.

In your victim's home, do not act like a blundering thief driven by resentment to wreck and destroy.

Treat the site of your burglary as though it were your own home. Do not hurt the feelings of others by violating their privacies unless you must prevent them reporting what has happened.

Maintaining a respectful distance between yourself and those whose homes you invade ensures that you retain control over feelings that should not be allowed to guide you in those moments and thus spoil your work.

Mustafa Ismail
The Book of Safety

3

I AM THE CHANCE AT DELIVERANCE that Sawsan al-Kashef hoped for. I did not hang the photograph of her with her lover right beside her wedding portrait on the wall of her home simply in order to prevent her husband reporting the burglary. If that had been all I was after, I would have threatened him with other, more important documents. Was it a coincidence, his total absence from her secret album, from the pictures she'd stockpiled from different events: at school, on the beach, trips to Europe, alone in a bar with only a glass of beer for company, dancing with a friend at a wedding while the newlyweds' relatives looked on grimly?

It was my decision to restore her to how she had looked at no more than seventeen, two fingers placed in her mouth (most likely an attempt to whistle); and up above, on one of the balconies, a figure pointing down to her; and on the balcony opposite, a man and woman sitting close together, his arm around her neck, and in front of them two cups of tea on a small table. The Seventies—I reckoned it from the clothes and a freedom whose fragrant breeze I almost scented as I studied the details. Sawsan al-Kashef's secret album, and its incongruity beside the scowling portraits on the walls, ushered me into her story. How was it that life had changed for her to such a degree?

To protect the reputation of the al-Adl family, what Mustafa testified to that day was not to be made public, a secret preserved by three who kept their pledge: the thief, the interrogator, and the transcriber. But I'm an author now. What do they expect? It means nothing to the writer that you make him swear by honor, integrity, or ethics. Writing, for those initiated into its secrets, means nothing if not the betrayal of what is stable and immutable. And why should Nabil al-Adl believe that his family is so exalted that any mention of it should be scrubbed from the transcript of the interviews? More importantly, Sawsan al-Kashef's story and what happened to her are vital in clarifying the reasons that led Mustafa Ismail to embark on his project as a whole. And so: I spill.

Mustafa knew nothing of the link that bound my boss to that home. His *Book of Safety* didn't cover coincidences like that. And so he didn't understand why the interrogator was so vexed that he'd exposed that woman's secrets to her husband in such a ruthless fashion. But as I saw it, he wouldn't have cared even had he known. He had his convictions, and these made him a believer in what he embodied.

Every home I entered brought me one step closer to what I did not know.

The only sentence concerning that incident that I entered into the transcript of his confessions. Al-Adl made his wishes quite clear as he left his desk for the sofa in the room's far corner. He plucked the pen from my hand, capped it, and laid it on the paper before me. To the page that would remain blank, I apologized. That evening I was to enjoy being an audience and nothing else—a child whose father reads him a story before bed. But what about my fingers? I laid them against my thigh, tapped out a tune that was buzzing around my head, whose title and composer I'd forgotten.

Nabil's voice, apologizing to Mustafa for the interruption: "Please go on. Sorry."

Several jobs in, my comrades had their instructions off by heart—what we wanted and what we couldn't use; what we mustn't touch; what, if we took it, would implicate us in a situation we couldn't deal with. There are some things whose loss people are unable to forgive, usually when under some form of compulsion: important documents, guns. We steal what can, with a little menacing, be forgotten. My colleagues carry out their tasks as befits a contemptible band of thieves, while I wander monk-like through the home, feeling out its detail. At first, this involved no more than the search for documents—blackmail material—but it soon became an end in itself. I came to love these close inspections of how our victims lived, and the experience taught me to make quick and accurate judgments of their homes. Here, with its predominantly feminine touch, the woman is in charge. This one is devoid of love, evident from the absence of the harmony that affection brings. There are homes you're at ease in, that bewitch you the moment you enter. Have you heard about thieves who doze off in the homes they enter, only to be surprised by the return of the owners? I used to think this was the stupidest kind of larceny, and the laziest, until I had perfected my trade and experienced the same thing myself—the sense that this is my home, this woman who's hung her picture on the wall is my wife; her underwear, left lying with typical negligence on the bed or in the bathroom, keeps her body present.

My companions left me to my own devices, knowing that my presence was a guarantee of our safe departure. It was as though we were guests to whom the generous owners had gifted some of their possessions—poor relatives to rich folk who gave clothes to us and our children, saying that they were unused, and yet they weren't quite right for us. But we would accept them, convincing ourselves that we were exchanging gifts.

"Exchange gifts and exchange love."

And yet we were recalcitrant paupers, mature enough to admit that we were resentful for our lesser standing, that this resentment would spur us to gift them, too, something to keep us in their hearts—something hurtful and painful that would perhaps upset their code of values and principles. They would stop receiving poor relatives and wouldn't give them gifts. Not so freely. No call for tenderness.

I told you that every home I entered brought me a step closer to myself. Everything I stole led me to a part of myself and what I wanted. It was more like therapy than anything else, which is why I became addicted to living within the lives of others.

I no longer cared what we came away with. My treasure was the details. Unlike that woman, I possess almost no photographs from childhood.

Photography was another expense whose cost we couldn't bear. The camera I inherited from my father he had rarely used himself, and after his passing we kept it only for special occasions, the kind that are carefully prepared for precisely because they will be photographed. Which is why I cannot remember how I looked, except by relying on a memory that shifts about according to the whim of the moment. Among the papers left by my father, reserve officer Ismail al-Sayyid—the majority of which were comprised of official documents, letters addressed to him from military command, and a few photographs of landscapes, there was a single picture—one single solitary picture—from which I know what he looked like. Standing on the seashore in Alexandria (so he'd written on it) with a group of colleagues, all aping the pose of bodybuilding champs: one arm bowed out from their sides, the other held skyward in a straight line, the face turned with it, out as far as it would go. Little gods who fell and never knew why.

I lost myself in Sawsan's life. Compare these hidden pictures with the official portraits on the wall: the bearded husband, the young women in hijabs, the son who looks more like his father than her. And then an exception, a group shot: her with a little girl at the seaside. The little girl is pouring a bucket of water over her mother's head. Of the three children, she seems to be the closest to Sawsan. Alone among the pictures on the wall, their expressions hold some kind of rebelliousness, while those of the father, son, and other daughter possess a serenity and placidity in keeping with the piety hinted at by numerous small details scattered around the apartment.

Mustafa reclined on a big, black leather chair in a pose that matched his self-confidence, his hands on the armrests, talking languidly as though seated in his own office with old friends who could discuss without embarrassment the smallest details of their lives. I was sitting on a similar chair, but drowning in it. I tried sitting according to the image I had of myself, but it came off as distinctly forced. What we think of ourselves does not always pan out in reality. He saw greatness in himself, as I did in myself, but the practical application of this thought proved his vision to be the correct one. Was I deceived, then, or was it just a question of practicing to make the idea correspond with reality?

Practicing greatness!

An excellent title for a book dealing with the difficulties of a certain class of person looking for solutions to predicaments like mine: in search of that harmony between the idea of oneself and the passage of that self through life. I made do with perching on the edge of the chair, leaning slightly forward: a student in his teacher's chambers patiently absorbing his lessons until he'd formed sufficient convictions to leave him puffed up and proud.

When the thieving first began, it was driven by an anger that I could only expend in that particular way. This does not constitute any admission of error—quite the opposite! It's just that I was not conscious, exactly, of the factors that were making me act this way. But it was in this woman's home in particular that I realized I was in possession of a message, and one that I must carry out. Call me a devil if you must, but I have the power to expose the fakery in whose prison we pass our lives.

Nothing is done except at my signal. I am involved from beginning to end. The true leader goes at the head of troops, and this is what ensures that he keeps his position.

 My presence on the ground during operations safeguards my project. No matter how adept and well-trained your foot soldiers, they cannot cope with surprises.

 Leadership means swift reactions, calm in the face of crises, reassuring the men that they will always be protected from things they have no idea how to handle.

Mustafa Ismail
The Book of Safety

4

"WOULD YOU LIKE TO KNOW your end, then arrange your life accordingly?"

I directed the question at Dmitri, owner of the Sappho bookshop, and his friends, still and silent, arrayed in the ancient photograph's tableau. I had been coming to the bookshop with my father since I was little, and not one detail had altered, every figure in the picture holding position. With this photo, Dmitri had made the most beautiful period of his life immutable. There he stood in his suit, white and cut in the Forties style— were it not for the red handkerchief in his breast pocket, he would have looked like a little puddle of milk. To his right and left respectively, Maria and Helene, and on the opposite side of the picture his friend with the tricky name I couldn't remember.

Dmitri's reticence about personal matters opened the floor to speculation. From time to time, I would dream up different explanations for this picture, for this four-way tie that ended with three off to Greece and Dmitri staying behind. The authentic Shubra kid, passionate about Egypt. That friend of his was bound to leave; the sharply masculine features and athletic body, his simultaneously simple and elegant clothes, spoke of ambitions that no longer belonged in the burgeoning dictatorship. The girl on the other side of the picture had traveled with him, that much seemed certain. Today's backstory was that she had been his lover. Her casually parted legs went with his liberated air, while her companion's conservative posture suited Dmitri's commitment to dapper formality on an occasion that didn't warrant the effort. But unable to endure his reticence she had chosen to follow her friends.

In front of the pyramids and the Sphinx: two men and two women mounted on four camels gazing at the horizon, trying to mirror the still-majestic statue. Yet they fell short of the effect they strove for. A pharaonic curse had slipped out from the pyramids and into the four camels, lending them a satirical spirit that spurred them to lampoon their riders: gazing, like them, defiantly into the distance.

Yes indeed, Mustafa. I would like—would long—to know how it will end for me and to arrange my life accordingly.

Dmitri heaved his body out of the storeroom I had never been permitted to enter. There was no longer any resemblance between him and his portrait, but beginnings tend to lead to endings, and he had answered a propensity for fatness, doubling the size of every cell in his body. He raised his glasses to his eyes and wiped away beads of sweat. Huge effort was expended in the storeroom, which was why, to obtain a book, lengthy negotiations were unavoidable. The book was a rare edition, he would insist: unobtainable, even from the National Library, which—like every square foot of this country—had succumbed to neglect! I smiled to myself. Then:

"You were speaking to me?"

"No, no, Uncle Dmitri, be well."

Always suspicious and never troubled to hide it. Innocent behavior could take on quite inappropriate significance with him, and so to prevent his misgivings spreading I pretended to study the book in his hand.

He had not accommodated himself to the frailties imposed by his age, working around the clock to prove he was up to it. More than anything, he loathed his faculties being called into question, as though he were some pitiable pensioner. I had made a mistake. I should have told him straight that my habit of speaking to myself had slipped out of my control; then he would have smiled, wheeling out that brand of empathy with which he maintained a distance between himself and others. The point being that he would have been reassured no defects had been detected in any of his faculties, for that would signal that the breakdown had begun.

He set the book on a stack of lowbrow crime novels, the ones he had refused to trade in when they first became popular, hating the idea of them, the way they were written, even their covers—then weakening when confronted with the lure of their profits. He concealed the title of the book he held from me, determined to spin out the game of enticement that he played so well.

"Cryptography is like magic. It first requires you to believe that reality does not exist. A fundamental requirement, this: without it you will see only signs and symbols."

He fell silent to catch his breath, preparing for the next sentence which was to be considerably longer. It would incorporate, perhaps, the difference between cryptography, a science, and magic, a supernatural force on which one should never be so rash as to rely entirely. How could one combine the two?

Then the conclusion: "Thus all innovation throughout history."

This was Dmitri's motto, which he would shape and shunt into any topic, even food. I often thought to myself that he existed in a room only he was allowed to enter. He would invent things to accommodate this theory of his, but I was unable to guess at the nature of the mutually incompatible elements he was combining—nor, I believe, could anyone else. For Dmitri was a living, breathing dictionary, with effrontery enough to learn everything about everything by reading a book about it. And yet, because he who excels in speech finds it difficult to act, things never panned out for his theory as they should. Ever since our relationship had become properly established, I would hear him talk of it—maybe as my father had before me. We exist in a mesh of unchanging sentences, then seek out new ones, fleeing the tedium of repetition and uniformity. Take the strategy adopted by a close friend of mine, Lotfi Zadeh: unable to bear his father's oft-repeated line on freedom, he had voluntarily joined the ranks of a group that regarded such things as heresy.

Behind me, the sound of panpipes trilled. One of the constants in my life. As a child, I would go ahead of my father to shove the door, which would knock the machine mounted behind it and make it play a tune. Many times, I'd leave the pair of them and go back out into the street, then return to push the door and hear the music once again. My father would tell me off, tell me to mind my manners, and Dmitri would cry, "No, no, *parakalo*, please, *parakalo*, let the boy have fun."

With uncertain steps, accompanied by the tune, a young woman came in. Her dress was covered with flowers, and her hair so thick that I was quite entranced and didn't even glance at her face. She looked about, then stood there, a few paces off, her head bowed and as still as though turned to stone by Medusa. This is what Dmitri looked for—all his customers were different in some way, somehow dreamy and disoriented; summoned by the sad sound of his panpipes, they never regained themselves thereafter.

Seeing him distracted with the girl, I made to leave. He wasn't so insistent that I stay.

"We must finish our conversation. . . ."

"I've got an important appointment."

Out I went, hugging the book—*Enigma*—to my chest and hoping it would help me find my way to a starting line. Mustafa's confessions were a web of riddles. He quoted from books, quotes that were sometimes quite beside the point. Among his words lay a message of some kind, perhaps one that transcended reality—but not, as Dmitri would put it, to the extent of negating it.

No one who knew my good-hearted Greek friend would subject the views he expressed to intense scrutiny, nor blame themselves for seeking to escape the chatter of a lonely old man, devoted to his customers, who wanted nothing more than someone to listen to him for a while.

From home to the bookshop was fifteen minutes on foot, more or less the same distance that separated the bookshop from the café—a full quarter of an hour which, until that moment, I'd never before considered how to spend. (But considering late is better than never at all). I stood outside Sappho, the book-store whose golden anniversary we'd shortly be celebrating, its signage over my head. Beside it stood Golden Shoe Footwear, then Koshari Delight. This was not as incongruous as it might seem, quite the opposite: when the sun begins to set, Sappho steps out to don her golden shoe, singing to the pipes of Dmitri's door as she goes to meet her students.

This was not the Shubra Street laid out by Muhammad Ali, the ruler who forged the modern state. We were now on Lesbos, land of love and beauty. Structures of similar heights and styles harmoniously coexisting with their inhabitants, who contentedly live out an undisrupted and orderly life, spoilt by nothing—nothing save one of the newer buildings, which towered over the rest: the Pharaoh Building, so-called by its neighbors. This was their redress for the arrogance of its wealthy owner—who lived with his family on the first four floors—and that of its other residents, its high priesthood (some of whom owned famous stores in the district, others returnees from the Gulf), bound together by wealth and shared pride in inhabiting the highest and most luxurious building in the neighborhood.

I marked it as my primary target for when I put my planned mutiny into action. Years from now, a young man would come seeking the reason for my transformation from the ranks of the powers-that-be into a bold thief.

I was gathering information that most likely was useless. Was I determined enough to walk in the footsteps of Mustafa Ismail?

The girl emerged from the bookshop, surprised to see me. Ah, how I love these undisguised reactions. Did she think that I was waiting for her? Rest easy now, my thick-haired friend, there is a covenant between myself and Sappho: that I shall never visit harm on her possessions. But at least allow me a sight of that surprised and childlike face.

I watched her walk away with quick, resolute steps, more like a boy trying to act the man, taller than was womanly. She didn't sway when she walked like other women—that severe body had it in it to rebel against her—and so she had let her hair grow thick, and cultivated flowers on her dress: signs by which she hinted at a hidden softness. The scant breeze plastered the fabric to her body, molding to the lines of her small, rounded buttocks. Every inch of her frame suggested a man somehow possessed by a female spirit—I would only discover how once I'd visited her village and seen the place where she'd been raised.

At the end of Khulousi Street, she stood in a daze, looking left and right. I scampered across to the other side, keen she not catch sight of me a third time. I turned right down Bulaq Canal Street toward the café, fighting the urge to look back and see if my suspicion was correct: that our roles were reversed and she was now scrutinizing me. How did my buttocks look to her? The very thought made them hang heavier. I came to a halt, flustered, making a pantomime of lighting a cigarette, and trying to get a fix on her out of the corner of my eye. At that angle, she was nowhere to be seen. Bolder, I looked around, but she had vanished. I walked on to the café, luxuriating in daydreams that had me a king who cared less for his subjects than for stockpiling women. This girl would be the latest addition to a collection which already included Lotfi's girlfriend Manal, and Huda, made my girlfriend by some witch's curse. Taking a scientific approach, setting lust aside, I compared the bodies of all three.

The mission I'd left home specifically to perform had been a failure. I had collected very little information. Who guarded the Pharaoh Building? When was he absent? How to get upstairs without arousing suspicion? And, most importantly, which apartment was currently free of its occupants?

I would have to wait years before I understood what Mustafa's experiment meant. Young as I was, I'd listened spellbound to what I took to be an adventure story, and because I was learning its details from its leading man this had given me the impression that I had a role to play myself. The missing sixth man of his gang. The mind to match his own, which itself solicited this balance so as to avoid coming to some foolish end that ran against the course of the tale. I had taken on his personality—scouting out locations, going over guard rosters, befriending and bonding with doormen and shopkeepers, making plans to burgle a target (getting in and out, making plan Bs)—enjoying the movement between two contradictory roles. I had regarded it as a chess match, but now I was playing on the primary board. I wasn't selfish, though. I made sure to initiate certain friends into certain details, stressing that should these details find their way outside our gathering it would mean troubles there'd be no avoiding.

The loser toppled his king and for a few seconds we held him, pityingly, in our gaze. To us, the boards were kingdoms, with soldiers, rulers, and ministers. No one had the right to talk during a match. Brief, concise comments from an early leaver, if he had something worth saying. The moment the king fell, the murmurs would rise up: match analysis, the reasons for victory and defeat, replaying critical moves to avoid making the same mistakes, and, on the margins of it all, the study of openings and recently published books. Our stars. Our heroes. The senior chess players. Great minds denied their birthright, to take their place at the top board.

Ustaz Fakhri moved the café's cheap board to a table behind him. Some of the pieces fell to the floor, and Lotfi rushed to help. The bishop lay by my foot, head nibbled by the passing years. I fought a powerful urge to stamp down on it and on Lotfi's fingers, about to pick it up. Soon I'd be needing a visit to a psychologist to find out what lay behind these irrational urges.

Fakhri laid the Samsonite case across his thighs. His eyes narrowed and his thick eyebrows drew together. One of Satan's avatars: sinister, bulging eyes, the heavy brows almost meeting in the middle, a face held taut by a hidden anger—but a passive devil, too idle to perform his duties; eschewing temptation.

He ran his fingers over the tumblers beside the locks on either side. We stared at him in apprehension and held our breath, waiting for the familiar click that proclaimed the treasure was to hand.

He'd once forgotten the numbers. All efforts to recall them had failed—the suggestion, gloatingly advanced by Anwar al-Waraqi, that he smash the case open had only left him tenser and more irritable. The way to the royal ivory pieces ran through him. We had suggested dozens of numbers based on important dates from his life—his birth, the day he met the king, his visit to Russia—but to no avail. He had asked to be left alone for a moment. The proprietor, Ashraf al-Suweifi, had made a gift to him of his own favorite corner, that he might be alone with his case—a great sacrifice, but the goal was greater still: the royal chess set, symbol of the café and its clientele. And Fakhri would not resort to smashing the case, for that would be an insult to his intelligence and his memory. He would rather the pieces remain imprisoned: an ill omen should it come to pass. It had taken half an hour of total silence before the trial came to an end.

"Want to play?"

I refused, pleading a headache. Ustaz Fakhri offered a game to Lotfi. Moved to the chair facing him, and gave him white straight out. Lotfi concealed his irritation at being thought a lesser player behind the smoke from his cigarette. Anwar al-Waraqi, sitting next to Lotfi, made no effort to conceal the derision on his face. Then he leaned forward to get closer to me:

"So?"

The only Egyptian who made sure to pronounce his Arabic letters properly, a habit he'd picked up living among the Arabs of the Gulf.

"The Egyptians are an idle people," he would say, "So idle that they can't be bothered to speak their language the right way."

He pressed me to tell him about the latest developments in the case. This was his favorite game now. He wanted to leave Shubra for a better life, but he knew that what he sought was not simply a change in location but something that called for a different approach altogether, one that would help him acclimatize to his new environment. And in Mustafa Ismail's story, he had found what he was looking for. But he needn't have asked, for I could not free myself from Mustafa's grip. I would pass on what I saw, in the hope of increasing the numbers of his admirers, carrying out his unspoken wish that his story be preserved against the authorities' limitless capacity to erase what it wants of memory.

As I explained, Nabil al-Adl had made no secret of his surprise; nothing in his records could explain Mustafa's violent transformation. Why would a university professor sacrifice all he had and turn to crime? And, more importantly, how and when did he come by the expertise that had made a legend of him? Money wasn't the motive. He had enough of it, and his qualifications and abilities allowed him to get more in ways that would never have led him to this end. In any case, he didn't seem hungry for cash. So what had led him to risk all that he'd achieved?

From his seat beside me, Ustaz Fakhri glanced reprovingly at me out of the corner of his eye. He didn't need to concentrate on his game with Lotfi, but he wished to hear no more. A growing desire to provoke him came over me. I crossed one leg over another. Mustafa's words filled me with a sense of greatness.

"The reasons are so diverse that they disappear, leaving the crime an act committed for its own sake. Simply put, when 'safe' methods fail to guide you to yourself, you have no choice but to try out a set of actions proscribed by convention. And all the dangers this path may bring are preferable to living and dying without discovering who you are. What is it people do, save wake, and sleep, and eat, and fuck?"

Nabil al-Adl had broken in: "And this list of actions is improved when we add steal and blackmail?"

"You view the crime through a filter that your job imposes on you. Such things do not apply to me. I am free of job titles and the need to comply. If you could only obtain your freedom, then we could discuss those actions that are categorized as forbidden, and our right to engage in them.'"

"That's philosophy, not crime," was Lotfi's comment. His eyes were on Ustaz Fakhri: a transparent attempt to curry favor. His position didn't satisfy him. His desire would bring him down. I had brought him along to help him restore his lost memories of poetry. His knowledge of chess went no further than the general outlines: the pawns, eight identical pieces, the first to be sacrificed. Move by move, the game revealed its secrets and his most salient memories returned, enabling a pawn to reach the far end of the board and be promoted into a thoroughly respectable rook patrolling the northern border of Fakhri's kingdom. What now?

Long hours I would spend here, seated alongside Ustaz Fakhri, the café's chief elder and a nationally ranked chess player. If some idiot back in the Sixties hadn't barred him from traveling on the grounds that engaging with a hostile nation was forbidden, he would have been one of the international stars of the game. Fakhri and I were two sides of the same coin: father and son, as the rest of the group would joke. A resemblance that stemmed from our characters, and the stern countenances that sought to set the world at arm's length. Two individuals from a now extinct stock who cared nothing for what went on around them: looking on and not getting involved. But I admit that Fakhri was an extreme case. I never fought for long and, full of regret for what I'd lost, would return to reality. He had lived his life without being prey, even for a moment, to such a feeling. He had seemed pitying when I informed him of my decision, and though I was careful to maintain our relationship and return to the old habits whenever time allowed, what had been broken was greater than any attempt to restore it.

A changeless backdrop. We bestowed but fleeting glances on the world. The glass blocked most of the sound, and what reached us did so purged of its degradation. If people only realized how beautiful they were when they shut their mouths. Fakhri had sat here for twenty years—every day except Fridays, which he would spend rambling about the city for hours, following this with a specially prepared meal and then bed. The walking cleared the cigarette smoke that clung to his lungs, and emptied his dreams of any unwonted words or deeds he had been forced to engage in. This was a program that admitted no outside participation; should it so happen—and it had happened many times—that he encounter one of the café's customers, he would cut them dead without the slightest attempt to soften the blow. His acquaintances had grown accustomed to this. That the man should have maintained his solitary existence for all these years. Well, something must have affected his mind. Loneliness leaves you mad or a genius, and he oscillated between the two. But it seemed most probable, with the greater part of his life behind him, that madness was the closer. Maybe it was the Friday ritual alone that held his breakdown at bay.

I was a Trojan horse brought to life. I wasn't sufficiently aware at the time to perceive that the virus first took root when I began to recount the stories that had suddenly unfurled before me out of a cave whose existence I had never guessed at. A gullible traitor, handing over the keys and only understanding what he was embarked on once his mission was at an end. I spoke with pride: what are we but a set of stories we tell or hear? And as I weakened before temptation, the crack in the window widened, and the street, with all its myriad details, slipped in to claim more territory for itself.

When did I first become aware of my betrayal? From the breadstick seller! That's it! That half-turn, that look he gave me. Around five o'clock, quite unhurried, he would open the café door (one quarter wooden, the remainder glass), the rasp it made disturbing those present, who would plead with him to hurry it up, some waiting for that moment to test out newly minted wisecracks about the man's lack of speed. The robe and headdress never changed. Maybe he had more than one outfit in the same faded hues, the same coarse fabric, the same length that granted sight of a skinny shank terminating in a vast and flattened foot trussed up in a peculiar kind of sandal that seemed to have been plaited from strips of a hide which had lost its color and whose original nature could not be guessed at. Similar strips were tied to the basket of breadsticks and roundels, passing across his chest while the basket itself swayed on his back. He'd lift these straps, the basket would lift over him and, as he turned with a dancer's grace, would suddenly be in front. He would hold it, lower it to the ground, and set to: moving around the café's tables, distributing his wares to the customers without a word being spoken. Not a day went by without my observing the whole performance. Before plunging in he would stand by the door for a few seconds, as though tallying up his enemies before the charge. Spellbinding, the slow pace at which he proceeded. It wasn't frailty or weakness. It wasn't age forcing him to keep that beat. He was healthy enough—you saw it in the rigid, upright body and the two sweating hands: it was just that he was like a man walking through a graveyard, taking care lest he wake the dead. A sinister rhythm that brought back fears I'd long discarded: of death and what comes after.

When the man was done, and everyone had taken their share of breadsticks, he would sit alone in a corner and sip the tea that Amm Sayyid brought him. Half an hour, then he'd set off again. He'd perfected all this an age ago, and every motion now took place according to a system and routine that none dared contemplate altering, each one of us operating in his private world, satisfied with his appointed station.

Ashraf al-Suweifi would watch the breadstick seller for the time it took him to close the door, then return to his papers, a stack comprising almost every sheet of print journalism that had ever been published. It was an assignment he had taken on sincerely and devotedly after completing his studies in the faculty of engineering. He'd gotten the message early on, but his father would continue to repeat the famous line in his hearing: "Finish your studies, and after that you're free."

Now Amm Sayyid's voice rose up to puncture the tranquil calm, telling al-Suweifi of his discovery of a suspicious shortfall in the storeroom's sugar supply, and making insinuations about his nemesis Fathi, who stood at the counter reckoning up the orders. Al-Suweifi had no liking for the particulars that Sayyid was obliged to share with him—the supplies running out, the number of cups they'd lost. He lacked his father's ability to discuss work-related matters without getting dragged in. His response brought the conversation to an end.

"Please, Sayyid, don't bother me with these silly things."

And once Sayyid had withdrawn, thrilled with this further proof that his word held sway in the café, al-Suweifi let out an exasperated sigh:

"Haven't I lost years enough to stupid trifles?"

The customers sympathized with his bitterness. They would attempt to soothe him by suggesting that they, too, had lost many years against their will. Most things in life were stupid trifles.

"God'll make it up. Others have lost more."

Anwar al-Waraqi would voice despair at his circumstances, and at the eons he'd spent in marital disputes, which had at times prevented him coming to the café—until the separation had set him free.

And what was it they did, to make them regret this lost time? The question preoccupied me, and the breadstick seller had sensed it, telling me, "You don't belong here. . . ."

I spent nights plotting to get rid of him before he exposed me. I'd murder him in one of Shubra's serene nighttime streets and around his body I'd spell out some devastating line of Mustafa's—in breadsticks. The patrons dealt gravely with anything that concerned mixing with the outside world. A shared faith with no prior consultation and no proselytizing necessary.

Ashraf al-Suweifi had returned home, disgusted, from the faculty of engineering to find his father preparing to leave his office and take his siesta, a routine only altered in exceptional circumstances, irresistible circumstances before which one could only surrender to the rhythm of the outside world. For instance, that one's son had fallen into a fresh trap.

The father had never protested his son's absences. What was left to him in this world was too precious to waste in argument. In his private corner, which he would subsequently bequeath to his offspring, he had made use of every minute. He was not far from the window, but the daylight didn't reach him and the passersby couldn't see him: a miraculous spot, as though a giant creature were shielding him with its shadow. Of course, closer inspection was enough to solve the riddle: that corner was the beginning of a long, dark passage at the end of which lay a large room for storing the café's supplies. The corridor's shadow cast its full weight on the father's corner to set the daylight, no matter how bright it became, at defiance. A space like this had to be used for the purpose it was made for, and he would sit in silence for hours, watching, his memory picking out millions of images for use in his report to the heavens on what went on down here. He was the founder of the League of Watchers, and the memory of him and his like had to be preserved.

When he passed from this world, his son immortalized him in one corner of his corner:

The al-Suweifi Museum for the Defiance of Death and Forgetting

To wit, a wooden cabinet containing his possessions: some books and old magazines, his spectacles, a tarboosh missing its tassel, an antique radio, and—at the heart of the display—a small statue by a long-forgotten artist, a patron of the café, notable for a Mona Lisa-like gaze of exaggerated effect. Such a distinctive feature in such a poor piece got on the nerves of the customers: it seemed to be observing their presence. Indeed, it started to affect them after they'd departed.

"It's following me in my sleep."

Before tributes turned into an endless orgy of satire at 'Big Brother's' expense, al-Suweifi shifted the cabinet so that it was facing the street, explaining to his deceased father that since his gaze had always extended to the outside world, he could now continue doing what he had loved. All thought the idea a good one, avoiding the statue's gaze as they walked past and reveling in the discomfort of the passersby.

The younger al-Suweifi inherited his father's faith, but expressed through a different rite whose performance he never shirked; he scorned criticism till he had proved that it was not worldly concerns that interested him, unlike those professional perusers of newspapers and magazines who become machines that churn out information and analysis. Al-Suweifi never spoke of what he'd read. No explosions of irritation from him. The politics page, the crossword, the obituaries: the same calm, the same posture for each. No sooner finishing one paper than dropping it at his feet to start the next—without a pause: a grueling marathon.

I'd arrive at noon to find a respectably sized heap on the floor. If time was pressing, he'd speed up, adjusting his pace to a biological alarm clock that let him know when his next appointment was approaching. When not a single newspaper or magazine was left, and once the cuttings were pasted up on the wall, Amm Sayyid would wipe away the dirty trace of ink—of words—and set the backgammon and a ginger and cinnamon upon the table. The drink was the secret behind al-Suweifi's unflagging energy, and with its arrival, unavoidably, the topic of women would be broached, the topic on which he would address us with any man who had experiences to share welcome to contribute his advice. Al-Suweifi's friend would sit facing him in silence, not breaking the flow of talk, greeting none of us. He would open the board and arrange the pieces, taking white because al-Suweifi favored black. They were the only two exempted from the café's rule forbidding all games but chess, embarking on their match with the shyness of someone taking what does not belong to them. Should enthusiasm get the better of them, al-Suweifi would apologize to the others who were sunk in thought:

"Sorry about that, your excellencies. It's just that he will slap those pieces!"

His friend, who by some miracle we hadn't yet poisoned, would point at al-Suweifi, intending to give an impression of superiority:

"A kid. What can you do?"

But it would rebound on him and leave him looking foolish.

Their racket did no harm in any case, for their stamina lasted no longer than a single round, after which they'd depart.

I always wanted to leave a card for those I visited, like Arsène Lupin, but with a different inscription for every home:
"To you, and your exquisite taste."
"One day you'll thank me for what I have done."

Mustafa Ismail
The Book of Safety

5

I SLOWED, WANTING TO SEE the mechanism complete the operation, but fear of failure spurred me to throw my body through the narrowing gap. I didn't calculate whether it was wide enough or not, whether it would crush me, or chop me in two, or maybe give free rein to its cruelty and sever a foot, leaving me to live out a life dragging what was left of me along the highways and byways.

God in His mercy was watching over me, and I made it through in one piece. I dropped into emptiness, then water detonated, as I broke my fall in a pond filled with plants. I cared nothing for myself: all my senses were trained on the giant petals folding shut. I had observed them many a time from the desert sands, and this was the one and only occasion that I would have the opportunity to be a part of their structure. The gap admitting light thinned gradually till I was lost in an endless darkness, stretched out on my back in a watery grave, no torch to hand. It had been a spur-of-the-moment decision to jump in. The perfect symmetry of the outer shell had overwhelmed me and, distracted by it, the chance had nearly passed me by. The sun had been setting and with the last of its rays, the sound of machinery had begun to swell, and the golden petals had risen up. Here I could search for a different starting point for myself, something other than my own mad project, returning home to live in harmony with my quotidian routines.

Before regret could come, a sign that I was on the right path: a dazzling white light that pushed back against the pitch dark; hundreds of small creatures flitting by so fast I could not immediately tell what they were, but my heart was glad. Even if they turned out to be carnivorous and tore the flesh from my bones, I'd consider their pricks a prize that I had earned. The lotus leaves onto which I'd fallen were struggling to shake off my weight. It was like they were cradling me. A comforting thought, though I leapt up in alarm when it occurred to me that they, too, were closing as their larger iterations had before them.

The water soaked me through. I was being purified that I might deserve this honor. On down a narrow corridor, built wide enough for one. All the space on offer had been given over to plants, in shapes and colors I hadn't known existed: blue, red, white, and gold, some with elongated leaves, others with leaves round and flattened, some with beating hearts, some coyly folded, some gazing out with brazen hunger.

Never would I have guessed that Amgad al-Douqli, owner of the Lotus House, was quite this crazy. A jamboree so carefully coordinated that no one element overwhelmed another and then, as the space widened, it became clear that it would be impossible to take in the scene in its entirety. Luminous larvae lent an air of magic and mystery. They squirmed around me, investigating the creature who had invaded their sanctuary, and turning me into something sacred. The profane was non-existent. We shall spend the night alone together, glowing friends.

The living quarters were tiny. Al-Douqli had wanted a lotus plant to enclose him like a womb, but he couldn't get one large enough. Forced to build, he'd drawn inspiration from the idea of a Buddha's statue and had erected a house, just a bedroom and bathroom on a base constructed from lotus leaves. The end result was a giant and sinister lotus that closed tight shut, with no way to make it open other than the dawning sun.

My dear Amgad al-Douqli,
I shall not write at length, for we share no bond by which I might compel you to endure the companionship of my thoughts. I wanted to write to you simply because of this wondrous home of yours, the target I selected as the starting point in a new life, whose essence shall be movement rather than immobility. All I have learned and trust in shall be put to the test. There is no need for me to stress that I am a decent man and not a thieving crook. Not yet. And certainly you will know that a man's

proximity to decency has nothing to do with the trade he plies. I have no doubt that you will guess what kind of person I am from the way I phrase this letter, but I am not obliged to explicate and explain. We are not friends, in any case, though I am currently sitting at your desk and using your paper and pen.

Permit me to express my admiration of your genius in designing this house and its garden. This genius was what summoned me, insistently, to view it up close.

You will find nothing missing. The safe is untouched. I haven't looked in any potential hiding places for money or jewelry. That is not why I came. I do not know if this will cushion the blow of having your home invaded, but, whatever the case, I would like to inform you of the following: to me, your house is nothing but a station on the way, a door from one world to another. All I have permitted myself to take is a picture of you with a young woman who, I happen to know, is not your wife. Consider it a down payment on a friendship that may one day bloom. And so I might set your heart at ease, be certain that the picture will occupy the most prominent place on the wall of my modest home, as though it depicted my own brother.

Accept my thanks and appreciation for your understanding, which I regard as an unavoidable necessity.

Your devoted servant,
Mustafa Ismail

Anwar al-Waraqi lifted his eyes from the page. He stayed staring at me, and I didn't care for it. I don't believe in what they call the language of the eyes—what was said on the subject I had always considered misguided hyperbole. Nevertheless, I held firm; if this was a test, I wouldn't turn tail. I tried amplifying my inner thoughts and transmitting them through my gaze:

You're a fool.

And you're full of it.

He broke off eye contact to confirm—as though he were a real publisher and not a mere printer—that this beginning left him unimpressed.

"Doesn't work," he said. "The flights of fancy don't fit with the real story."

Anger at what I took to be an insult was tempered by a suspicion that he might be right. I had been led on, bewitched by the possibility that such sorcery could be real. Even so, Mustafa's first rule had to be defended:

You are always right. You are sacred. You must believe this before making your move, the vital first step to making your miracle a reality. Within us all, alongside what might be described as the fleetingly mortal, is something more elevated, and to lay your hands on this thing entails being transported to a higher plane than those around you.

So affecting was the idea that my voice grew fervent, silencing the voice of reason, of doubt.

"I didn't believe the Lotus House existed," I said, "and al-Adl strengthened my doubts—he had no time for wonders and marvels. He put it down to Mustafa losing his grip on reality, to him confusing fact and fantasy. He would gloatingly declare that Mustafa's mind couldn't cope with the perversity of his thoughts. He asked me to look into his claims and redraw that missing boundary line, which is why he never bothered looking for Amgad al-Douqli. However, I believed that the truth of Mustafa's tale, its entire value, rested on al-Douqli and his hideout in the heart of the desert—it was the key to the man—and so I began my private quest to locate it."

"And?"

We were in a Chinese restaurant in Cairo's Heliopolis district, empty but for us. It was a boast of al-Waraqi's that he knew somewhere to go on every street in Heliopolis. He was talking of how his father had had the opportunity to upgrade his business activities and the lives of his children. He'd been offered a printing press for a trifling sum in the Seventies, but hadn't wanted to leave Shubra.

"Shubra's the sea and I'm a fish," he had said. "I could never leave."

Al-Waraqi never tired of sighing over the chance let slip.

"I could have been something else altogether, God forgive him. A fish! What a metaphor, I ask you. . . . The Abdel-Nasser generation drove him out of his senses."

"Topographically speaking, you'd have trouble comparing Shubra to the sea. Maybe you've noticed how its streets all run south to north. I mean, it's more accurate to compare it to a river."

He knocked back what was left in his wine glass and rode roughshod over what I'd said, as though he hadn't heard, ordering another bottle from the young waiter leaning over him.

The rice: lost in its own dazzling whiteness.

"They steam it. Very healthy."

Given the way he gobbled it down, 'healthy' seemed like a stretch. His presence was at odds with everything about the restaurant, down to the smallest detail: the staff with their contrived air of politeness, the pair of scrupulously carved red dragons, the color scheme of vivid but inoffensive crimson and yellow, the soft music pitched for murmuring patrons. I was suddenly struck by revulsion at what he stood for, his hopes and dreams of social elevation. I still hadn't learned to read a letter before opening it. As Ustaz Fakhri had once advised me, justifying his driving a café regular from his chair:

"Never expect good things from a man whose smile never leaves his lips."

An odd reason to commit an unkindness against someone who seemed civil enough, but seated with al-Waraqi I longed to be able to love and hate based on motives like these. I waited for Dutch courage to come, but wine is the same as masturbation: the illusion of ecstasy, then the letdown.

Even going out into the desert with Amgad al-Douqli and his driver, my doubts accompanied me. The Saqqara pyramid was the last thing I could make out. After that, it was all desert with no landmarks to tell one part from the next. Yet the dark-skinned driver, his master's equal in decrepitude, drove the powerful, fitted-out car with the self-confident prescience of Zarqa, blue-eyed sibyl of ancient Nejd, and did not give in to my attempts to draw him out of his silence. He slid in a cassette at al-Douqli's request, a ponderous symphony by Haydn with no choral parts. It was among the most beautiful pieces the Santa Cecilia Orchestra had ever played, he said, and I was lucky: his son had sent it to him just yesterday from England, where he lived. Enkland—he pronounced it as the Arabs did, with the 'k,' and made it sound like a country he had been the first to discover. The melancholy music and the vast tan expanse around us woke within me an obscure fear. Maybe I was getting involved in something I lacked the ability to deal with. What if he was Mustafa's partner, and the Lotus House a warehouse for their ill-gotten gains and a tomb for the curious?

Eyes closed, he nodded his head faintly in time. He appeared to have nothing to do with crime, but my work had taught me that those who seem furthest from it are often the closest. Mustafa again:

The one you discount is precisely the one you're after.

If he decided to murder me, then nobody would find out what had become of me, and who would care? Or notice? Huda might have tried if I'd shown her a little love, but her limited intelligence would make her of no use. Her search would stop at the little gang in the café, who'd persuade her that each of us has a journey that he or she must make.

I distracted myself from the fear by indulging my despair at a loneliness more profound than that of Fakhri. His choices in life (though I mocked them) had at least, I now decided, been made of his own free will, and were not guided by the will of others as mine were.

Most of what Mustafa had said was true. From afar, the flower appeared vast and golden, the sunlight reflecting off its petals and burning like a shard of fire. A lair for indulging lusts or the symbol of some secret cult. Having opened the iron gate for us and let the massive chain drop with a clang, the driver returned to the vehicle. Al-Douqli ordered him to stay there, saying that we wouldn't be long—an order that inflamed my curiosity.

We had to duck to pass through a little door which was initially impossible to make out. Al-Douqli let me enter first so that I could help him through. To conceive of a place like this, set out here in the lifeless wastes, would have been impossible. Bewitched by the sight, my mind drifted and I failed to notice the crutch held out for me to grasp. Al-Douqli was forced to shout, poor fellow. We wandered about for a few minutes while he explained to me about the machine that managed the irrigation: pipes, reaching out underground to a subterranean reservoir, supplied the plants with the water they required at prescribed times. It was a system set up to run for years without need of human intervention.

"The only problem is that it's going to turn into a jungle."

And in something phrased close to an apology, as he clipped the leaves of plants that had spilled over the lip of their planter and onto the ground, he added, "The whole thing's starting to wear me down."

Did the house close up on itself at sunset and reopen in the morning? Were there glowing larvae? He laughed for a long time when I asked him, but gave no answer, leading me to believe that at night some miracle took place which no one but Mustafa had seen.

Anwar al-Waraqi tipped what was left of the wine into our glasses, moving the bottle back and forth between them in an attempt to serve us equal measures. He showed excessive interest in the final drop, which stubbornly refused to fall into his glass. He didn't want what he was about to say to come across as an order.

"No getting around it, things happen in real life that are hard to believe. Just days ago, I saw a djinn leaving a girl's body. I don't mean the usual cliché, that she started speaking in tongues—I mean exactly what I say: after the sheikh had held negotiations to convince the demon to set her free, her body lurched upright and out stepped this weird figure. Just like us, but somehow see-through."

He laughed.

"The spitting image of your friend Fakhri. An extraordinary resemblance! So similar that I thought the fellow who sits with us at the café must be a djinn himself. No way could that be a man. You won't believe me, but at the same time you must understand that people no longer believe in fiction and they don't value it. Aren't you literary types always saying that reality's now stranger than fiction? So make do with reality. All I ask is that you amend the introduction so it's in keeping with what people expect from a book like this. After that, you write what you want."

Getting the timing right is the most important step in the whole operation. The plan can be perfect, the victim ideal, and then the timing ruins everything.

Though the issue of timing can never be inflexible, there are rules on which one can base one's calculations, at least most of the time.

The best time during the working week: between ten a.m. and twelve noon (when attendance for public and private employment is at its height).

The best season: winter.

The best day: Friday in summer.

Mustafa Ismail
The Book of Safety

6

"Talia."

With a conviction that carried her over the incongruity between her unconventional name and her appearance, she introduced herself to us.

Since she'd first rung Dmitri's bell, I'd been sure that we would meet again—and not a chance encounter, not a fleeting glance and a greeting. But she had gone about it the wrong way. She should have followed me, so as not to waste weeks on a journey whose final destination had lain only ten minutes away. Yet her tardiness in joining us didn't detract from her achievement. She had the right to list her name as the first woman to penetrate this male world, beating every feminist group to it and thereby being the paragon they could boast of. What *did* cast doubt on Talia's achievement, however, was that it might not have been an entirely solitary effort. I draw attention to this somewhat reluctantly, since I am not the type to deny people their accomplishments based on unsubstantiated rumor. But anyway, even supposing she *was* Ashraf al-Suweifi's lover, does that mean we only accepted her as a favor to him? Certainly not. What kind of people would we be if that were the case?

Ustaz Fakhri waited for one of those moments when she was watching us, unable to turn her face quickly enough to the street (which she did whenever one of us took notice of her):

"Please join us."

She thanked him with a slight nod of the head, failing to appreciate the sheer scale of the concession he had made with such an invitation. His vanity and pride knew no bounds, and he was no lover of womankind to put the status quo at risk for the sake of a female who was more girl than grown adult. Even so, he would subsequently prove her champion, defending her rights before the waiter:

"It doesn't matter whether she drinks it or not, Sayyid, she's free to do as she pleases!"

In the normal course of events, an argument to determine the fate of a new customer was unavoidable. As a member of the inner circle here, there was no need to go to the trouble of ordering. Your drink would come minutes after your arrival, as though you were some creaking aristocrat in a gentleman's club, whose every habit the barman knew like the back of his hand. But of course you were no aristocrat, and this was no gentleman's club. That understood, and so long as you were here, you were expected to show keen awareness that all the money in the world did not give you the right to impose your own rhythm.

"Just make up your mind what you want to drink and give us a break."

With such unmistakable hostility had the waiter addressed the dapper fellow who'd walked in the week before and failed to accommodate himself to the system, no sooner finishing one drink than his voice would be raised for another, switching his orders so that Amm Sayyid was quite unable to guess what his next one would be. The customer, paralyzed by shock and incapable of answering, had sought refuge with the owner, buried in his papers. But what had he expected, interrupting al-Suweifi as he pursued his historic mission?

"See, your worship's voice is far louder than it need be. . . ."

Al-Suweifi, burning to get back to what he was reading, had spoken coldly, and before the poor customer could get a word in, the matter had been settled: "This clearly isn't the place for you."

Contrary to what the customer might have thought, al-Suweifi hadn't set out to humiliate him; he had simply been conveying the decision of the café, which possessed a will of its own when it came to selection and rejection. And this fellow who cared so about his clothes—this failed customer—was a mere mortal.

Or such was the judgment of Ustaz Fakhri, who'd seized the chance to turn a barb against Anwar al-Waraqi:

"Dressing well is just a trick idiots employ to conceal their lack of comprehension."

Al-Waraqi might well have been an idiot, but he was at least possessed of a great self-confidence that allowed him to shrug off Fakhri's pompous declarations delivered as though he were apprised of the single immutable principle from which all others flow: the prime law, long forgotten. With a theatrical gesture, he'd brushed down his Versace jacket with his fingertips.

"To every action, a reaction, my friend. . . . We're governed by the laws of physics."

He was right, for the customer, denied the mercy of madness, had considered what had happened a humiliation. Speechless, he had withdrawn, but his plans for revenge had smoldered at leisure. Many subsequent incidents connected him with the stone that smashed the pane of glass and let the barbarians in.

There were many more like him who tried to join our ranks, seeking the honor of becoming a member of the Café of Lunatics, as it was known in Shubra. They were the mentally unstable who, still bound to normal people by a faint thread of sanity, still cherished their dignity. Each brought his own madness, his own rhythm, heedless of the difficulties ahead. Most were unable to keep time with the complex symphony here. They would stay as long as they wanted and, although things didn't run as usual while they were around, we wouldn't turn them away. The betting would start as soon as one of them appeared. How long he'd stay, how he'd behave, and—the big question—how he'd cope with Sayyid's diverse range of taunts, a preliminary test eagerly anticipated by the regulars because it gave the first clue to the newcomer's character.

Talia, we made an exception for. We exempted her from the test and supported her in her encounter with Sayyid, who, though he doubtless felt betrayed, could do nothing but surrender to circumstance. He was complicit enough himself to know that "laws are made to be broken."

Was it pity? Perhaps, for her face wore an expression of confusion and suffering only emphasized by her unbroken silence—a dumb canvas that refused to allow visitors to contemplate it at leisure. But we never could have accepted her like that; she had to be placed in some context, and the cup of tea came to bind her to our circle.

If she really was al-Suweifi's lover, then he would be facing fierce competition. He needed to cut down on the newspapers and keep an eye on Anwar al-Waraqi's behavior. Loud and obnoxious it might be, but some women like their cockerels with ruffled plumage, and al-Waraqi spared no effort, fluffing up everything he had. He evinced excessive eagerness in defending her right to hang on to her teacup as long as she wanted. He did not hide his masculinity or his masculine desires under a bushel, and she took note of his intentions.

For the year she came, this habit of hers never altered—having made firm friends with everyone, she would move from place to place, her teacup with its never-diminishing contents accompanying her like a talisman. We did not ask her for any explanations, for her real name, or where she'd come from, or the reason she was so attached to those dresses covered with flowers—in all these things, she offered us justifications for her existence. Little was said, and the margin for speculation was wide, and if she wasn't different then what was the point of accepting her? Particularly as she was a woman (or woman-like, to be precise). Yet information does leak out, borne by the breeze to shape an outline of every individual that is not necessarily the reality.

She worked in a sweetshop in Shubra Street, and had a mysterious relationship with Dmitri, the old Greek who owned the Sappho bookshop. His neighbors had been taken aback to witness him leaving his store, bringing the self-imposed isolation of years to an end, walking ponderously along in the company of a young woman who resembled a boy. They'd never seen her before, and their curiosity was insatiable. To their questions, he indifferently replied that she was from Kafr al-Sheikh and had recently moved to Cairo, thereafter ignoring them as he related to her the history of the land on which they both stood. She, meanwhile, was completely captivated by his exposition, and paid attention neither to those who spoke to her nor to the neighbors' attempts to ferret out information during their little sightseeing expedition.

"Shubra, Talia, was originally called Elephant Island, a little piece of land in the Nile, and Muhammad Ali leveled it and turned it into a thoroughfare."

A field trip: once she'd gleaned the basic facts from his photographs and rare books. And since Shubra was an island that had grown from nothing, it was, as he said, mixing myth with reality: "Land borne up on the hands of djinn, which we have overburdened, and soon they shall set it down to become once again just an island with a spit like an elephant's trunk."

What Dmitri said was true, perhaps. Who could say for sure? Shubra is a district of marvels, and there was no greater evidence for this than his rambles in Talia's company, beginning each afternoon and becoming nothing more nor less than an integral part of the neighborhood's day.

The tour over, he would return to his bookshop to prepare for the next place they would visit, while she would come to the café to spend an hour or more until her friends arrived: the girls she roomed with nearby. She couldn't bear to be alone. Or so she said, though she spent most of her time that way, even when she sat with us: distant and out of reach, no matter how much she spoke or joined in. Yet for all that, her effect, her presence, was the most deeply felt.

Things came to her without her asking. She took my place at Ustaz Fakhri's side without making any kind of effort—with an ease that left me doubting my relationship with the man who, for a time, I'd regarded as my mentor. Indeed, I began to seriously question the worth of his principles, which now quivered beneath the hammer blows of desire and lust. Did he crave her because she looked like a young boy, or did he view her as the protégée most fitting to receive his legacy? Contrary to habit, his explanations were given with none of the usual signs of disgust or vexation:

"I cannot advise you to do better than use the Philosophical Defense, a form of defense that can be deployed against both experienced players and beginners alike. Complex and straightforward at one and the same time, I mean. The novice can use it to answer threats without having to consider his opponent's long-term plans, and won't have to plan more than a couple of moves ahead. In one masterful game, the Cuban champion Capablanca found himself in an extremely tricky position, and should by rights have conceded—but he resorted to the Philosophical Defense, exploited it with great skill, and was able to obtain a draw that had the flavor of a victory. Let me show you what he did. . . ."

Was she so very seductive, or just the only representative of her sex in a café no woman had entered since the day it was founded? I found myself competing, comparing the reception he accorded me with the one he gave her. How was I supposed to endure his coldness? If it hadn't been for Dmitri and his bookshop, I would never have discovered the things Fakhri was now telling her, without her having made the slightest effort. On the contrary, he was trying to keep it simple so she wouldn't grow tired of him.

I sat beside him. He paid no attention to me, but nor did he object, absorbed as he was in a five-minute match. After every move, a hand would shift of its own accord and stop its player's clock to set the clock of their opponent spontaneously tick-tocking. No time to think. The game? To outfox time. And Fakhri dealt skillfully with time. In my estimation, he was the best. I'm no professional, but the board yields up its secrets to anyone who inspects it carefully from the sidelines.

They shook hands, and he turned to me with hostility.

"All well?"

It was winter, but not so cold that it required the wearing of such a heavy overcoat. All his clothes were the same kind of odd. Most were wool or cotton, purchased during his lone trip to the Soviet Union, and he cared for them as he cared for his life, washing them himself and storing them in individual wrappers (not hanging them up, as that would make them like hanged men, dragged down toward death by the weight of their bodies). For all that time treated them more mercifully, they were still subject to the same laws as those who wore them—destined to fall apart, for which reason it was better to lay them out. More importantly, he kept his weight steady so they would fit him his whole life long, and then, in accordance with his will, accompany him to the grave.

"Just so you know," he would say: "the Russians make things to last forever. All you have to do is work out the proper way to look after them. If you're one of those consumerists, you'll never get it."

He was the only one to bear the title 'Ustaz,' and the moment you joined his little gang in the café you would become his pupil. No experience or knowledge was sufficient to raise you a peg higher than this. Anything anyone else might think? "Heard it before."

71

All human progress was merely the reproduction of what he'd learned himself in a different form. The relationship governing master and pupil would inevitably stop your tongue should you catch him attributing your stories to himself, glossing over what you'd failed to realize were marginal details which distorted meaning and interrupted the flow.

Talia talked, and he listened. Shamelessly, she ripped off Dmitri. Years of acquaintanceship meant that I had his lines by heart, could tell them the moment I heard them, even when the person parroting them possessed Talia's astonishing powers of assimilation. Like him, she would start with an obscure and mysterious piece of information, as though she now shared with him the task of overseeing the trove where the world's secrets were stored.

"Can Tusun Pasha really have killed himself in his palace?"

At the mention of the royal family, Fakhri pricked up his ears. The famous frown departed his brow, and the pair of them came together to try to answer her question (likewise stolen from Dmitri): how had the decline come about? I listened to details that I'd heard dozens of times before in Sappho: how Shubra was first a resort for the cream of society, then a pleasant residential neighborhood set amid verdant groves, then a refuge for respectable officials, before the hordes had come. The only difference, that I didn't hear Dmitri's traditional conclusion to his tale:

"Extraordinary what's become of you lot!"

That 'you lot' a distancing, a denial that he had anything to do with the decline. He was nothing more than an observer, come from Greece to document the deliberate destruction we had visited on an entire culture.

Talia watched the street and its people through the café's window, seeking after an answer to Dmitri's question—or for something simpler. Which of the two men around whom her life revolved would she choose? Al-Waraqi, ceaselessly flattering and engaging, or al-Suweifi, who went on pretending that she wasn't there, though everyone knew about their connection? We treated it as incontrovertible fact. They never spoke, but there was some covert communication taking place without a doubt—it could be guessed at from the way he ignored her and she avoided him.

Based on statistics compiled by one of our branch associations, we concluded that Fridays in wintertime were not popular days on which to work.

The figures showed that in 95 percent of homes, the owners were present during this period, whereas for the same day in summer the results were completely different, with 80 percent of homes unoccupied.

Mustafa Ismail
The Book of Safety

7

"WHEN I DISAPPEAR, YOU COME for me."

The second sentence Talia had heard Ashraf al-Suweifi deliver in the short span of their acquaintanceship, and confirmation of the conclusion she'd come to when they met: that her liking him did not mean they had anything in common, quite the opposite—it was the 'liking' that would ruin the relationship.

Her upbringing had been more Sufi than anything else. From a young age, she'd learned not to take what she wanted till she could do without it; nor was poverty the reason for this. Her family was among the few well-off households in her village, but neither she, her siblings, nor her father were permitted to enjoy what was given them, because it was not theirs: the things of this earth belong to no man, and he who accepts them as such bears a curse. The earth and all that is upon it is sinful, and to know this is to flee from it. This, according to Talia's mother, who, until her marriage, would travel from village to village with her father, following the festival of Sheikh al-Desouqi (to whose order her father belonged) and, dazzled by the green banners, chanting in time with the praise singers: "I am the Lodestar, / Timelord to every school and creed. / I am the Master, the Testament, the Sheikh of Truth."

Talia's mother would sit in the zikr with the men, a young girl who—blessed by the saint—never wearied or wept. A young girl overcome by the chaste Presence. And no man objected to her being there, even once she had left childhood behind and her body began to display its difference. Her sex meant nothing to her. She disavowed it, was ashamed of it— she erased her breasts by binding them cruelly with a length of cloth. This they saw, and treated her as a brother in the Way and in Love, holding dear the fact that her feet had cracked and split as she strove after their sheikh. And all the while whispering to one another that her being here this way wasn't proper, but without a word from their leader ordering her to leave, they didn't dare go further.

But even Sufis marry and breed, and Talia's mother pursued the Calling no further than most, stepping from the Way to rest and water her mortal frame. She never forsook what she had learned and experienced, however, and held fast to the creeds she'd learned from her sheikh: first and foremost that those who thirst for the world shall never be quenched, a principle that led her to treat herself and her family most severely and austerely.

As a child, Talia forgot her real name and would walk for hours juggling her flights of imagination with reality, grew accustomed both to wanting things and to hearing from her mother the single refrain on which the life of every Sufi was based: "Every time you want something, do you buy it?"

Talia would persist, but, when she got her hands on it, the shimmer that had seduced her would depart the coveted object. She would turn it in her hands, searching for what had made her desire it so.

Al-Suweifi imagined that he was master and commander, He Who Is Obeyed. The first sentence he spoke had had this effect on her. She'd been standing outside the shop where she worked, mulling over whether or not she wanted to stay on in her job: how long she would sell sweets, had she left behind everything she knew for *this*? When, possibly in answer to these questions, he had suddenly materialized before her with his blond hair and similarly blond beard, radiant as the ice cream sandwiches she assembled in the shop. And when he'd said, boldly and spontaneously, "All right, sweetie? Waiting for someone?" she had struggled not to laugh from sheer happiness.

Despite being careful to maintain secrecy, his proclivities were well known, and his shock had been very great when Talia later carelessly broached the topic of his adventures—of the women he went with, which of them had kept him company for a while, and which had walked out on him? He felt embarrassed that his mother, and father, and relatives, and the inhabitants of the two apartments on the top floor—and who knew how many other neighbors on his street?—were up on all his secrets. A shame which forced him to consider that he might have been a fool and not known it; and if he hadn't been, with all those plans and stratagems so artfully devised, then what *was* foolishness?

Still, precautionary measures had to be rigorously adhered to. The basic rule was to leave the quarry a suitable distance from the apartment, having first described it to her in detail: "It's an old building with a carved head of Nefertiti over the entrance. Next door is Dapper Shoes, and the Sappho bookshop's across the street."

The rest he could leave to the crowds, provided by the building's location along a main road. He maintained the social standing of a rich family respected by its neighbors, but it was the hidden side of such plans that drew attention. To the ones he chose he left the freedom of choice: to decide whether they wanted what he was offering or not. This left him in a stronger position when it came to the negotiations. Usually, he fixed on a price the moment he saw them. The first words they spoke determined how long they'd spend in his apartment. Were they worth it? The deciding factor here was whether he felt any misgivings or anxiety when he left them alone in the house. He couldn't stand feeling like that. He'd experienced it with one girl—he had been nervous the whole time he was at the café, and for no tangible reason. She had seemed perfectly innocent. But a sense of impending catastrophe had nagged at him, and at last he'd heeded it, to find that she had indeed departed, along with his most valuable possession: the twin cassette deck—the thing of myth, the latest thing on the market, bought just weeks before. Thereafter he never dared doubt his instincts, and never gave in, no matter how great the temptation. Some of them, with their female charms and capacity for giving pleasure, would be worth keeping around for months, but, as he was wont to say when speaking of his experiences with women, "Without trust, it's like sleeping with a snake. You never know when you might be betrayed."

Most of the time, the hunt was easy. All he had to do was draw up to the prey, flaunting the European skin he'd exploited from childhood—a vanity implanted by his mother over the course of hundreds of stories about her origins, and one he used in order to extend his authority over the victim so that she would accept what he offered with greater gratitude. Confronted by his folder of lecture notes, the scale ruler, and the assistance he offered to help them find work, none put up much resistance, and would end up in the apartment set aside for him in his father's building. Most spent no more than a few hours. Most likely they were no strangers to this sort of thing. Very few of those who stayed in the apartment for days at a time took seriously his warnings to remain quiet and not go outside.

With Talia, though, it was different, for all that she didn't seem worth the candle. He'd even walked straight past her after giving her the fleeting glance she'd failed to notice— though that wasn't why he went back; his confidence in his abilities wasn't easily shaken. No, he just wanted to get a closer look: the height of her, the solid body. Something out of the ordinary, as it seemed to him.

She replied spontaneously and artlessly:

"Trying to make up my mind if I should stay on in my job."

"Shouldn't need all that thought."

His dismissiveness provoked her, as it would whenever they spoke, but the provocation was a trap of whose workings she was wholly ignorant.

Time ticked by, the man before her waiting for any response aside from the piercing stare. Finally, she said, "What's that supposed to mean?"

That hadn't been the answer she'd wanted to give. She could have matched his tone, if not been more aggressive still, but her issue was an inability to convert what was in her head into sentences fit for bandying.

She would walk for around ten minutes before emerging from the narrow lane where she lived. It was calm and still, somehow reassuring, as though she were still in her village—unlike the streets that lay before her now, their buildings clumped together, the street's dust that turned to mud in winter, and nothing to break the spell but the crude advances of the young men who were yet to grow used to her presence and refused to treat her as a neighbor. Some of the overtures seemed like insults, shaping her relationship with the place and its people: "A bone that quarreled with its flesh!"

Petty irritants that would blend with the roar from Shubra Street, her trepidation growing till she resolved, as she did daily, to gather up what little she owned and go home. But her next step would take her away from such thoughts. Curiosity was stronger than fear. The desire to see. Her family home stood for silence and emptiness, while fear (though she loathed it) was adventure and sensations she'd never dreamed of.

On the street corner facing her was a building whose vast, grimy sign proclaimed "North Cairo Educational Department." She would stand before it like someone who'd come down to the sea and was preparing to dive in. Dozens of people entered and exited, all with their heads bowed and seemingly weighed down with cares, plodding past a woman who carpeted the sidewalk with wares that had nothing in common: paper tissues, pliers, glasses, plastic plates, halwa, combs. The woman would lean against the wall of the building, motionless, as though carved from it. Talia had sworn by the tomb of her mother's master, Sheikh al-Desouqi, that whatever happened she would never end up like this woman, but a terror would grip her as she wondered just how she might avoid that fate. It was during just one such moment that al-Suweifi had materialized before her with his pale European face, like a message from the heavens.

It was just as she'd dreamed it: the chance encounter. He was carrying a folder and a scale ruler, his blond hair and beard alerting anyone who might have missed his skin color.

Later, Talia would hear the whole story from his mother, Ilham al-Said: about her Turkish roots, and the 'lousy luck' that landed her with a peasant from the common herd. Petite and reckless, the fashion of her day had seen the classes mingle, but that fashion had gone up in smoke and the facts remained: the robustly olive skin that her daughter inherited had severed all remaining links with Ilham's family. However, before she could die, heartsore and grief-stricken, she had been blessed with a son (the proof of her elevated standing) who would carry her story forward, that it might not be lost as her life had been amid peasant customs that permitted neither dance parties nor cocktails.

The 'Madam,' as Talia called her, spoke of her son with a fervor that overstepped the bounds of motherhood, from which the young woman could tell that the mother— so down-to-earth and capable, single-handedly managing her domestic affairs—lived, when alone with herself, in another world, as though by an act of will she was able to move between rationality and madness. Only the maids were allowed to share their mistress's delusions. Her son was her sweetheart, and a descendant of great men, and Talia the poor serving girl bedded by a young buck notorious for his tendencies. Ilham reassured her that she'd find her a good husband. The so-called serving girl found herself beguiled by this histrionic gush, and overlooked the insult. She did her best to come up with a performance to fit Ilham's assumptions, but left faced with the older woman's musings on what she didn't know, on the scenes she struggled to visualize, she fell short:

Where do you meet? Does he steal into the kitchen where you sleep? But that's beneath him. . . . Does he invite you into his room? Take you to his love nest? What does he give you in return? How does he look naked? His performance—rough or tender? And after he's finished? Does he immediately roll away and smoke, or does he stay in your arms? Does he mention me?

The mother's delusions, confusing her son with a former lover, alerted Talia to the place she occupied in this world: a maid. She wasn't a maid, but the realization made her to understand that she must change her behavior to fit her urban name, rid herself of the fear the city triggered in her, the guileless dress, the thick hair left untended—everything that placed her in the frame. She decided to keep the flower-covered dresses, though, spurning a change that would be no more than superficial, and in exchange she opened her senses to the city and trained herself to hide her fear, a first step toward self-confidence.

From the first word al-Suweifi uttered, she had decided to agree, hoping that it wouldn't begin and end at her body. She would give him what he wanted, but not right away, not before he'd tired of asking, not before she'd repeated in his earshot, time and time again, "Every time you want something, do you fuck it?" And when he got hold of her, he would turn her in his hands, searching for what it was that made him pursue her.

She wanted him to have the opportunity to try to convince her, but it wasn't to be. He seemed to be enjoying himself, and he wouldn't be completely happy unless she was out of bounds, making his quarry all the more valuable in his eyes. Were all men this simple? Ashraf al-Suweifi was neither the first nor the last to have persuaded her it might be so; after him came al-Waraqi, and prior to them both, her father, a simpleton when compared to her mother's wisdom.

When al-Suweifi had started to repeat the building's description so that she would remember it, she'd stopped him with a wave of her hand.

"I've got it. No problem."

She memorized the map on the spot. There were places she had been without visiting them. Mysteries. Revelations and blessings from a sheikh she didn't believe in, but who had chosen her. She exploited her innate talent for determining the next step, following after whatever found an echo in her own soul. Her departure from home had been based on a message, and from that day forward the threads had been leading one to another. She had been spared the choice. A prophet would come, bearing a sentence in which lay a command— commanded by which, she would set out, and the path would open up before her.

Her childhood obsession with departure formed the backbone of late-night discussions. No one could recall how it had started, who'd taught her the terminology of travel; it wasn't her mother's tales, in any case, for *she* would never speak of such things in case they provoked a charge of boastfulness. Indeed, she had never rushed to show appreciation or admiration for anything, not even her children, whose upbringing followed the well-attested approach of inculcating awe and terror of their elders so that they might receive their instructions all the easier.

Talia, who at that time had a traditional name, had grown—and the more she grew, the more she resembled her mother. She loved to sit alone. Her womanliness was late in arriving. She was exercised by the thought of what lay beyond her village, often repeating that she was going to go 'there.' It was only later that people realized that they had helped to fix the idea in her head by suggesting various destinations; only later that they understood the consequences of taking pleasure in a child's imagination. They promptly stopped.

Aged twelve, she left home and walked the tar road that linked the villages. Hours passed before her absence was noticed, and yet more hours were spent searching around the walls of Tell al-Faraeen—the Hill of Pharaohs—carrying lanterns, shouting her name, more or less convinced that her blood was at that instant watering that cursed ground. In the end, urged on by her mother, they set out for the highway. It was hard to believe she had covered such a distance on her two skinny legs. She had no answers for them, beyond a tale of the spectral voice she'd trailed after like a sleepwalker.

Al-Suweifi took her hand as she lifted her leg over the low metal railing that ringed the building. The lechery in the look he gave her leg annoyed her. It irritated her to imagine the effort she would have to make to alter his view of her as the naïf, the easy girl. Where did she get her certainty that what they had would last that long?

Leaning on the bus stop's post, she had watched him walk off with his wide stride, trousers tight across his buttocks. She had looked away, then back again, compelled by an attraction that would become, from that moment on, a hobby, her riposte to sexual harassment.

Ashamed, she thought of her underwear. She hadn't the time or space—or the lack of worries—that she needed to look after them, and the freedom she'd dreamed of was clearly a mirage. Nothing changed except the faces, which never gave one a chance to settle down. She couldn't stand facing the wanton window display to inspect the dress: translucent nylon with three precisely placed rosettes and nothing else. She wanted to see it on her body, but she didn't buy it. Where would she wear it? Around the girls she roomed with? They didn't accept her as it was. The neighbors were the same. They treated her like an enemy, and felt that her long silences were directed against them. And so a snatched glance when circumstances permitted would have to do, every morning and evening increasing her store of details, careful not to draw close enough to the display to excite the suspicions of the passersby. What kind of girl would buy something so immodest? A few seconds were all she needed to imprint it on her mind, from where it would come back to her each time she closed her eyes. She still wore what her mother had habituated her to, clothes closer to garments for boys. Many a time she'd gotten mixed up and dressed in items belonging to her brothers. Aside from the folded triangular flap in front—left open for them, stitched shut for her—there was no noticeable difference: the same heavy cloth, the same cheap white yellowed by use.

Two years after their first meeting and days before their marriage, she would decide to give him part of what he wanted, and return to the clothes in which he'd first seen her, including the rarely worn cheap panties. And when she did, his lust—for what she was ashamed of, for the buttocks clad in boys' clothes—would be ungovernable, and she would only later understand that what he'd been mumbling had come from al-Waraqi, from whose example she would learn that sex was not the simple activity she'd imagined. She would come to understand just what an unmapped jungle she'd been ignorant of, and that she would reap the benefit when she behaved in keeping with what she'd been given: the body of a boy, brimful of girl.

Al-Suweifi had reached the point where she could no longer make him out, which was the moment she'd have to move.

"When I disappear, you come for me," he had said.

But she stayed where she was, motionless like the stern-faced woman beside her, two carvings on the wall. What decided her was the desire to see him again, to feel that confidence with which he conducted himself, and see the theatrical, mocking smile he brought with him.

Soon, she stood outside the promised building, inspecting Nefertiti's bust. She couldn't be sure that this was the one who had devoured the children from her village, but as far as she was concerned anything to do with the pharaohs was an unmitigated evil—and because of this, she mistrusted what awaited her within. The kid from the shoe shop next door, leaning against the glass frontage, saw something in her that distracted him from the routine sight of passersby. Her rigidity gave him room to stare. He raised his face to the bust. For years he'd worked here and had never noticed it. He shifted his gaze back and forth between them. After a few minutes, she turned to him. Her fixity startled him. He nearly retreated into the shop.

"Does Bashmohandis Ashraf live here?"

At her question, his confidence was restored—one of al-Suweifi's women and not, say, a witch. But she was younger and more innocent than the usual. Suitable for a sweetheart. He became disgruntled at al-Suweifi—soon there wouldn't be a girl in the country that he hadn't brought home! Who'd be left for him?

"Al-Suweifi or his mother?"

His tone made no secret of his irritation. The message hit home, and she was mortified.

"His mother, of course."

"Fourth floor. Both the apartments are hers."

Then, trying to draw the conversation out:

"And he's on the fifth. Apartment ten."

She withdrew rapidly, hiding her disquiet in the vast, cool lobby. Very slowly, she mounted the stairs, counting the steps. At fifty-six, she stopped. The fourth floor. Another twenty-eight would see her elevated to a quite different level: boyfriend acquired, a man she could go to when the troubles pressed in.

Thrilling to the thought of him burning in anticipation, she went back down the stairs.

The spider's-web structure includes all the benefits of large groups, such as their ability to spread, carry out operations, gather information, and rapidly dispose of their haul over a wide area, making them hard to track.

This formation also avoids the drawbacks of these large groups, which are difficult to control.

Our organization currently consists of more than ten cells, unknown to one another and in contact with myself alone via their leaders. Each cell has its own distinct objectives and tasks.

Mustafa Ismail
The Book of Safety

8

With the soul of an art lover, Mustafa Ismail examined the photograph of Sawsan al-Kashef and her lover in great detail. Their eyes, afire with booze and the sex they'd sought to commemorate. Mustafa sat slumped, nearly empty glass in hand, examining the contents of the bottle of wine beside them in the picture.

The glass in her hand was full, its base not quite steady on her bare leg, her elbow between her thighs, resting on a green pillow stitched with a great heart in garish red which hid her shame, high breasts set off by the scarf tied about her neck, and hanging down. The photo ended where the thighs bent back against her belly, at the faint black scrub. The man's thumb marked the frame's edge on the right-hand side, one's attention immediately drawn to a ring worn with bohemian disregard for formal placement, then to the small metal ring at the woman's belly button. The two objects, ring and ring, manifested a sensual symmetry that encouraged speculation about what it was the other fingers, concealed behind her body and away from the camera's spying eye, were up to.

Every picture in Sawsan's album bore on its back the date and a single word; a young woman using pictures to learn the meanings of things, to recover sensations she'd almost forgotten. This photograph was inscribed: *Delight*.

Not *Sex*. With her lover, she had been emancipated from her traditional relationship with her husband, from the captivity of customs become a noose that tightened as, each dawn, the drop's trapdoor cracked open its prescribed fraction beneath her. Eagerly, she would await the end of the morning ritual, monitoring the children as they made ready for school, seeing them off from the balcony—with a gesture that was an indivisible part of their lives: the robotic wave—waking her husband an hour after they'd left, breakfasting with him (accompanied by the brief, rote conversation), reassuring him that everything was running as it should be and that the spirit of her old rebelliousness was fading fast.

She would return to the secret album, purging herself of the dull rites that murdered her mutinous soul, free of the daunting family traditions that fettered whoever submitted, leaving no option but to believe that this was the ideal life to lead, no choice but contentment unto death. It wasn't a case of betrayal, of sullying honor, as her husband had described it when they came home to find the house burgled and her naked portrait gracing the wall. It was a turning to the principle that needs must.

In truth, it was the answer to the prospect of dull routine. The boy in the picture had made no effort to seduce her. The opposite was true: it was she who'd striven and planned, who'd shamelessly admitted to him that he was too good to let slip and, with a mockery that amazed her, her words coming out as laughter, had said, "Swear to God, your mother raised you right!"

Her husband pronounced his judgment, reciting the verse that prescribed the punishment for adultery. It seemed to her that by labeling it adultery he increased the gravity of what she'd done. That to describe it thus made it a scandal. She wished that he would choose a gentler expression when he informed their families, if only, "She slept with another man."

'Sleeping with' held the possibility of quite innocent interpretations, whereas 'adultery' and its synonyms were unambiguous and conclusive. His grandiloquence alerted her to the fact that he had no serious evidence of her adultery. Neither he nor anyone else had seen anything they could use to tarnish her reputation. That would be her defense if he spoke out: "But did you see the feather in the kohl pot?"

'Feather' was a good word for her boy, and 'kohl pot' suited her. The difference in their ages made it so: her experience, his vigor. He'd told her that straight out, and she hadn't been as upset as she should have been. She loved to take the lead, and her boy had been led astray by her approach, her tenderness concealed behind a mask, unbending as his mother's: "What are you up to, my boy? You've slept with your own mother!"

Contentment clothed her face, and her husband—manhood, honor, and pride shaken—slapped it. An attempt to obtain redress, but the slap and the blows that followed weren't enough. He contemplated killing her—came very close to stabbing her sinful flesh, but the knife, which he dashed off to fetch from the kitchen, halted halfway to her body. Destroy his own life on her account? He'd loved her once, but what he'd loved was what had driven him to hate her, a hatred magnified by her unconcealed aversion to him following the rise of religiosity in his soul. He couldn't accept her position. If he could set aside the fact that his way was the Way and the Truth, then the least she could do. . . .

But then there was "My personal freedom!"

Not enough that he didn't force her to wear the hijab, even though she was more or less the only woman he knew that didn't. The hijab was the wall against which all criticism broke and foundered. With a paternal open-mindedness, he'd accepted her strange behavior, including the ring she had put in her belly button when they'd traveled to Europe. However, and despite his belief in the values of personal liberty, he was obliged as a man to warn her.

He had tried outflanking her: "Don't we want to be together in paradise afterward?"

Anyone who turned *that* down would have to be crazy. Breathlessly he had told her of a vision he'd been granted, of the inundating happiness that stretched away in ever-flowing cascades, but then, looking around, he'd found that she wasn't there beside him.

She didn't want his paradise. His presence there beside her was enough to negate its essence. Plus, he who'd turned this earth into a hell would have no share of the blessed life to come. She was anyway astonished at the growing number of people who dreamed of paradise, the ones who neglected their lives for the sake of something that could not be guaranteed. Who could guarantee anything after death? The possibilities were many and various, and each one deserved consideration, which meant you had to live according to your convictions. Betrayal was forbidden, but then what of "The punishment is life itself."

And what of the humiliation? Just as he had treated her so basely with his stick ("The slave is beaten with a staff. For the free man, humiliation is sufficient"), so she would respond in kind; which was why, despite her tremor of fear, a feeling of strength and defiance had given her confidence when she'd found herself face to face with her naked form. She had examined the picture with him as though they were at a museum. Indeed, she had been possessed by a desire to reach and take his hand, that they might share the moment, but he was utterly motionless, leading her to think that he might faint. That's if he wasn't hit by a heart attack or paralysis; a fit end for a character like his. His conversion, she was sure, had been feigned—a creed he leaned on to shrug off his weakness before her.

The knife terrified her, as did the death that would surely be a long time in coming; he was no good at carving and jointing, and the knife hadn't been sharpened since it was bought. Would a serpent come to torment her in her tomb, as the sheikhs promised for the guilty? Her flesh crawled. She toyed with the idea of asking him to carry out the religiously prescribed punishment, a diversion to buy time. While he dug a pit and fetched the stones with which to pelt her, she might find a way out. But her intimate knowledge of the man bent over her body gave her what she needed to pull herself together: he wouldn't sacrifice his reputation as a trader, he wouldn't risk prison.

For all his enraptured talk of the comfortless lives of the first Muslims, he had become accustomed to comfortable living and he was too soft to kill. He'd fled from the offer of power his father had made to him. A follower doesn't lead. He knew himself: that was his strength. She'd gotten with him because of it. The very existence of a man who wasn't a fraud had dazzled her. She had given her blessing to his mutiny against his father and family, and his rejection of the identities that brought them wealth and power. But she hadn't realized that his choice had not been truly his; that he was being effaced by her own rebelliousness. Like all leaders, she'd been unable to turn down a devoted follower—and like them, too, had failed to attend to the fact that faith waxes and wanes, vanishes even. Hadn't taken into account what would happen when he came to, never imagining she would hear words like, "I'm not prepared to lose this world and the next just so you can have your fancy lifestyle! Who cares about a villa on the north coast? What's wrong with a nice little place in Alexandria?"

It was like she was inside some movie that had been churned out in hundreds of iterations until it was no longer a fit subject for a treatment. She tried dissuading him from selling the land he owned so cheaply, but he was determined, and she girded herself for poverty. But to her astonishment, it never happened. Some of his new friends partnered with him in a business he described as 'godly.' More astonishing still, its profits were considerable.

"Perfumes and textiles." He said no more.

The money didn't make her happy, though, for alongside it grew his attachment to the implacable religiosity that mirrored the tendencies of his partners. Driven to it by his obsessive fears of the torments awaiting bareheaded women, his two daughters donned the hijab, conforming to the habits of their friends and female relatives. He forbad her intervening to make the choice theirs. He was resolute, making it clear that her authority extended no further than herself, and that he, as head of the family, would be the one called to account at the last. And when her stubbornness grew, he gave proof of his determination with ten blows of a cane pulled from his wardrobe. A disciplinary tactic prepared in advance, which only intensified her anger. She shuddered at each blow and was sunk in humiliation and by the time he'd finished punishing her—as his business partners had advised him—what they'd had was lost. She was no longer his rebel captain, and he her devoted follower no more.

Though certain that she was in the wrong, he was sure her obstinacy would prevent her from submitting. Their only hope of getting back to how they'd been was for the roles to be reversed. And where was the harm in that? It was his turn to take charge. Hadn't he let her run the game for long enough?

The only thing that saddened her now was that their final moments would never be captured by the camera: her, stretched out on the ground, hands raised as if to block the blow, shirt riding up off her belly, exposing the ring that had so maddened him and driven him to avoid all intimacy with her after she'd refused to get rid of it under any pretext—except to help liquidate his assets. The lens would be drawn to the gleam from the knife and the ring, she was certain of it. In the picture it would seem as though a line of light ran between them, the law of lustful attraction in whose orbit all things revolved.

Rod and Circle. The title she would give to the never-to-be-taken picture.

It had been her idea to set up the camera and take the pictures. She'd scolded the young man, who had been afraid to record the occasion for posterity. It was only through the camera that she could apprehend the things that happened to her. A new photo in her album was the equivalent of many lifetimes which she could live again and again until her eyes were sated. Her notebook, meant to contain scattered words about these pictures, began: *Man was only aware of himself when he invented the camera.*

An orphan sentence in a journal fated to be incomplete, its whole purpose the pictures themselves. She would take out her box, scatter the pictures on the floor, and open the notebook. Pick up the pen. But she never wrote a thing—each picture she chose opening a door in her mind to fantasies of dreams unrealized, and she would only come to when it was time for the children to be home from school.

The subjects of her pictures changed in ways that frightened her, as though they had become different people. Even her brother, a friend back in the Seventies, had imprisoned himself in a dull job and routine existence. It was he who'd once talked to her, overawed, of Guevara, of Ho Chi Minh, of the student demonstrations in Paris, and of the dream of equality—no rich, no poor. A time of rebellion and flowerings.

The daughter who was closest to her, and the only one of them to have seen the secret album, would sometimes sit with her, giggling at the clothes and hairstyles, but she would never know how sweet the world had tasted back then. Poor girl, from an era run by fanatics; she'd never live as her mother had done. Never have young male friends beneath whose balconies she had stood and loosed the whistle she was famed for, there in the late afternoons as the women sat with their husbands on the balconies to take their tea. She almost wept whenever she saw the picture her brother had taken of her placing two fingers in her mouth, whistling to summon the friend and neighbor with whom she used to roam.

Walking through the town, driven by a desire to explore, wearing what she liked with no heed paid to where she went or who might object, trailing after the posters pasted up on the walls, the advertisements placed there by humble citizens: *Rooms for rent. Women's hairstylist: Latest fashions. Salesmen and saleswomen required. For the ambitious and those with the desire: work to suit your abilities.* Prayers for Nasser and curses on Sadat. Words of love. Others sexual. She'd lose herself in every sentence. Peer at the handwriting, the font, the materials used. To prying questions, she'd respond that she was a journalist—the job she'd always wanted. They would offer to tell her the secrets that lay behind these lines. Subsequently she read that the compulsion to strip bare was an echo of the self's desire to be discovered. A sound explanation.

She never lost her love of her hobby, but she had become more prudent after someone in a working-class district had taken her to a darkened alley to show her words carved long ago in a language the neighborhood's residents had failed to decipher. And then, as she peered at the walls in search of the promised grail, he had carefully looked around and assaulted her from behind, holding his knife to her neck to stop her screaming. She'd consented on the condition that she didn't lose her virginity. Had it been fear, or had she been infected by the madness of the crude sexual slogans and sketches?

On her instructions, her husband would take his car around the streets, her gaze fixed on the passing scenery, on the religious posters and catchphrases: *Put on the hijab before judgment comes, my devout sister! Allah uber alles! Islam is the solution!* These she'd quickly turn away from. Something about them made her tense up—she wasn't sure why, unless her husband was right when he said some devil possessed her.

He chose to listen to the Quran at high volume while they drove. Once, when she asked him not to force his preferences on others, he'd answered in a strange tone, with a defiance she wasn't used to: "I'm stronger than the one who stole your soul."

Even so, and though the idea of the devil who'd taken possession of her remained something for her to look into, she was sure that her husband's religious fervor and these writings represented the start of an era quite different from the one in which she'd been raised, resembling what had gone before in that it harbored repressed desires, but of a sort that did not tempt her: a repression that sought to trap her with it.

The problem for thieves is not the alertness of the security services. The true dilemma is the pressing desire of each individual to become a hero, to find a story that he can tell and boast of for the rest of his life, even if its most significant event is that he shouted "Thief!" at the top of his voice and joined a mob which imagined it was in some running race.

One of the fundamental issues that must be taken into account at all times is how to keep people neutral should persuading them to join up prove impossible.

Mustafa Ismail
The Book of Safety

9

"It's just that, Ustaz Khaled—if you'll permit me—don't you think that this chapter might be . . . unconnected to the original story? I mean, what does the story of Sawsan al-Kashef add here? Not that I mean to impose any particular point of view on you—quite the opposite! I think the woman's character will be appreciated by some, the intellectuals perhaps, but most readers will reject her. Let me be frank with you. I'm not religious in the traditional sense, as you can see from what we're doing now."

He raised his glass and the light trembled on its surface, corroborating his words. He fell quiet for a few moments. Silently imploring God's forgiveness most likely. His arm straightened, pushing the glass to the edge of the table and out of his line of sight, then traveled back toward him to take a piece of bread, dip it in one of the dishes, and lift it to his mouth, which devoured it in a single gulp. He was the whale, and the wretched crust was Jonah: it would face a stern test inside. He talked on, even as I had closed my ears to what he said, hoping for a change of subject.

"There's no need for me to stress how keen I am to bring the book out, but we must be realists. Religion's an international trend these days, and it deserves its chance in the sun like the others—liberty, liberalism, revolution. I don't understand what's preventing you from seeing this basic truth, dealing with it, and maybe exploiting it to get yourself a following. Please don't tell me that it restricts your freedom of thought and speech. That's just a failing of yours. You can say what you like without creating shockwaves, unless that's what you're going for, in which case things are different. Like, I haven't finished reading it yet, but my sense is that it's not going to get any better."

"God protect—"

"You reminded me of Egypt thirty years ago. I was a young man. The country was very different, just like that friend of yours says. . . . And by the way, is she a real person? Do you have that photograph? How did you get hold of it? Shouldn't it be evidence in the case file? Did you steal it from the file? Did Mustafa really put it there on purpose so her husband would see it? I didn't buy that. How could he set out to do things like that? A thief, sure, but from the stories you tell, I'd thought he was kinder."

"Al-Khidr."

"Al-Khidr? What about him? Oh no, I beg you, don't start down that path. Al-Khidr's a prophet, Ustaz, and you—who's supposed to be good with words, blessed by God with the gift of eloquence—you go around saying things like that? Comparing a thief to a prophet? Now that's a bit of a shock, I have to tell you. I've seen you go off course before, but I never expected you'd take it this far. By the way, do you believe in the existence of God? Forgive me, I don't usually question people about their religion and beliefs. That's every individual's private business. My objection isn't based on religious grounds, but what you say goes against logic and reason. And I'm not asking you out of curiosity, or because we're friends—though that also concerns me on purely practical grounds. Imagine the al-Waraqi Publishing House releasing a book which took a line like that."

Since putting the sign up over his printing shop, he had treated his 'Publishing House' as something real, frequently mentioning its name as if in this way he could grant it legitimacy and the requisite fame.

The wine had lit his fuse and he chattered on.

"We might do well off the back of the uproar it'll provoke, but I don't want that sort of money. Never forget that the Arab market no longer tolerates views like those. Incidentally, did you know that for a while I worked in Jordan as an agent for a major publisher, and it was my time there that gave me the experience to be able to tell what the market will accept and what it will reject. Answer the question. Actually, don't. I don't want an answer from you. It's your affair.

"Only, you have to promise the following: that the conclusion of the book will affirm certain truths—most importantly, that God exists. We shan't disagree over that, I don't think. Then there's what all the revealed religions tell us concerning the subject of your book: that stealing is wrong, and that the sinner shall find his punishment first in this world and then a greater torment in the next. That's a human value system, first and foremost, and only then a religious one. You won't find anyone to support you in your foolishness. If you're confused, then follow the confused and be at peace."

"Hash is the solution," I said.

The disagreements between myself and Anwar al-Waraqi over the book were never-ending. Every chapter represented a problem. Mustafa's ideas alarmed him, and the greatest crisis—as he had said repeatedly in various different ways—was my position regarding these ideas. My prejudice for them and defense of them. He was, as he put it, "genuinely keen" to bring out the book, but he did not trust that I would play the role required of me as author. There was a long tradition of writing here, and I stood foursquare against the standards it had established. To be different was vital, and important, and he quite understood the need for that, but it shouldn't come at the cost of what everybody agreed to be true.

"Ask anyone, genius or everyman—he'll tell you what I'm telling you. You're out on a limb doing this."

Al-Waraqi was simply one strain of authoritarianism. It believed what you believed, wanted what you wanted, and if it was to try to contain Mustafa Ismail's insurrection in the real world, then it would achieve this by preventing its completion on the page.

I tried to go along with the amendments he requested, enough to keep him happy and not harm the book, but his appetite for change, for deletions and additions, swelled with each concession I made, stripping the book and Mustafa's character of everything that made it distinctive. In the end, I was left with no choice but to back down from the idea of publication, or otherwise to accept the compromise he'd suggested at the outset: a foreword in the publisher's name in which he gave his own perspective on the case, along with his personal analysis of what had led to the collapse of social values and customs.

A shameful addition, but I agreed to it on condition that he not touch what I wrote. In his mind, his foreword was sufficient to balance out the views expressed in the book. I didn't care what he thought. This solution would spare me lengthy debates over every particular—and his chatter (and maybe, too, my consent) stemmed from a hunch that his foreword, his conventional words, would shield me from the consequences of what I wrote. But then, who reads the publisher's foreword in any case?

Days after consenting to this introduction, the first edition of *The Book of Safety* came on to the market accompanied by a modest advertising campaign, driven by blaring commercial taglines.

Daytime, despite its crowds and many problems, is safer than night.

Slaves to the law believe that the daytime belongs to them, while the night is for the system's apostates. Defying this assumption makes theft easier, relatively speaking, especially if you are able to master your nerves, and appear calm and confident about what you are doing. That achieved, theft appears no different from any other daytime activity.

Mustafa Ismail
The Book of Safety

10

JUST AS HE HAD GROWN used to the sting of bees and their ceaseless buzzing in his ears, Nabil al-Adl was quite content to have life start at four in the afternoon every day. It was at this time that the pain and his bad temper would leave him: at four precisely, not a minute less or more. Hard to guess if the bee stings had so altered his genes that he possessed the organizational capacities of their well-ordered kingdom, or if he had managed, somehow, to instruct his body to collude with him over those things that he believed true.

It had been around four o'clock on just such a day that he'd been looking in from the desert district of Medinat Nasr, whose features he deliberately ignored, toward Heliopolis. He had been on the point of refusing the excellent placement his father had found for him through his contacts, because it would oblige him to be in a place he thought the ugliest he'd ever seen.

If it hadn't been for the fact that he couldn't find a logical justification, he would have made his apologies, for his father, the very man who'd taught him his devotion to Heliopolis, would have regarded this degree of passionate attachment as pure madness. Nabil had considered various ways to phrase the apology to match his father's pragmatic personality. For instance:

"The problem, sir, with Medinat Nasr is that the smell of sand out there is quite hateful. It's unbearable. Unlike where we live."

But did sand have a smell in the first place? That's what his father would ask him, gravely, not mockingly, for he believed only in what was real. And not just him: the whole family placed no faith in metaphor. Truth was defined by the five senses. And Nabil was no different. But whenever he was in Medinat Nasr he could smell the sand. It came over him till he choked, till it had laid him low with chronic depression. And then on top of it all, the illness, which he cured by exposing himself to the bees and their stings.

Four p.m. on a winter's day, the sun breaking over the classical facades and prompting Nabil to examine afresh the mythic face of his desert city. He was in his car, bewitched by the buildings' power to remake their tones to match the light. Harmony, not ostentation or minimalism, was the essential quality here: a moderation, a balance between the surfaces of building, and street, and green expanse. No protuberance assailed the eye, no garish or jarring hue. The observation of thirty years had left him well informed enough to take a post as an architectural authority, should he have cared for it, but like a true lover he preferred to keep his lover's gifts—shared with no one else but the Baron—close to his chest.

Unlike everybody else, he didn't take the shortest route back home. He could get there from his place of work in no more than twenty minutes, but would add another thirty to accommodate the journey of purification that began when he passed the Baron's palace. As its turret appeared in the distance, he would feel the irritation and distaste provoked in him by Medinat Nasr start to subside, and wouldn't bother to twist around and check behind him as he slowed the car almost to a halt.

It seemed he'd earned a nickname: Madman of the Palace.

He hardly heard the horns exhorting him to drive on, wholly absorbed by the buddhas on the Cambodian dome, the elephants hunkered down on the balconies, the mythic creatures whose origins and names he'd spent his teenage years tracking down. All this he'd seen and scrutinized a thousand times, and from every different angle, but his ardor never cooled, knowing that to lose himself in love was the necessary condition for Helena's return—that she might once more materialize, calling out to him instead of to her husband, who had been too dazed by the turret's revolutions and the changing vistas whirling around him to save her from falling.

"Nabiiiiiiiiil!"

He didn't hear his name, preoccupied as he was with preparations for the pain he put himself through thrice weekly. He was sitting, bare arm stretched out atop the metal table, unable to tell if it was the metal's chill that had transferred into his body, or fear. He braced himself against the impending shudder, while the buzzing sound from within the jar could be heard to grow and gather in response to the healer's attempts to pick out a bee with his tweezers. Ten bees and ten stings, a ten-minute break between each one and the next in which to catch his breath. One hundred long minutes to endure, and hardest of all the time spent waiting for the insect in its plastic cup to realize that its only way was down, to where his flesh lay, and to sink right in.

"Nabiiiiiiiiil!"

A cry for help, but not free of the aristocratic ring that emphasized the gulf between them. Yes, he was the grandson of al-Adl the Elder, the only Egyptian to enjoy a standing in Heliopolis equal to that of the foreigners—one of the founding fathers, the man who'd helped transform the desert into Eden. All of which was fine, and good, and a source of overweening pride, but only in front of Egyptians like himself, who didn't know their history, who trusted in photographs without weighing the circumstances in which they were created.

As for Helena, he definitely couldn't deceive her, wife of the scholar of magic and misdirection. Faced with her, things returned to their original state, unenhanced: a common-and-garden Egyptian grandson with no titles to his name but the least elevated, received for services rendered, and never rising a single degree higher despite his ambitions, till it clung to him like a slur: al-Adl Effendi.

Unusually for him, he left the immediate vicinity of the palace in a hurry, crushed by her mocking laughter at his weakness. The princess and the humble laborer's son, a tale that would be repeated endlessly even when the princesses had quit their palaces, which the poor, with an eye to vengeance, had then transformed into wastelands roamed by restless spirits. But astonishingly, these tales, though fantasy, generated the very feelings they would have provoked had they been real. Nabil's relationship with Helena negotiated all the twists and turns customary in comparable cases from real life.

She had been with him from his first awareness. Not a child in all Heliopolis from whom the knowledge of Terrifying Helena and Marianne, Eater of Souls, was kept hidden. They were not afraid, as the children of other neighborhoods were, of the traditional monsters, of The Ghoul, Skinned-Leg, or The Mother of Hair. They thought them ridiculous creatures. But when they pictured Marianne starting out on their trail, their tender souls the only thing sure to bring her any peace before she turned to drag her damaged leg back to the palace's entrance hall, emerging dripping with blood from the pink, forbidden room, in search of suitable prey. . . , while the lucky boy who managed to escape her would find no less terrible a fate in store: Helena, dropping from her bedroom balcony like a bird of prey, swooping up with him, then letting him fall, shattered, on the marble floor. They were the clock's pendulum to whose tempo the lives of the upper-class neighborhood's children moved—Helena dropping down in the morning, taking with her the dawdler, too lazy to heed the school bell, and Marianne abroad at night, in search of the wakeful child, tempering her solitude with the hunt for his soul.

Romances come from nowhere, their causes and explanations undefined, their enjoyment predicated on avoiding attempts to rationalize. And anyway, Nabil's age at the time of his affair with Helena did not equip him to think with any kind of logic.

"A child of ten! Can you credit it?"

So he'd stress to his friends when giving his favored account of his virility, something he sought to assert with the fact that he'd reached maturity earlier than usual. He still calibrated present happiness against his feelings at the time: a faint tremor between his thighs, the dawning awareness that this placid companion took its own view of what he was going through—from that moment on, he was to consult it on all important decisions: a process he referred to as democracy, not lust. And how could he ignore it, when its guidance had shaped the contours of his life? It had been what had alerted him to the fact that Helena was not as frightening as his cousin had made out.

His cousin, his mother's sister's daughter, boastful of having left childhood behind, attempted to frighten a boy still in its clutches:

"As every morning, the Baron was out on his magical balcony. Beneath this balcony stood demons in chains. Their master was the Baron, and they were unable to disobey him as long as, each day before sunrise, he had seated himself on the balcony and screamed a particular word at them. At this, they would begin to move the balcony about: a single hour in which he'd circle the whole world and survey it. But one dark day, he forgot the word. He tried everything he could to remember, terrified lest the sun come up, yet it was no good: he'd forgotten. The demons had anyway grown tired of him, and when their chains were loosed they took their revenge. The first thing they did was to throw Helena from the balcony. She tried calling out to him, but he was preoccupied by his problem. She fell to the palace's tiled floor, wracked by agonies until she passed away. That done, the demons chased after her sister, Marianne . . . , and the same story has repeated itself every day since, but now it is Helena and Marianne who revenge themselves on us."

Except the cousin's aim would not be achieved. For some reason, Nabil was not frightened by the story. To the contrary, he saw, in rising to the palace's highest point and plummeting from it in the embrace of a woman (beautiful, as children see these things), an experience no less wonderful than a trip to the Merryland arcades.

His lack of fear was impossible to explain. Why hadn't he trembled at the thought that his bones might be smashed to smithereens on the floor? Why did he believe that she wouldn't just abandon him to thin air, that she would ascend with him to repeat their journey again and again? No way of knowing, now, with his childhood behind him. What was certain, however—so Nabil assured his friends—was that Helena's story was answered by a strange thrill within him, alerting him, a boy of ten, to his cousin's compact chest, her nipples pushing against her blouse. Spontaneously he reached out a finger to touch one, and the poor girl, quite ambushed, didn't recover herself till he had her pressed to his breast. Her cry rallied the mothers who had been in the kitchen where—the usual Friday routine—they were preparing food for the extended family.

The crisis passed with the collusion of the women, but the young men, strapping and proud of their manhood, were not content with silence. His cousin's brother, criticized for what had happened to his sister, planned a special revenge and lured him to one of the parks.

"They say you're all grown up, Nabil."

And before the child, so proud of his maturity, had worked out what it was his cousin had in store, his trousers had been yanked off and the mocking laughter rang out.

"Let me show you what a big boy looks like."

And he hadn't made do with showing the lad the size of his little companion—which had frightened him—but had forced him to hold it. To grip it hard.

"Your hand is soft and sweet, lover boy."

He hadn't said a word. Hadn't absorbed what was going on. What upset him was his cousin's possessing such a massive member. Size provokes resentment even before it's clear what the benefit might be. Tension from the other boys had transmitted itself to him, and one of them had asked his cousin to leave it at that before it became a scandal.

"Not till he's learned his lesson."

His hand had reached out to the buttocks being caressed by the cold air. Gripped them hard.

"Lord, the boy's a shame to waste."

And amid loud laughter, the cousin's digit wedged into his anus. A first experience of degradation.

"A finger for a finger, mommy's boy."

The sentence had stuck with him as he'd fled weeping from the park, and the pain in his backside had never been effaced, revisiting him with every inconvenience he ever encountered, and always accompanied by that sentence, its gloating echo. He'd wanted to pay a visit to a psychologist, to stretch out before him and tell him what had happened, but to be cured meant losing Helena and how could he forget her when it was she who'd taken his revenge and afforded him protection?

He had run to the palace, where, clinging to its wall like a beggar, he'd recovered his breath. He was still an innocent—let us not forget that he was a child of ten—and moreover could think of no one in his family worth summoning or asking for help; but there was that instinct which, since man first trod this earth, has directed him to turn his pleas to the heavens. And like all the great miracles in human history, Helena had descended from her balcony, had alighted on the ground, and walked upon it, with her tender face and a diaphanous gown through which he could see her body gently rocking like the jelly he loved. She had stroked his hair. Allowed him to reach out and touch her breasts, squeeze one of the nipples that jutted so proudly compared to those of his cousin. And in her embrace, his little companion had unfurled from its nest with a sense of delight he was only able to express in the words "A flower opening. . . ."

It had been added to his phrasebook. It hadn't occurred to him that opening flowers applied to women—belonged to them alone, like the pangs of pregnancy and birth, or the sensations known as motherhood. Men don't open like a flower. They soar like mountains. Like tall buildings, they tower aloft. Like swords, they stab.

Given these facts, shouldn't Nabil have become a deviant in later life? The thought bothered him. The humiliation he suffered, and his feminine response to the princess's presence, should—he knew—have rigged up an association in his mind between the form his pleasure took and certain tendencies. Except it hadn't happened. Clearly then, people can triumph over the circumstances of their upbringing; yet in so heroically overcoming the obstacles purposefully strewn in their path, they gain difference. Thus Nabil: he had prevailed over his problems. By force of will, he had defeated the societal conditions that had conspired to afflict him with homosexuality. He had emerged from the struggle a man in every sense, but with a feminine sensibility.

The day after Nabil's vigil by the palace wall, an incident had taken place that had left his cousin bedridden for a month with a double fracture in his leg. Out of nowhere, a car had loomed up in front of him, struck him, and vanished. So the family had thought, but the truth of what had happened was known only to three, named in a fairytale banned by the censor for sexual content unfit for its intended audience: *The Princess of the Palace, the Innocent Child, and the Evil Cousin.*

Helena hadn't needed Nabil to ask for revenge. From the balcony where she amused herself watching the ways of man, she had seen what had happened in the park, had wanted to intervene, but had chosen instead to wait and see the whole thing unfold. If she hadn't been so curious, then things would never have become so complicated, yet neither would what happened later, have happened. And she, to relieve herself of the whole burden, had turned to her fairytale solution, happy to find that ghosts had other options aside from frightening people—she could take possession of souls to compensate herself for the life she'd been denied.

Nabil was the first worshipper she'd purchased, and though he was inappropriately temperamental for someone in his position she granted him partial freedom for two reasons: in recognition of the fact that he had more or less volunteered to serve her; and because he was the muse of her transformation—a ghostly act of kindness that proved what she did could not possibly be described as evil. Her many devoted subjects benefited her nothing. The opposite in fact: the pleasant times she'd spend out on the balcony—feeling sorry for herself and replaying her fall, screaming to her husband the Baron to come and save her—these times grew fewer and further between, which her husband's sister took as a perfect excuse to criticize her for upsetting the palace's routine; for her devotees, like the Hebrews of old, had turned away from the message she had intended to be spiritually elevating. When she had ascended to her balcony to be alone, they took to worshipping what they imagined to be her terrible cry, but which was in fact her sister's anger at the irksome and disagreeable music to whose rhythm the worshippers would dance.

And yet, for all that her followers were irritating and trivial, the sincerity of Nabil's love compelled her forgiveness. Ever since she had flown off with his cousin and deposited him in front of the car, she had become the thing dearest to his heart. She saw her servant's love, and it made her glad. No woman could approach the standing in which he held her, her allure the standard by which he judged all women. This one might have her voice, and that one her walk, or a body similar to hers, but in none other did he encounter someone who could speak his name the way he heard it from her. She had made him into her own, personal Nabil.

This pure and childlike love! Setting aside his blasphemy, his sometimes rabid desire to bed his goddess, the only cloud on the horizon was his terror of Marianne; and, though he never saw her when he'd enter the palace, the sound of her footfall on the tiles—coming after him, to keep him away from Helena—provided a distinctive backing to the time he spent there. And as things are not, in the usual course of events, distinct and separate, so his love for Helena grew in tandem with his terror of her twin—and as the love persisted, so the terror.

Years later, his skin crawling with that of his kids as his wife told her sinister stories; and yet he never honored the pledge he'd once made to himself, that his children would not suffer (as he'd done) from the nightmares stirred by those tales that aristocratic dames excel in telling in the belief that the women alone are responsible for rectifying what their menfolk's indulgence has spoiled. Well, true, he had tried once, but the disapproval on his wife's face had been enough for him to let it slide.

The heritage of Heliopolis: one of the pillars on which their marriage was founded. Rarely do you find a man and woman set on marriage for a nobler purpose than Reham and Nabil, and they richly deserved to share a spotlight. But humanity was yet to reach the stage when it could appreciate minds quite free of the romantic fancies that produce nothing but brute satisfaction. They would mock such clichéd tales of love, agreeing that those who lived them out, those who were this way, would be better to mate in public, in the bestial style that suited them.

What brought Reham and Nabil together was more refined than love. What worth has love when placed alongside science and history? It was a gimcrack word, they believed, befitting the lower classes, who had no idea how to express what it was that bound them to their partners and so called it 'love' for convenience. More exact to say: I am attached to. Yes, that's the description that went with them, that went with their neighborhood, that was in harmony with the time-honored upbringing they'd both enjoyed and which they'd taken as a template for their lives.

Nabil al-Adl became attached to his cousin because she was the only girl in the extended family who was a match for the men when it came to memorizing the history of Heliopolis and the characters that had passed through it. Their relationship evolved in a unique fashion, through the walking tours they took as part of their project to document the neighborhood's history using the stories of its oldest inhabitants. They exchanged their first kiss when together they arrived at the connection between the spread of street cats and the legend on which the city was founded. Not a sentimental clinch, but the kiss of two lab-bound researchers who have arrived at a scientific discovery.

The old lady who'd been telling them her tale was the first to point out, slyly, "You're both so alike, like a married couple."

Their uncompleted project was the base on which they built a sensual relationship, breaking the covenant of siblinghood that normally develops between girls and boys who are raised in freely mingling households. The file grew fatter, and zeal blinded them to their lack of rigor when it came to research techniques, but they brushed aside any uncertainties with a firm agreement that fictional work was of a lower order. If not for their determination to make something of them, they would have been quite content with just listening to the oldsters' stories, in pursuit of which they'd frittered away two college summer breaks. And in the end it hadn't taken any kind of effort, for the stories were vibrant enough to ignore style, and structure, and things of that sort.

But flip the coin, and on failure's verso is success. At last they had become typecast within the family. In their individuality, they seemed weak when compared to the identities being carved out by the remainder of their cousins. One learned the guitar in imitation of Omar Khorshid, a vast portrait of whom hung in his bedroom; another traveled to Europe with his club to compete in the World Swimming Championships—coming in last but, when all was said and done, having elevated the name of his neighborhood and street in the eyes of the whole city, and drawn attention to the al-Adl family, confirming their high breeding (and thanks to him, his sister and a friend of hers secured two top-notch marriages).

Nabil and Reham, meanwhile, were bywords for inconsequentiality, enthused by what was fundamentally unenthusing: reading, chess tournaments. Nor did their elevation to one such tournament—a national tournament—improve their standing, though they played one another in the final, and took first and second places. Who would sit motionless for an hour or more to watch two people sunk in thought? It was an event that was only of wider interest after they'd come home: to check the accuracy of predictions that she would trump him.

It was precisely this inconsequentiality of theirs that helped them penetrate to the hidden heart of Heliopolis. None of those whose doors they knocked at barred their way—they were a boy and girl, just out of childhood, thirsting for experience and wonder, features clothed in bashfulness like beggars hoping for alms.

While others of a similar age were hooked on the products of the free-market boom, they were preoccupied with the city's vanishing history. They married to preserve their beliefs and pass them to another generation; and if marital cares and responsibilities had seen their file set to one side, it remained the central pillar of their sacred memory. From time to time, out would come the carefully preserved pages, and they would remember these or those things, the adventure they had that day. Out of pity, he'd pretend to have forgotten, for nothing of her old fire was left save a memory she'd match against his.

And because, as many tales from history tell us, the noblest ends melt man's differences away, their marriage was a paragon.

It preserved their social success. After their interest in the project had waned, and their forgetting had almost brought them back to the point where they'd begun, they made their return.

They were the al-Adl family's most celebrated domestic success, and one often on people's lips whenever newlyweds found themselves faced with multiplying problems. At any dispute, the family would gather at one of their homes to reach a solution, and—amid screams and stabs at a settlement—the couple's posture would inevitably attract attention: conjoined, her hand in his, whispering to one another from time to time. At which one of the assembly would fix on what it was the troubled couple needed:

"Learn from Reham and Nabil."

They would smile with a modesty that could not conceal their pleasure, and Nabil would choke back the hurt prompted by a question to which he had no answer. *Why does her name always come first?*

Questions that before had spurred him to fight all the harder were now too heavy to be borne. He wandered lost, unable to fight off a leaden sense—grown stronger in recent times—that his city had grown narrow and could no more suffice him. Walking its streets no longer set him at ease, and this alarmed him to the point of terror, for this wasn't simply the neighborhood where he lived. It was his City of the Sun. His fifth humor. His father had it pat in the maxim he'd passed down: "Heliopolis is not a homeland we inhabit, but one that lives in us."

Since boyhood, the literal meaning of Heliopolis's Arabic name, Masr al-Gadida, had stuck in his mind: New Egypt. The implication: that there were two Egypts, one old and another new. The name's vainglory he saw as justifiable and natural. It was no corner store to be compared to others, but should the subject arise he could see off all comers with the help of his extensive experience: he had its streets off by heart, and he could tell a resident by the way he looked. The locals had their own ways of talking, of explaining the world. They weren't chic like the inhabitants of Zamalek or frenchified like the denizens of

Maadi. They made no false claims to modesty. More European than American, they drew from a rich culture that gave them, when confronted with the barbarity of others, a calm that buffered rough conduct and aggravations, as though carried along on a pillow of air. So it was that he could pick out the intruders, a power he'd refined to the point where he could guess which area the alien hailed from, not just from dress and speech, but also from the body's movement, the movement that fundamentally set the residents of high-class districts apart from the others. For even if one of them were to perfect his disguise in terms of dress, his movements—characteristically marked by nervousness or embellishment—would betray his affiliation. It is critical to note, however, that Nabil harbored no prejudice against the poor or informal neighborhoods. He made no distinction between the newcomer from Zamalek and one from Imbaba. They were all 'Cairenes,' and in recent times their numbers had started a steady climb. Grieved, he observed that the differences between them and the indigenous inhabitants, once clear-cut, were now grown vague, especially with the emergence of generations who cared nothing for the Baron's legacy, and did not stand firm against the incomers' determination to destroy.

The arrival of Mustafa's case on Nabil's desk coincided with his sense that the display on his life's countdown clock had just lit up, that everything was going wrong, and that the dream on which he had shored himself up was slipping away. And this was no fleeting crisis to be overcome by staying up smoking hash and bringing himself back on track. Those all-nighters with childhood friends, his mind worrying at questions he'd consigned to a dark corner . . . , then the mists clearing, and he would return, light-footed and happy, ready to reengage with reality. The dark corner now claimed greater acreage in his mind, upsetting the balance, prompting the hash sessions to come more frequently, weekly and now without their former effect, so that he would resort to smoking in his car by day, breaking the rules by which he abided. It seemed that the problem he was facing had outgrown the drug's capacity to cure.

Just as it is our fate to wake in the morning and run straight into a bleached-out reality quite unlike our dreams, it was Mustafa's arrival that had marked Nabil's own awakening. He had dreaded this moment, but the fact that his fears did not transpire reassured him that his city and his dreams were proof against collapse. In this, Nabil regarded himself as the contemporary version of his grandfather, the one who would carry on his work.

Al-Adl the Elder had been the only Egyptian to have joined the Heliopolis Corporation as an administrator and not a worker. The only Egyptian among the sixty-five employees to enjoy the rights accorded to foreigners. While the company's Egyptians—the engineers, and clerks, and laborers—had ridden second class in the tram from Downtown to the new city, he'd been among the foreigners, enjoying, like them, the luxury of first class. And when the buildings had begun to rise, his had been a house in the finest district of all—the same house where the family's offspring were born and raised before setting up for themselves in houses next door.

No one knew why he was so close to the Baron. He was no architectural wonder like the French and Belgians, had no skill with accounts like the Germans and English, but the speculation (unconfirmed) was that he had mastered the arts of pharaonic sorcery, the most powerful of the various magics the Baron had studied in the course of his extensive travels. Counter-theories, based on the palace's lack of any pharaonic motifs, said otherwise. Their alternative explanation was that al-Adl had assisted the Baron in negotiating a tantrum by Khedive Abbas, who had designs on the wondrous palace and had been unsatisfied with substitutes he'd deemed not up to scratch. Subsequently al-Adl had become the Baron's advisor on the fine points of Egyptian affairs. Historically speaking, no evidence can be found regarding the nature of their relationship or its limits, but there be can be no doubting its existence and its strength. The photograph of them together outside the palace during the final stages of its construction silenced the doubters, and was the most precious object the al-Adl family possessed, with the original copy placed in a bank vault and copies distributed among the family homes.

Mustafa's arrival at the Palace of Confessions coincided with the intensification of the invaders' assault upon Nabil's neighborhood, as though the man was the heaven-sent rein- forcement who had rallied their troops.

Through the windshield of his car, Nabil observed the pair, astonished, as though a thief had broken into his home in the middle of the day. A boy and a girl, from a working-class neighborhood as borne out by their clothes (suitably garish for Eid)—the cut of his at least two years out of date—and the way she wore her hair. They were crossing at the red lights, hands linked, reveling in a rain shower in a revolting state of romance. Unforgivably conspicuous. He looked about to see if any of his fellow motorists in the neighboring cars would come to his aid, thinking: *O, ye who sit behind the wheels of the cars idling at the Korba Square lights! It is in our time that the walls, which have stood firm for a hundred years, are being breached. It is we who shall bear this shame!*

But his fellow motorists were busy waiting for the green light. He would find no help. It was his battle alone. He wanted to get out of the car and arrest them, but there was no charge called 'staggering about beneath the rain.' So be it, he'd deal with them *his* way: put them on the back seat, finish them off in the desert (one bullet each), then conceal the corpses in the palace of his master and teacher. No, he'd leave them out there, alive, dying of hunger, and thirst, and fear. A caution to intruders.

Instead he stayed motionless—allowed them to have their moment, knowing it meant that something had altered irrevo- cably; that these streets were no longer his; that the city would cease granting him its secrets; that he would have nowhere but his office in which to shelter until the invaders came. He would be ready, revolver against his thigh and hand ready to fire the bullet into his head. Or their heads, it made no difference.

Initially the presence of these unwelcome visitors had been confined to the morning, which was office hours. And, to some extent, he'd sympathized: they were working hard, had their own traditions that led them here; they showed deference to the neighborhood and its rightful owners; they accepted that their presence here was of limited duration, and never sought the miracle that might keep them here. Like a pill that has to be taken every morning, it was only once they left that the medicine took effect: the symptoms would vanish and things return to normal. He endured his illness, and he endured them: a daily penance for his sins. And the two things became bound up in one another, till he came to believe that they were the cause of his suffering, the hazy gauze falling over his eyes and the tiny electric jolts running through his body. He had taken to shrugging it off in the morning, as though the malady wasn't his, though the illness steered him through an invisible seizure of which he showed no symptoms save a scowl that occupied his whole face—for which reason, he appeared unbearably tense early in the day. Those who knew him were in the habit of avoiding him then.

He would slump on his comfy chair, put his feet up on the desk, lean his head back, close his eyes, and let his imagination take him away. Standing on the field after the battle was over, surrounded by the dead and wounded, the only one, for fateful reasons, destined to survive. Had he hidden as the slaughter raged? Turned up too late, the orders that he brought with him no longer worth a thing?

He peered out of the window at the passersby. Dead people. He was filled with the feeling that he was hugely blessed not to have fallen like them. An eye turned aloft and murmured thanks, but the words wouldn't leave his throat. He made do with a gesture. During these sessions, he would go back over the details of his day, scenes stilled and silenced which he watched without emotion. Pleading and breaking down in the face of the ghosts to which he was bound, in the impossible hope that they might find peace and leave him. Much of the pain was feigned, but lately he had been unable to find good reason to bear any of it. He felt the narrowness and congestion of the road that they were going down.

Nabil al-Adl was aware that every aspect of the collapse he was going through had coincided with the Mustafa Ismail case coming to him. He put it out of his head, out of pride, and in order that the man in question not become a ghost to haunt him—crouching in his mind—but he did not have much power to influence Ismail's effect. The moment his eyes had fallen on the file squatting on his desktop, he'd suffered an attack, quite out of place, and from that day the dossier had been associated with catastrophe. Its arrival had wrecked his routines. He fought his fear of taking the case any further only to discover, unprepared, that Mustafa had broken into, robbed, and plundered the homes of his nearest and dearest. He was, at the very least, the main cause of the collapse of his brother's household. Nabil applied himself to avoiding awkward and painful questions that might bring a return of the malady he almost had contained by means of the bees. Had Mustafa entered his house, too? Discovered that his wife kept the household budget among her folded underwear?

Was that why his face wore that mocking look while he questioned him?

Appropriately attired, we penetrated many levels of society. We have friends in a wide variety of fields, including security: a mutually beneficial relationship. We are businessmen. We have the finances, and they have the power. They boast of the things they've been through. We have come to hear of our exploits from the other point of view, have learned that we would have fallen into their hands on more than one occasion were it not for luck.

The stories I hear help me plug the gaps.

Mustafa Ismail
The Book of Safety

11

LOOKING FOR A BREAK IN the case, Nabil al-Adl summoned witnesses (who were potentially new names for the charge sheet, too). Sometimes they were pertinent to the course of the investigation, but frequently they were selected simply to satisfy his curiosity. He burned to see how those not like him lived. The journey he'd undertaken with his wife to discover their city had stirred in him an obsession with comparisons, and up until Mustafa's case had come to him no one he'd ever met had failed to confirm his contentment with his lot and his beliefs. It wasn't simply a question of passion for the neighborhood where he lived. It went much further, that was for sure. Nabil al-Adl was no shallow classist. Like others, he noted the collapse that the country was going through, but as far as he was concerned Heliopolis was the exception. He never spoke of this to anyone but himself, because his love of the district wouldn't be understood. Even his wife, who'd shared this love of his, had subsequently turned her back on it—so what of others? When he spoke to her of the invaders, she would hear him out, then plead with him to be careful lest the suburb claim his sanity. And when in protest he referenced their project and their discussions of the Baron and his genius, their pledge sworn outside his palace to remain eternally loyal to his principles, she'd reply, astonished, "We were young and fooling around, Nabil."

But he hadn't been young, and he hadn't been fooling. Or the second supposition: that he would go on being young and foolish; that he'd remain a boy of ten, clinging to the wall of the Baron's Palace and waiting for the descent of Helena, consort of his waking dreams, to protect him from the taunts of the other children. From that day onward, he placed his wife on the list of potential fifth columnists, determined, as he kept an eye on her behavior, not to weaken should the time come to brand her one of the traitors whose actions and indifference had opened the gates to the horde. That day they'd had their first quarrel since getting married, but he'd been quick to apologize. Not because he had lost his temper for no reason, nor to keep their love untainted by disputes, as he had whispered in her ear between kisses. No. He was, quite simply, lying, resorting to trickery to save a reputation he sensed was under threat. The family would gather as it usually did to smooth over discord and achieve a rapprochement. They would listen, as had happened in similar cases, to the opposing points of view, ten minutes each, then anyone who had an opinion would speak, and finally the eldest elder would pass comment.

Of course, Reham would tell the story of his obsession with the neighborhood and they would listen in astonishment, trying to control their laughter. He couldn't bear derision. Their diagnosis of his condition alone would drive him to madness. As she rushed weeping to the phone to summon her mother's help, he pictured himself seated beside the palace wall mumbling unintelligibly to passersby—the names of mythic beasts—and from time to time calling out to Princess Helena.

The Baron's Madman: that would be his name in his own town, stories told of a man whose love for the Baron's wife, the princess who'd died in mysterious circumstances, led him to haunt the walls of her palace and place an eminently respectable social standing in jeopardy. This fate was not as frightening to Nabil as was the process of convincingly playing the part for his wife, leading her to the bed to celebrate their first experience of falling out and making up. He was more terrified of the central issue of his life being sullied.

Swept away by his thoughts, he quite forgot the person beneath him and drifted, and were it not for the moans she made he would have lost the ability to keep going. But she never noticed his distraction. He tried performing as he should, entertained by the thought of being a spy in the enemy camp who'd successfully seduced one of their women in order to bring back the necessary information. Emotionless, as was proper to a man whose nation's fate rested on the vigor of his erection—just a machine going back and forth inside her, not stilling till she'd reached her pleasure's peak, to become his property.

"If I'd known arguing had this kind of effect on you, I'd have started fighting with you long ago!"

On her face, a look of gratitude, the first since they'd been married. All previous attempts to control the premature ejaculation that plagued him had failed, and now, by chance, he found that hatred was the answer.

Al-Adl had been observing his wife's behavior for a long time now, but it was not until this confrontation that he put it in its proper context. For years, he'd watched her exploit the relationships they'd formed through their summer holiday investigations, building a following first among the town's old-timers and then their children. Many of those they'd met she'd made close friends of, dropping in to the Heliopolis Club, answering the greetings of this one or that, and frequently thanking God for giving her the gift of people's love. She would say, "Whom God loves, people love," never for an instant ceasing to puzzle over the difference between that self-sufficient love, where lovers are like creatures free of ulterior motives, and that founded squarely on self-interest. The question troubled her, but might just as conceivably never have occurred to her, being so out of keeping with a nature characterized by a considerable innocence.

"Sweetheart, come and help me choose a gift for Muhammad al-Maboudi, our friend from the club. He's a lovely man and he's been good to us."

And to himself he would nod over and over at her sentence, replacing 'gift' with 'bribe' and 'good to us' with 'he can make a deal for the printing press.' Actions and objects were defined by their naming, and things could be easy or hard depending on one's desire to make them so. And this was the fundamental difference between them: he had turned Heliopolis into a cause that weighed him down without respite, while she saw in it only an adventure and a game.

His wife's words might not have prompted such a negative response, but their falling out coincided with a peak in his doubts over his convictions. Until Mustafa's case came along, he had believed that his town was as well as could be under the aegis of its own special religion, while those without lived in a bewilderment.

While Mustafa himself might not have been able to shift his certainties over good and evil, it was his many sidekicks who had cast his beliefs into turmoil—the doormen, security guards, shopkeepers, employees at the phone exchange, the post office, and the electricity department. All had trusted Mustafa and happily handed over the information he wanted, never considering for one moment why he wanted it, even though one had to have doubts about anyone who'd make the request. Why would someone want to know, for instance, the average electricity consumption of an apartment, without being connected in any clear way with the people who lived there? Or when they'd last paid their phone bill? But they didn't care.

Maybe he'd given them money, but that wasn't what they were after; Nabil's experience allowed him to distinguish those with criminal tendencies from people with principles, and all of these individuals resembled Mustafa. All those he called for questioning, all those with connections to the case had something of the man's spirit, his obstinacy, his belief that he was right.

And so he was now obliged to reexamine the conclusions he'd reached in the course of his research. He no longer much trusted his feeling that Baron Empain, builder of the Baron's Palace, had worked to fortify the neighborhood against the native affinity for destruction. At first, he had believed that the Baron had achieved this using the magic he'd mastered during a lifetime in India, and then he'd established a scientific basis for his theory.

The interviews he'd continued to hold with the town's inhabitants (far from his wife's gaze) had led him to one of the oldest residents of all, who had passed on to him stories he'd learned from his grandparents, and from which Nabil understood that the Egyptians' choice to settle here had not been an arbitrary one. There had been a committee whose task it was to assess to what extent the applicants met the conditions laid down by the Baron. The committee comprised a group of Arabic-speaking foreigners, and the selection process was not as difficult or complex as one might think.

It went as follows: a committee member would sit with the 'client' and engage him in a discussion, in which he'd explain about the construction plans, and prices, and so on, while his colleagues, apparently occupied with other business, would be watching the candidate out of the corner of their eyes—the way he spoke, his clothes, the information he gave about his circumstances, financial, domestic, and social. And the essential reason why the business went without a hitch was that anyone pursuing accommodation in Heliopolis at that period possessed, by definition, a culture that meant they had what it took to set out into the Dream of the Phoenix, which was rising anew.

Nabil only sometimes left his suburb—two days a week at most—on trips that gave him a top-up dose of pride and faith in what he had. He was returning to the same places he'd once visited possessed by fear, searching for what he'd missed, mixing with those others he'd once thought to be nothings—destroyers, wreckers—only for it to become clear that they were not quite that. Fridays he set aside to discover how life was led elsewhere, driving directionless from morning onward, and breakfasting somewhere preferably working class: Sayyida Zeinab, al-Hussein, Shubra. He preferred the places whose history had some echo in his memory, not those that had sprung up on the sly. Finishing breakfast, he would wander in search of a mosque for the Friday prayers. Back and forth between many sheikhs until he grew skilled in identifying the approach and method of each preacher from his opening words, from the way he mounted the minbar even, distinguishing the disingenuous from the sincere in no time. It was a weekly ritual of purification that he undertook in the belief that, as the saying went, "Friday to Friday cancels what comes between."

Arriving early, he would spend the time reading the Quran, and, when the preacher began, would lend his full attention, aching for the moment of understanding. Yet week after week, he began to see that the words all revolved in the same galaxy. He would sit restlessly, waiting for the show to be over and, after a while, realized that he had the right to deliver his verdict on what the preacher said, albeit passively, like the audience member who may leave the auditorium when he grows bored—walking, heedless of censorious eyes, from the front rows of worshippers where he'd been sitting to the door, then out to the car and away.

He drove from Heliopolis to the Corniche, the only thing his own city lacked. But this was no bad thing, quite the opposite—the Nile only appeared beautiful from the top-floor apartments where a few of his friends lived; otherwise it was a magnet for every kind of filth. He stopped at Cairo's old grain dock, a memory surfacing of having come here back when the ships would moor and the swarm of porters descend singly, each humping grain sacks, poor and crook-backed, their labor overseen by rough, ruthless men primed for the slightest slip.

His memory was playing tricks with him. He'd just visited the place as a boy, that was all, a school trip, and the tour guide introduced to them by their teacher had stuck in his mind. Standing by the nearby water purification plant, he had watched as the children of his school, he among them, were introduced to the image of the powerful nation-state that the soldiers had forged. His own boy had never gone on similar excursions: they had replaced that approach with trips to resorts where they presented them with artificial sights and sounds.

He left the car and went on foot, crossed to the other side of the river: old buildings in the Arab style—doorways, lattice screens, and wooden balconies—and alongside them others, ugly, in red brick. A market for fodder, spices, and dates, and a fish market, too. The smells ran into one another, a sensory storm to which the locals had grown accustomed, but which battered every one of his senses. Scent blent with scent, and he could no longer tell if it was revulsion that held sway over him or hunger, a voracious need for street food and a tumble with one of the women whose bodies jounced inside black robes. At the obscure promptings of memory, he turned right into a long street filled with car-repair workshops. Seemingly unimpressed young men looked him insolently up and down. He became conscious that he shouldn't have come here quite so elegantly attired. His presence constituted a breach in the scene.

Outside one of the buildings a man sat, cigarette in hand. Nabil walked past him, and the pungent reek of hash reached him. The sound of powerful blows against a chassis stripped down to nothing. They bought wrecked cars and reassembled them. The tree he'd seen as a boy by the purification plant's wall had grown gigantic, home now to hundreds of sparrows. Was it the one he'd watered that day by his own hand, or was his memory still playing tricks? The merry voices of young women grew louder the closer he got, and with them the plash of water. Did the station pour forth its water in gushing torrents where the neighborhood's residents gamboled? The

closer he got, the more certain he was that he would see something to spoil his contentment, yet he didn't have it in him
to fall back. The women's voices were a call that set him in
motion against his will. That careless laughter made, with the
sound of birds in his tree and the dinning crash of car metal,
an enchanting medley. For the first time, he did not feel fortunate to possess what had been given him, or despair for those
stationed lower.

When he reached the public pump, his first instinct was
confirmed. The scene struck to his soul. The women were
fighting over the water, clothes wet and sticking to their bodies, and they didn't care. He paused, to store away as many
impressions as he could. They put on their show, guarded
by the men, who smoked and chatted. He paid no heed to
glances, and the girls, having spied a well-dressed stranger
stricken with longing, shrugged off the burden of social obligation and summoned their ancient nature—sorceresses of
the Iliad—knowing full well that they would haunt his imagination; their special revenge cooked up for such as him.

Mustafa's case was simply the alarm that woke some part
of him—a part which, after years of repression, he had
thought to be inauthentic—and that notion he'd taken from
crime thrillers as a child had returned: that there are no rigid
definitions of good and evil, just roles the protagonists play
for the reader's entertainment. And just as he had moved
between the two roles as a child, he now wished to do the
same as an adult. He had tired of playing the hunter. The
whole thing was a game.

"Life's so much simpler than that."

His favorite line, and a lesson he'd never applied himself.
There was a dimension here he couldn't see, but he no longer
had the strength for adventure, for traveling from neighborhood to neighborhood—and him the one who'd wanted above
all to be a traveler, to leave the country to learn and discover.

But his ambitions had not been backed by arguments robust enough to stand up to his mother and her plans for him. *You think you'll find a woman over there who'll take care of you as I do?* The very thought of moving away from her and Heliopolis rendered him supine when faced with his other parent's wish that he enroll in a specialized training course, which would equip him for a job that his father described as a compromise between their desires. Both their dreams would be realized.

After all these years, his life built on the time-honored code of his family, along had come Mustafa Ismail to force a rethink of every detail. For the first time, he had encountered evil as he conceived and wanted it to be: elegant, rational, unshaken by the other point of view for all that it claimed possession of the truth. His respect and appreciation of the man's difference crept into his thoughts.

Respect. The motto on which his father had raised him and the basis of his whole existence:

"Respect yourself and others will respect you."

His father had never clarified his understanding of the principle of self-respect. It had been enough—at various times, on different occasions—simply to convey what he meant through passing comment on some outfit or behavior he deemed inappropriate, or someone speaking in some unseemly way. The impression formed that the intended principle had to do with being out of order, that a species of self-discipline produced the desired result: the respect of others.

The whole clan put the rule into practice with hermitic rigor, as befitted their total loyalty to the regime. Nearly all the men worked in various departments of the Interior Ministry. They proceeded from a basis of blind faith, samurais sworn to defend the king. But close acquaintance with the family revealed the worldly concerns that drove this faith and kept it burning ever brightly in the souls of the faithful. With quite spontaneous adroitness, the family had split itself in two, the first half making do with government employment and its modest salaries, while the second busied itself with commerce, the wellspring of vast, never-ending, guaranteed-in-advance profits. Nabil's maternal uncle was the ministry's largest supplier of foodstuffs. The paternal uncle with his printing press who'd won the tender for the ministry's posters, which achievement—despite his failing in a fiercely fought battle to secure rights for printing its educational booklets, monopolized by a newspaper foundation—was no small thing in itself. Enough that the posters enabled him to purchase the next-door press after its owner went bankrupt, and to relocate from an apartment to a private villa. In his father's family, there were intertwined interests and relationships that could only be unpicked by revolution. His wife was his cousin. His brother was partner to his wife's father, his paternal uncle, at the printing press—a secret partner, because at the same time he worked as an accountant at the ministry. Perhaps no regulation forbad it, but things were better like this, for the sake of the golden rule: respect.

And as in the mafia, if you do what you're told, you get what you want. He had no idea where the money that entered his household came from, nor where it went. Reham, responsible for the running of her father's printing press, assumed responsibility for their domestic finances. She had cannily demanded that this be the case at the outset of their union, and he'd put up no serious objection. Some indefinable thing had made him bow to her wish and, after all these years of happy marriage, he was now certain she'd been right. He admired a woman who worked, just as long as it was work that did no damage to her womanliness or transformed her into some distorted female facsimile of a man fighting for the next opportunity. A woman's job was just another of the accessories she wore—no harm in boasting about it with friends or at family gatherings. All this made it perfectly natural for him to respond to her request that he intervene in a matter that concerned the press:

"Sweetheart, we've got this idiot who's objecting to the work we've sent him. He says it's not up to standard. Could you please do something? We're going to get screwed, and you know I'm run ragged between the job and home."

He made some calls, all had ended well, and his reward was not just a night of sex but a greater share of the domestic budget, which she kept in the cupboard—folded between her underwear, to be precise. An odd choice, but he'd gotten used to it; in his mind, money was linked to the smell of his wife's body, to creams and perfumes, to the fragrance of her pussy. Was she so wicked as to declare her power in this way? His mind betrayed him, and convinced him that the same thing had happened to his father. His mother's responses had been as ready as his wife's:

"I deduct from both our salaries and I make deals with Papa, and may God see us good."

Reham's ability to invent reasons for the presence of all this cash in the house was inexhaustible. And why should he want to check? Why couldn't he be more like his father, the major general? And what did it matter that his wife was like his mother, daughter of an undistinguished seller of fruit and vegetable who had risen on the coattails of his child's husband, their journeys yoked together and both profiting, the frequency of promotions quickening here, income doubling there, and everyone taken care of and content?

In time, he came around to his father's outlook, which once he'd seen as old-fashioned:

"Strength or weakness, killer or victim, there's no space for a third choice. The third choice is a catastrophe. We weren't put on earth to be artists, we came here to fight it out, with victory for the strongest. And no judgments—the judgments come at the end."

Nabil sympathized with Sawsan, his youngest brother's bride-to-be, and was content to watch her argue with his father from afar, as each did their utmost to provoke the other.

During the engagement, she'd come around to their place in Heliopolis carrying a book, something to pass the time en route. The distance between Shubra and their home, she'd say, was "about half a decent-sized novel." For a while, his father had observed good etiquette in the face of her views— so offensive to the patriarchal system by which he governed the family—but all of them, while firmly wedded to the dignity of social standing, were dazzled by her lack of restraint. That was what had attracted his brother. The father, confronted by her wild assault on his fiat, had not fought back, but had made his son choose between the family's cozy familiarity and her rebellion, saying, "We'll find you a Heliopolis girl who knows how to behave."

The briefest acquaintance with human history and his son's personality would have told the father to avoid placing the family ties at risk. Nabil's brother's choices were all too limited; the story, written long before and reproducing itself, was destined to play out again—the rebel fated to break out of paradise, to put himself and his desires to the test.

Am I now confusing things? Certainly I am. That's what I've always done.
And why?
It is what I do.

Mustafa Ismail
The Book of Safety

12

WITH A FORCE BORN OF rage at what she considered a distortion of every true fact she'd ever known, Hasna Ismail hurled her recently purchased first edition of the *Book of Safety* from her open bedroom window. For an instant, it hung in place. The breeze turned its pages. Turned them into wings, and it tried to fly. A miracle: proving the error of her assumptions about it. She didn't care if it fell on someone's head.

An irresistible compulsion had directed her from the moment she had begun to read it. Every line provoked her; before she was done with a page, she'd be blind with rage, and the letters and words would run together. She was reading a fantasy about her father that depicted him as someone other than the man she knew, a romantic hero from days of yore, heedless of the law. If he was brought to heel, then everything he'd acquired would be sacrificed, but he was safe and secure in his individualism.

She would close the book and drift back to scenes from the past in which he figured. She was almost overwhelmed by tears, but fought them back down. She'd wept once and never again, coming around from her whimpering to find that some of the anger that she wished to keep kindled—puffing on it to bolster her resolve—had been lost.

The first reading left her assailed by doubts that she had erred in her own judgment. At the sound of steps in the still street, she would start up, just as used to happen when his footfall had suddenly come to her ears. Years of listening out had taught her to tell them apart: heavy and assured. About a hundred meters separated their home from the main road. At the expected hour of his arrival, she would train her ears on the cars' roars, uninterested in any vehicle which peeled off from the noise into their street, for he wouldn't be among the passengers. He would leave the taxi in advance of his destination—one of his habits, whose secret purpose she hadn't penetrated.

"Just here, please."

Decisive, forcing the driver to jam his foot onto the brakes. Distance remaining? Five minutes on foot. He'd once forced Hasna to walk through the heat to where they were going, prompting her to demand an explanation for this premature disembarkation. He hadn't answered her. He had lengthened his stride, her short frame straining to catch up. Afterward he'd brought her a book on al-Khidr. She wasn't interested in what he might have meant by this; her desire for freedom conceived it as a pledge that he would depart after her three questions had been answered. She had endured what the patience of Moses could not, had suffered, uncomplaining, her possession of a gift that raised her to the rank of the prophets. She had consented to his wish to shape her at his whim, and in her lonely cell shrugged off what he had planted in her head. She had blended her desires with his and resisted the thing she sensed coming into being, till the parting had come about and he had disappeared behind bars.

From the moment of his disembarkation to his arrival, she would have five golden minutes, enough to conceal the self that freed itself following his departure, and to make her way back to what he expected of her. She would hide what she was prohibited from partaking of and pretend to be doing the daily chores. So long as the stream of cars kept flowing, she was safe; only when one stopped did she pay attention, her senses coming to life like an animal's. Fear had given her the gift of attention. She could pick out the car door's slam even if a tram passed by at the selfsame moment. Every sound had its own field in which it moved, and training left the ear capable of separating out every movement along each wavelength. She wouldn't hear his steps straight away; she'd have to wait nearly two minutes for the first tread, distant as a dream, a few seconds more to be sure—the second footfall clearer, after which there was no call for uncertainty (her senses hadn't the courage to deceive her)—then a minute to put on the clothes stacked in order so as not to waste time (underwear, then a set of the pajamas she always wore around the house), and then she'd stuff her magazine, bought on the sly, behind the row of books lined up on the floor. Before he had crossed the threshold, she'd have settled down, the book they'd chosen together in her hand and, with every step he ascended, working hard to bring her exasperation under control so that nothing of what went on inside her would show.

Despite the loathing, Hasna still lived by his instructions: "A first reading is to make an acquaintanceship that can only grow deeper with further encounters." So she went back over the details, starting with the dedication, in which she perceived a fraudulent claim to special insight: *Would you like to know your end, then arrange your life accordingly?*

Yet in the instant before her feelings boiled over, she was unable to follow her father's rational path and read on. The scale of the imposture was beyond endurance. Jettisoning the book this way was just a way to express her rejection of the facts being so brazenly disarranged. To believe it would mean, quite simply, that her ideas were in error, and that wasn't the case. If she was to live as she chose, she had no choice but to correct the deception practiced by this *Khaled*.

Her father had made his return just as Hasna was approaching seventeen. She had woken to the assault of his male reek. Standing there in the middle of the living room, stiff as a lance. The pale light meant she hadn't been able to see his face too well, but he'd been tired, something she'd sensed from his clothes, which had borne the clear signs of a long journey. And the bag at his feet, wasn't it the same one that had accompanied him the day he'd gone away? Wasn't this the selfsame scene: the naturally bright girl who understood what was going on her around her, the mother gazing imploringly at the departing man, hoping her romantic appeal would make him go back on his decision? And now, was she imploring him to return whence he'd come?

Seven whole years of cloudless female calm. A home out of bounds to men.

"We don't need anyone."

The line much more than a grieving female's pride: like a vow, and this apartment their convent, keeping themselves apart until he should come to crown their patience with his blessing and break their fast.

Hasna had noticed that her top button was undone and had fastened it up to try to appear normal. Her father—his relationship to her would never change its name, no matter how far apart the years had set them. Was it really him? Could she be wrong? Were the darkness and the late hour conspiring to deceive her? One of her relatives, for instance? A relative who resembled him? And why was longing not breaking her down? In a situation such as this, shouldn't an instinctive joy possess her, produce a cocktail of hugs, kisses, and tears?

If there was anything about her father's tale that deserved to be retold, then she was the one to tell it. Hasna knew him better than anybody, better than her own mother, that poor soul who'd never understood why he had left, why all news of him had stopped from the day of his departure right up until the moment he'd surprised her at the door, holding the same suitcase he'd left with. Had it been a sign from him, a pointed suggestion that yesterday was the same as today, and that just as the suitcase had come through unscathed, had returned as it had left, so they, too, had it in them to be a happy family once again? But who would consent? Her mother's heart had thumped, fearful for a body and soul accustomed to the calm of solitude.

The day he had come back she had pulled herself together, but she hadn't lasted a year by his side.

"Your mother's passed away."

Sitting fully dressed on the balcony, before him the cup of warm water with which he began his day. Since the night before, she'd been dreaming of a scene:

> Him sitting thus and her before him, escaping his scrutiny by staring at the water, whose level dropped just a touch every two minutes, or examining the few passersby, the cars—a Mercedes, a taxi, an old Peugeot inside which she thought she saw a young girl wave to her behind the glass, the glass that lay between herself and her father, and which had shattered the morning that she'd caught the smell of winter approaching after a burning summer.

But of the dream only his posture and the smell of winter had come true. The chill glass between them had thickened, become bulletproof. Well-meaning snipers shot at it from the roofs of neighboring buildings, and the bullets ricocheted back, a warning to those who might be tempted by gallantry to come between them.

"She died in her sleep."

Passing on the news like a presenter positioned equidistant from all parties, leaving her to gather what she would from the report. It was the way he'd told her that astounded her, not the news itself. She withdrew without saying a word, fear muddling her mind. There would be no one to distract him from her now. She went into her mother's room with an impossible wish: that this new label, 'the late,' might not place her out of reach of her daughter's assistance.

She was stretched out on the bed, her face seemingly free of death. Hasna examined her mother with pity. She sat next to her on the edge of the bed. Arranged her hair. Was it appropriate that she pass away in her nightgown? What place was she in now? Her death hadn't come as a shock. Hasna had expected it—it was the logical conclusion of surrendering her life to him without thought for herself.

For the first two years of his absence, she had devoted herself to her love, and the memories he'd left behind had sufficed her. She would speak of her hero: the romantic, the savior, the talented. Little details retold the same way, in the same tones, and yet certain events and dates would be changed, suggesting a memory going under at an ever increasing rate—or otherwise, that the events were not wholly true, and fantasy was making merry between the lines.

In the third year, the pitch of her mother's ardor had gone into gradual decline. She would halt halfway through a story as though rethinking it, and as the fourth year came around it appeared that she had taken a decision, had decided to abolish the annual ceremony the pair of them staged to mark the date of his disappearance. No more sacraments. September 4 was no longer an official holiday from work and school. His picture, hanging in its gilt frame, would never again be taken down or candles counting off the years of his absence lit before it. No more prayers and supplications for his return.

"If he'd wanted to come back, he would have."

Firm words that closed the door to debate and any talk of him. An angry decree from a wife whose sense of dignity had awoken after realizing that there was no reason left to defer the orgy of grief. She dropped the part of the devotedly waiting Pining Lover, and in its place performed an expansively romantic role, the Abandoned Wife. She cared not that the rituals by which she'd sought to summon him formed the only bond with her unflagging 'audience,' her daughter—who (it had slipped the mother's mind) could rightfully claim a share of her misfortunes.

Hasna prepared for the evening schedule that she had followed since her father had gone to prison, retrieving the day's victims from her desk: *One Hundred Years of Solitude*, *The Sleepwalkers*, *The Drunkards*, *The Fool*, *The Dove's Necklace*, a volume of poetry by Ahmed Abdel-Muati Hegazi, another by Mahmoud Darwish, and finally, *Love in the Time of Cholera*.

She fought her personal feelings of distaste toward this last book. It took an idiot to believe that any man would dedicate his life to waiting for one woman, and the ending was stupider still: a man and woman in their seventies floating out to sea on a boat. She couldn't comprehend the reverential aura that surrounded it. The baby with the pig's tail in *One Hundred Years of Solitude* she could accept; she could see arguments for calling that city Macondo. This book, though? No, and a thousand times no. But she was aware enough to realize that she would never realize the humanitarian goal that lay behind her project unless she opened herself to all tastes.

With a skill built up over what was now forty days of ripping and cutting, she removed the pages from between the black covers of her chosen books, then tossed them, naked, into the middle of the room to land beside a large cardboard box, the tenth such brought up to her by the building's doorman for her to fill with shredded pages. She returned the covers to their places. She gloated over the golden letters of the title and author's name, then the name of her father, which he'd made sure to add as though he had played a part in writing each and every one of them. The covers took up less room now, male members that had lost their perkiness after a fierce battle, their blood flowing from desk to floor. They'd call her a killer and she would go to join her father, to sit at his feet and learn.

The initial plan had been to get rid of the books, to create a little space where once she had been entombed in their midst. It was a solution to the problem they both suffered—they were living here as guests of the books. Since her mother's death, any sense of reserve over the books encroaching at their expense had vanished, yet she would pause for a long time before burning them or tearing them up. She might have been forced to live side by side with the protagonists of these books, but she sympathized with them, too. Like her, they'd been imprisoned, cellmates toward whom her rancor had mellowed now that the prison governor was gone. At this thought, a most excellent idea had occurred. A compromise between destruction and preservation.

Each night, she would heap ten books before her and, to the rhythm of banned tunes, would liberate their pages—particular pages from each book, her own reading guiding her choice. She had in mind, more or less, the passages that she needed to compile to complete a thousand-page tome. What she didn't want, she ripped to bits and chucked in the box. She'd shuffle the chosen pages together, once, then twice, then three times, before rearranging her gleanings from previous nights and slipping them all between black covers.

The Final Truth.

And beneath the title, in her father's golden lettering:

Hasna Mustafa Ismail.

It is not the case that life is either hunt or be hunted. Many possibilities lie between the two.

Mustafa Ismail
The Book of Safety

13

"WE MEET AT FIVE, AT the Body Shop."

I stood where it suited me, outside a store that celebrated machismo: lighters, chunky watches, tough leather boots, silver rings set with stones on which snakes and crocodiles were etched. My relationship with Hasna had awoken in me a masculine sensibility which I had never before experienced so shamelessly. I looked at the goods, dithering over whether to buy, and kept one eye on the passageway, trying to imagine how she'd look this time: hair in hijab or uncovered? Fair or dark? Shy or defiant? It had been a month and a half, and that was time enough for her to have changed.

I hadn't considered that she might ride up in the lift as opposed to the escalator that we'd lately taken to using, and when she appeared beside me she looked at what held my attention. She had no need to say anything. Feminism made masculinity hateful, femininity effortlessly elevated to a supreme value, a status more asserted than earned.

She took her time in her favorite store. From her I'd learned that Woman is not one thing, but rather that each part of her has an independent existence, its own particular products—for hands, arms, stomach, and breasts, the legs and what's between them, the buttocks—and what works for one doesn't for another. There are products for slimming, darkening, lightening, peeling. Every so often, she'd alter. Be different. Like a fugitive, careful not to look the same way for long. The changes she'd enact didn't just affect her appearance but would come accompanied by appropriate alterations in behavior: as a blonde, she had to appear somewhat frivolous, more reliant on her femininity, while spectacles were suited to reserve and gravity. Clearly she belonged to an obscure government agency like the one where I worked, and it had planted her in my life following the book's publication, but I couldn't guess what her mission might be. Killing me? Why, and with what? And would that require such elaborate games? Or was it more likely that they wanted to smear Mustafa, something that would have greater impact if undertaken by the very man who had forged his legend? Better to suspect her than to think that these transformations were the product of mental disturbance. That was more alarming than the thought of her being an assassin.

At first, her ways had held me spellbound, but they were now a cause for hatred. I missed stability. I was a man from Shubra, a district that holds immutability and tradition in high regard, and however much I might have denied it I knew full well that this neighborhood was a part of me. And then again, just contemplating the time and money she spent on these changes was terrifying to me. What would you think of someone who spent most of their waking hours in front of a mirror performing minor cosmetic operations on themselves? How was it she hadn't gone mad?

We were sitting in one of the luxury hotels. She only felt at ease around luxury. One time, she'd consented to go to a café I liked, but she couldn't take the seedy courtships taking place around her, nor the waiter with his salacious glances. She would be accepted there, I'd told her, if she dropped the bourgeois act, but she had given the impression that her desire to deflate my pride in belonging there was not going to diminish, nor had I managed to convince her that many authors and artists sought the place out. People like that, she'd said with a certain hauteur, weren't the kind she cared to copy.

As soon as she sat, she took off her shoes, propped her feet on the chair opposite, and set the magazine on her leg, dividing the time we spent together between it and me. She would drink hardly any of her juice. I was unable to proceed at the same unflustered tempo. My drink would be done before I could tell what it tasted of. Once, mischievously, she informed me that one of the articles she was reading in her magazine said that the way a man sipped his drink symbolized his sexual performance (technique and duration). From then on, I worked hard to slow my rate of consumption.

When I'd almost forgotten the whole thing, I was compelled to retell the story, jettisoning essential details from the first edition of *The Book of Safety*. I went back to the notes I'd made, some pages yellowed, some letters bleached away, and yet others—thanks to an excess of speed in an effort to outpace forgetting—unintelligible, except that imagination would come to my aid in guessing at what was missing. I was preparing the second edition of the book, this time with the interpolation of his daughter's perspective, one based on their life together. She had offered to help me clear up any puzzles and reveal yet more secrets on condition that I not be constrained by anything I'd written before, no matter how stark the contradictions. I'd gone along with her wishes, delighting in her sound judgment and her astonishing ability to draw conclusions, to make connections between events and characters, and absorb the internal dynamics of said characters to generate attitudes and motives diametrically opposed to those I'd created for them. She appended modifications onto the character of Mustafa, lending it a human dimension which stripped it of the mythic stamp that had been my contribution. I would search through my original papers, on the hunt for sentences and signs that might support her view, to come out looking like I was just a pen for hire who'd had a story dictated to him with no basis in reality, its plot answering its ambitions, and dreams, and visions of what he *should* be, not what he *was*.

She was no less dangerous than her dad. The experience he had over her, young as she was, she matched with a feminine magic that she could deploy without any apparent effort. You could put her in your pocket, you felt, to use her whenever you wanted. But slight as she was, and despite the innocence in her features, she had a hardness that stopped you going ahead and taking advantage of her weakness, only to realize (if you were lucky and before it was too late) that said weakness was simply a staggering capacity for self-effacement. Like her father would say, quoting from one of his bibles, *The Art of War*, "When you are strong, pretend to be weak; and when you are weak, pretend to be strong."

We were sitting surrounded by Gulf Arabs, who were making their intentions clear.

"Arab mating season." Her insouciant commentary on the arousal that threaded her voice, carnal joy in her eyes—speaking in the name of others. No avoiding the thought that any one of those girls would shortly be stripped bare for one of these men. The young women declared their trade with the pride of true beauties, conjuring movements and laughter, holding gazes. An unforced display, maybe because it was still morning, the time when the nicer punters were about. Why did the bad boys never dare violate this custom? Would the sunlight burn them up like vampires?

"You know that most of your father's burglaries took place during the day, unlike the rest of God's criminals."

She pulled her lips thin and tight, all her senses engaged by the hunt currently in progress. "That girl's going to go off with the guy in the black T-shirt."

A few minutes later, the guy left, followed by the girl—and on Hasna's face the clear signs of triumph. Before I could say anything, her question came:

"You reckon the whore enjoys her job, or it's just business?"

The word 'whore' came as a shock. She was being vulgar to seem brave, shielding herself from callousness by steeling herself to violence. Pretending naiveté, I told her about my experience of sex for cash. It had been intolerably cold-blooded. She'd undressed in an instant, had demanded we do it right away while refusing to let me kiss her, and then, after being pressed, consented to one stupid, passionless clinch. She'd had a lover for whom she saved her heart—and kisses, as she saw it, were one of the signs of love. She had treated me as if I'd forced her to do it.

Hasna listened with interest, then said, "Silly girl."

Not the response I'd expected. Then she went further, emphasizing her point.

"That stuff about kissing was from back when romance was a thing, before women drew a distinction between the body and love. That's all over now, just like the business of poets searching for grace in the impurity of flesh. In Europe, porn's pretty much a profession like any other. Prostitution, of course, will continue to be a morally unacceptable industry, or so we'll pretend even as we surf through skin flicks. And if the chance comes along for a fuck, no problem, then it's back to your home and upstanding life. That prostitute of yours was old school, or maybe she was putting on an act for you because she guessed—and I reckon she's right—that you're a romantic. To be honest, I don't understand how you managed not to fall for the trap of the noble whore."

She took pleasure in the irritation on my face. She was so petite and harmless-looking that you weren't immediately aware that what she'd said had left any impression beyond its immediate meaning.

I had been readying myself to ditch writing and search for something else, but my desire for her had forced a return to square one in my relationship with Mustafa Ismail and my work. Hasna had dropped into my life out of the blue.

Al-Waraqi had asked to see me. A matter of urgency.

"Could we please meet up in my office as quickly as possible?"

The selfsame sentence whose every syllable he stressed whenever an important guest was with him.

I had arrived midway through a conversation which suggested to me they'd known each other, except before she left she had given him her phone number.

With a nod in her direction, he'd said, "Looks like we're going to bring out a second edition with new information."

Subsequently I was to be staggered by her views on al-Waraqi and his social aspirations. I couldn't believe there was anyone brave enough to pick apart the personalities of people they'd met just the once, and though I was unconvinced by many of her opinions of people, and uncomfortable with the judgments she used in deciding how to deal with them, this approach was to her advantage. In any gathering, she instantly became a center with its own gravitational pull. Positions took shape and hardened around her, and she didn't much care if anyone disliked her or took her as an enemy. Her excessive self-regard lent her the conviction that what she did was right and beyond dispute simply because it came from her.

She had Mustafa's bravery, his ability to form and make fast friendships, taking their benefit and none of their burden. Could genes really be this sly, continuing to reaffirm resemblances despite their bearer's rebellion against the source? For all her efforts, I was unable to banish her father's shadow from our relationship. The likeness that bound them was too great to be erased by words. I told her that I saw her father in her eyes, and she answered that he meant nothing to her and that the genes that had slipped across from him to her did not constrain her, but only pushed her harder to free herself. She didn't hide her anger at him—that he'd abandoned her as a little girl to the care of a weak mother and, on his return, had refused to contemplate his obligation to repay her with tenderness. Not a father, but rather a strict schoolmaster whose pupil's duty was unquestioning faith and surrender, and to forget what she might think and want. Her rage had bequeathed her a revulsion of all men of his type, which may be why our relationship stayed trapped in a cycle of defiance and tension. And despite her conviction that her father had deceived me, she was forever saying that I should neither have fallen for it nor gone on to deceive others in the same way.

"You must know that Robin Hood's not real."

I guessed what she was getting at. With a few arguments behind us, I'd become accustomed to her way of tearing down what I had written. It was a systematic approach, only strengthening my suspicions that she belonged to some agency that was feeding her instructions on how to deal with me.

"Well, no, the chances of him having existed are no weaker than the doubts that he did, which obviously favors those who claim he's real, on the principle that uncertainty must always be to the benefit of the accused. That's assuming he's being accused of being an imaginary character. . . ."

"Wrong. The majority of the sources are literary texts, and I think you'd agree that caution is called for when using literature to study history."

"All right then," I said. "Even though I don't concede your point, since contemporary chroniclers wrote about him, I've no desire to turn this into a historical discussion group. What's your point?"

"Your interpretation of Mustafa Ismail's personality and behavior rests on your outlandish theory about the Merry Men. If Robin Hood's not real, your theory's out the window, and so, by inference, is your interpretation of his personality."

"Even supposing what you say is right, that doesn't render the theory invalid. It's not my invention: it exists in psychology as one explanation for male behavior."

We agreed that it was as though we'd met in an earlier age. And we *believed*, for all that the word is misleading, in a slapdash method of plastering over those gaps which as soon as perceived should have obliged us to cut our ties.

It seems strange just how quickly my relationship with Hasna was forged. I should have paid attention to the fact that something was wrong, that the apparent agreement over certain issues did not necessarily mean that the pair who held these views could form a good relationship, particularly if they were a man and a woman. More importantly, I should have seen that her circumstances might well have left her ready to get with the first person to come along who met the bare minimum of her requirements. She was like a prisoner released unprepared, the present full of vexing incidents and an enigmatic future ahead, with no established facts to help her hypothesize what it might be like. Yet alongside all that, she possessed an undimming energy for discovery. She had the suppleness of mutability, and my ability to assimilate all this lagged behind.

What held me and Hasna together? Her father, Mr. Mustafa Ismail. The philosopher-thief, or thief turned philosopher. One and the same: true philosophy leads you to break the law. The man, his philosophy, and his crimes were the greatest things we had in common. That I loved him and she loathed him was neither here nor there, since what united us could not divide us . . . , right? And what heaven joins only death shall divide. Mustafa was the ring on which our names were engraved. And it was as though he'd rebelled for this purpose alone—it being the only thing, as far as I could see, that had resulted from his actions.

My experience of mathematics was limited. Women, it seemed, were drawn to the mathematical mind. Which is how Ustaz Ali, Lotfi's father, had ended up beating me and winning her heart, transcending the age difference between them. How that mathematical mind of his helped him bed her I couldn't imagine, but where there's a will. . . .

The math metaphor enables me to reevaluate what happened. She and I: an equation. Her father: a common denominator. And don't forget the presence of numerous other, minor, common denominators.

For example: like her, I'd been a prisoner, perhaps even for the same number of years. Different types of prisons, of course, as were the jailers and the torture techniques. Hers was a luxurious apartment near al-Tayaran Street in Medinat Nasr. And mine? A palace about an hour's drive distant. The irony came from the fact that her jailer had become one of my prisoners. But I was no jailer; I was tied to my chair, facing a stage whose curtains never fell. The actors trooped on one by one to tell their stories, in no fixed order, with no governing style, talking till their souls were spent and withdrawing lifeless shells. After a while, I became convinced that I was demateri- alizing in my chair, becoming the stories I listened to.

I couldn't be like Abdel-Qawi, who cared nothing for any story, no matter what it was about, immunized by what he had (and yearned) to tell. What *I* heard broke me up. My personal stories went up in flames. I would become a corpse flayed by memories that weren't its own. New scenes competed with the old, searched for a place to call their own. My mind was a rag- bag for whatever the confessors spat out. I had to get away. Day on day, hatred of that stage was building, the interrogations were bleeding me dry. I had a right to live some story-free days, where there weren't all these significations for the smallest actions.

Hasna and I had a shared desire to forget what had been, and to search for another memory.

"You'd like us to leave the whole past far behind?"

This was her question the fourth time we met. That day, she'd been like someone stepping out of the Seventies: on the loose and limitlessly romantic.

"It's hard to see this relationship lasting."

So she ruled on the fifth meeting, following an argu- ment that had concluded a discussion about the latest wave of popular music. I had championed the old in the face of what appeared to be a distortion of the most basic principles of composition and singing, in which position she had seen inflexibility and the adoption of a political attitude that feared change. How could liking messed-up music and singing amount to political opposition?

The smaller things we had in common were little creatures that pricked us with their stings, but we delighted in a relationship that had no stronger half and no sense of obligation dictated by social frameworks, both proud of our awareness, of our knowledge that the labels which bound people to one another—love, friendship, family—were an attempt to turn away from what could not be faced. Each individual was sunk within themselves, searching for a solution to their personal dilemma.

The barrier between us, however, had its roots in her sense of female superiority and her anger toward men. Is there a single woman who ever avoided falling into this trap? I didn't disagree with her over this, though, quite the opposite: I leaned toward the belief that our qualities, hers and mine, were none of them fully formed. I was not completely man, and she was not all woman. When we met, we'd slough off pretense and swap characteristics, play with them. She'd be rough and severe, and I would turn into a meek creature, absorbing her rage, and then, when we'd tired of this, we would return to our original roles. Yet, before we could be sucked into the snare of a traditional relationship between man and woman, between a passive object and an instigator, we would flip to another role and another game, would disgorge all the frustration we contained, would delight in our freedom—would be however we cared to be, with no impediments in our way. We would not be shy before each other, and despite the fights— too many to reckon in that short period—neither of us ever hurt the other. Perhaps that's why I wasn't angry at her for dumping me, and still yearned for her whenever she came to mind. Hasna was one of the few happy memories I woke up to and went to sleep with, maybe because her story and that of her father went beyond their respective personalities to play a part in all that I saw and lived.

All too late, I woke from the dream. The Hasna of my fancy was not the one present in reality. It was imperative to examine the signals she deliberately transmitted in the spaces between her words. She was sincere in her concern for me with regard to what she was planning, which is why she sought to focus my attention on her unforgiving side. Except that I'd been mesmerized by her, and still was, and my discovery that almost the entirety of her story was more or less a fabrication, and that she'd left me for a mentally unstable man, did not spur me to hatred. I really tried. I pictured her naked in his bed, but felt no jealousy. Should he succeed, it would be a cold prize. He'd never reach her as I'd done. It would never occur to him that sex repelled her.

"Men are more like animals than anything. No matter how civilized or how much they might claim to respect women, they're still brutes."

We were sitting in a bar in one of the big hotels, watching a girl. All I could see of her was her fully bare back, two thin crossed straps roping the lower half of the dress to the section about her neck. I was lost in a detailed scrutiny of the exposed expanse that ran down from the neck, fringed by her short hair, and ended just above her buttocks—barely concealed by a small flap of fabric—before the nakedness once more returned with her legs, challenging and beckoning her admirers. With two glasses of beer drunk, her desire was stirred stronger; there was no purpose to her body's exaggerated movements beyond freeing itself from its remaining bonds.

"All very well, but her tits are sagging," said Hasna.

Her comment delighted me. Rooted in jealousy, it pointed to the possibility of love. I was unable to contain my excitement, and some trace of this showed on my face. Hasna couldn't bear me to have any thought while we were together without me telling her. Was this a weakness? Possessiveness? One led to the other. And if she insisted that something was the case, then it must be, and I must deal with it accordingly—must devise, author, invent something that would drive her to anger, to laughter; something to provoke her according to my desire.

"My whole mind's busy imagining you naked," I said.

Unruffled, she replied, "Great. As long as you're happy."

However, she was seriously and decisively opposed to anything that might lay the foundation for a serious relationship.

"Why do men always think that one woman's jealousy of another means she's in love? For the most part, women's jealousy is groundless, without external cause. Point one. The other thing is that I'm telling you the truth; it's not based on jealousy. This girl's got saggy tits, but you and most of the guys here haven't noticed because your eyes go straight to the flesh. But I see what's *beneath* the clothes."

That was true. For the rest of the evening, I felt nauseous every time I caught sight of the girl, as though I'd been eating and had suddenly came across a strand of hair from the chef's head in the food.

I began to get a hunch about Hasna's preferences. She'd compete with me to spot the pretty and sexy ones, would look them up and down with me, and then we'd start to pick over the body of the chosen one. One of our little games, through which we'd discovered one another's taste in women. Naturally, it was all too easy to deduce that this inclination of hers was a reaction to what she'd been through with her father. Was psychology so very simple, or was I a genius? A woman, oppressed by a man, turns to those of her own sex.

"Masculinity is already insupportable enough, so imagine if your male adds violence to the mix. Men need to seriously consider the fact that they are creatures that go against nature. Their natures need to be brought into line. Like, say, gay men are distinctly creative."

"Being gay isn't just about having sex with men," I replied. "You can't just say it's a rebellion against maleness. It's a rebellion against femininity, too. Against the human context as a whole."

Though our relationship was close, she still refused to have sex. On those occasions when it almost happened, she'd take fright and ask me to leave, and that state of affairs only altered at her whim—one solitary time—after which our relationship ended.

We'd started hanging out at her apartment in Medinat Nasr because we were getting fed up with the swarms of inquisitive eyeballs and the pressure they brought.

"Why do people stare like that? It's really irritating. I can't get to sleep with all those eyes chasing me around at night," she said.

And I supported her decision, wanting to make the best of the opportunity.

"Egyptians have always poked their noses into each other's lives, but lately, with everyone packed into such small spaces together, the thing's taken on the shape of a mental illness."

I made my move, impelled by the thought that I was a man who must take the initiative. After all, she'd paved the way by moving our meetings to an enclosed space.

It was, however, a grave error.

"So you've come to the conclusion that I invited you over for filth? So sordid!"

"You think of sex as filth? You're seriously messed up."

"Your ideas about me and about women in general leave me no choice but to think of sex as filth."

In penance for my clumsy attempt, I was obliged to accustom myself to a brotherly companionship with her seductive body. After a while, my presence beside her became normal, as though we were husband and wife surrendered to the routine of their lives—yet the desire to move the relationship on never left me for an instant. Not just a hankering for sex, but for communication, for completion with her, for actualization through her, without which I had only what she said and what I saw. And language wasn't enough. How to tell her that my desire for her was not animal lust so much as an attempt to engage? I was gambling that she would take this as an ingenious method of seduction and would respond for that reason alone. Except, more likely, that wouldn't happen. She wouldn't believe it, of course. To her, all men were tarnished with inferiority:

"The heaviness between a man's thighs binds him to the ground. The woman's wound is light and rises to the sky, which is why, once a month, the Lord gives them fouled blood, so they might not fly away like angels from sheer weightlessness."

No less than her body, her ideas would arouse me, and I'd be drawn more firmly toward the ground. Like a radar, she could register the slightest uptick in my passions, and my constant desire for her enraged her. Shouldn't any woman be happy that her man is always thinking of her? She'd come across me daydreaming, draw close, and, with a spellbinding simplicity, she'd touch it—the faintest touch, as though she hadn't meant to, and whispering in my ear, "Can't you just be a human being and not an animal all the time?"

I'd try hard to take control of whatever was pushing the blood through my veins, to cool the heat, muttering spells to shrink it up—not, as she had it, in order to be a human being, but to drive her from my imagination, where she'd set up shop. I needed detachment to negotiate with her, just as her father had negotiated with the government and gotten out of jail—her body in return for the truth that she wished me to rewrite. It was easy for her to act all pure. Women's desire doesn't show as obviously as men's. We're shockingly unshielded. It's hard to guess what a woman wants unless she makes it plain, or if she's very uncynical and instinctive—something you're pretty much unlikely to encounter.

*

We spent most of our time in the street. Hasna always had somewhere new she wanted to go. She was skilled in discovering what I could never have believed existed. Outside Cairo, where the buildings hid away and the desert's edge began—as though the civilization we lived in were nothing more than an illusion—we would sit on the sand in a restaurant made ready for the likes of us, broken and scattered between two worlds, waiting for the sand-buried flesh to bake.

I think she meant it when she said she longed for a life like this—to be far from people, buildings, and cars, to wake and not be surrounded by news reports and songs. I'd assumed these were rambling obsessions, from the hash we'd sneaked a smoke of. Only later did I appreciate how profound had been the effect of the world she'd been raised in: the absolute stillness in an isolated apartment, nothing but books and classical music. It had taught her never to expect anything. Then the bewilderment when at last she'd been set free, a freedom she had craved, and yet what she'd gone through she still thought sweet, somehow—redemptive suffering: "We're like the smallest insect in the sight of the tremendous Power that watches us from the skies."

We drank beer in vast quantities. The hash had given us the ability to absorb it. Stretched out on the sand, surveying the night sky. It was the first time I'd seen it so clear. Dazzled by what I saw, I thought that this might be the turning point in my life, forcing me to confront what I'd previously avoided.

"What do you think we'll do after we die?" Hasna asked.

What can anyone do after they die? The question annoyed me, as though she'd directed some personal insult at me. "What? Are we going somewhere?"

The sarcasm incensed her.

"You're so shallow!"

The experience was too much for us: the meat cooked under the sand, the silent old woman serving us like the Angel of Death, beer, hash, the moon—the perfect recipe for a straight dive into depression. She asked to leave, which was what I wanted very much myself.

"I'd like it if we didn't meet up for a bit," she said.

"And I'd prefer it if we didn't get together for a while as well."

I thought seriously about ending this complicated relationship. What was it that had made me take up with a girl in need of resocialization? She was crazy, basically.

We went our separate ways.

A week later, she called and asked to meet. Amid pride at her submission and terror at what she might be planning, I was certain that our relationship was on the verge of some change.

It is almost impossible to carry out a burglary in a popular neighborhood and get away with it. The buildings are jammed together, and high population density is an impediment—there is constant movement, children playing in the street and on the stairs, the men indoors, the youths on the corners, not to mention a veritable army of doormen, worshippers, and vendors.

Surprises in popular neighborhoods are impossible to plan for. It is hard to establish the routines of those who live there, or to stick to a plan.

Safety means steering clear of the poor.

Mustafa Ismail
The Book of Safety

14

LOTFI HAD NO DARK SIDE at all. I was still sure that was the case, despite the doubts Hasna had sowed about my ability to form sound judgments: "The absolute judgments you resort to are comforting, but they aren't the slightest bit realistic."

Why hadn't I told her that she was the *queen* of absolute judgments, resorting to them with her father and now with me—her claim that *I* resorted to absolute judgments an absolute judgment itself.

I, like Talia, am no smooth-talker. It's one of my faults. There's no harm in confronting yourself with your faults; it's the best way to reform them, to straighten them out. But I did have a memory like a steel trap, which stored words and reviewed them before subjecting them to analysis. One of my strengths—it's also important to appreciate ourselves, so as not to sit around grimly beating ourselves up. Between narcissism and nihilism is where we find our psychological balance.

Lotfi and I continued our friendship; on different terms, but it was still possible to call it a friendship. Is there, my runaway darling, any better proof than this that I'm an excellent judge?

Lotfi was neither a narcissist nor a nihilist. Lotfi: *lotf-i,* 'my kindness.' A definition rather than a name. My very own *lotf.* The most transparent creature in all the world: you could see the thoughts scrolling through his mind, and all so childlike that I would feel, when with him, that I was the person who'd brought him down out of his heaven.

He was like my brother, and he did his best till he'd become a father to me, though maybe that was no more than coincidence. I was sticking to my room. No way was I going to leave it and move into my dead father's room just to assume command of the little family taking shape before my eyes. Leadership means being distracted from the pursuit of contentment, to become one of the instruments of its deliverance.

I'd known Lotfi since childhood—a friend imposed by family ties, and then, after I was left orphaned and alone, he'd persevered with our relationship until he earned the right to come around when he wanted and do what he pleased in the little apartment, which had grown comfortable when my father and mother departed this world at the propitious moment: two bedrooms, a small living room, a kitchen, and a bathroom. Visitors would be astounded that it had been divided into all of that, a single step enough to take you from one section to another. When they'd married, my father had promised to get my mother a bigger place, but crossing the threshold he'd grown lazy and they had stayed there in its trap their whole lives. They'd never had a second child, conceivably because they hadn't got enough space, and if it had been up to me I would have buried them here, because it was pretty much a tomb already.

Lotfi's girlfriend, Manal, with whom he shared his room, was like my mother. "Hey mama," I'd call to her, meaning nothing by it, but it would be enough to blind her to my patent lust. The times we weren't arguing, I'd feel her pity, a compassion for my loneliness that Huda had failed to fill.

What can one say about Huda? She's hard to make out through the shadows of loathing. This much is clear to me now: when it was too late, I realized that I had treated her with an unearned superiority. However, seeing as we're drawing up a list of my strengths and weaknesses, we should add that I never tried to alter reality (as others might see it), even if the charge be leveled against me. I was drawn to the enchantment of possibilities, and terrified of remaining alone, and she seemed kind and gentle. So I believed, before I found that she was pulling me with her into her world, and that was a world I didn't care for: completely still, and silent, and her inside it, that serene expression on her face and once a minute sliding those spectacles up her nose, even as they defied her and started to slip back down.

Her name fashioned the first barrier between us—*huda*: 'the one true way.' All I could think of when I heard it was praise poems to the Prophet and prayers.

"You remind me of Ramadan," I told her once.

I met the resulting look of disgust with silence, something I was to become addicted to. I'd say something dumb, and the expression would take shape.

"And there's something wrong with Ramadan, is there?"

That was Manal, and this was her first appearance onstage. Having the courage to confront me wasn't enough for her; she moved on to hard words and life lessons:

"In my opinion you need a little faith in your life."

Lotfi was next to her, laughing to lighten a situation he sensed was growing tense, yet simultaneously patting her shoulder in support—a man who believed in the tenets of feminism. It was at precisely this moment that the pattern of the relationship between the four of us was established: childish squabbles with which we'd relieve the guilt that weighed the two girls down.

"Hudhud!"

Manal's call, a squawk that accompanied the squeak of the opening door—the same squeak that would come once or twice a week when my parents had finished their business (the door was only ever shut to hide their shame). Manal would open the bedroom door from within, lingering inside to give us both sufficient time to rearrange ourselves, and her Hud-hud would get to her feet, happily or hurriedly according to the call's intonation, itself subject to her commander's mood.

Stretched out, emphatic, sing-song, sometimes split into two sections:

"Hud . . ."

Then seconds passing before the second half was set loose:

". . . hud!"

Hudhud's cue: "Manal's going to be here any second."

My attempts to persuade Huda that I'd heard the first strategic cry and the second warning one were in vain, and I'd know that in approximately two minutes there she'd be before us, teasing us with one of her immortal lines—"Song-birds of love!" or "My chicks!"—as though we were filming some cheap flick from the Seventies. Except that she—and more's the pity—never resorted to vulgarity. This wasn't some blue film. She didn't come in half-naked, say, so drunk she could barely hold the beer bottle, and Lotfi reeling in her wake. No, no. She'd come in fully clothed, showing no signs of what she'd been up to. And we'd be the same. We'd finish, Huda would immediately put on her clothes, and nothing would be said.

In any case, she never undressed completely, staying ready for any emergency. She was so well trained that she could probably win a race to determine the fastest ever to kick over the traces of lovemaking, setting straight the hijab that had slipped from her head, craning to open the door, then quickly sitting back on the bed's edge, plucking up any book her hand might fall on and busily leafing through it. As though for the last hour we'd been occupied educating ourselves.

God rot the Eighties and what they left us: no art, no fash-ion—the era of politics and culture ended, and that of piety and tradition dawning. We could do what we liked as long we gave an 'in God's name' with a 'no power but God's' to push it home.

One time, the two girls went off in a temper because I'd been unable to suppress my irritation at the coincidence that had led her to pluck up *Beyond Good and Evil*:

"Huda, I've got some Mickey Mouses that are much better. On the locked shelf in the library."

"You don't have to read all these books to be an intellectual. Culture comes from the world," said Manal, intervening to champion her follower's tear-filled eyes, and Lotfi playing his usual part—supporting his girlfriend in front of us, then mocking her without her knowledge. Though maybe she did know, but chose to ignore it in exchange for the space he gave her and his constant affirmations of respect for women and their role. Of course, this was placed in direct opposition to the role I found myself confined to and forced to play out to the end: the 'enemy of womankind.'

I took the book from Huda, who was shyly hanging onto it, opened it, and read. "'What, in spite of all fear, prompts pity for woman, for this dangerous and beautiful cat, is that she appears to suffer more, to be more vulnerable and more in need of love, more subject to disappointment than any other animal.'"

I didn't regret what I'd said—the words in any case weren't mine. If they felt so inclined, they could get cross with Nietzsche.

Ustaz Fakhri told me once that women don't like to take responsibility, for which reason, deep down, they gravitate to those who oppress them. Women, like our people, love a dictator—which is why we're all women. My relationship with Huda was forged by Nietzsche and Fakhri. I had no idea about Nietzsche's experiences with women, but I did know that I should think twice about listening to Ustaz Fakhri's views, because his relationship with those creatures should have afforded him no space to voice any opinions on the subject. Even so, I borrowed something from his relationship with his long-term lover.

I tried hard to turn Huda into a slave, who neither spoke, nor thought, nor dreamed. It doesn't work with some people. It was an experiment which gave our relationship a certain pep, but she wouldn't accept it and I couldn't respect her choice. Why wouldn't she treat her discipleship of Manal the same way? She finally stopped pretending to love reading, which she'd done to increase the common ground between us. That was for the best, because the slow hemorrhaging of my books now stopped and I was no longer obliged to listen to her shallow views on what she'd read. The Hudhud who once pretended to refinement now revealed a violent soul. She began meeting my hatred with hatred, making fun of my total isolation and depression—yet this, strange to say, only drove us to more enthusiastic sexual performances. We'd finished acting our love story and begun to see the true nature of the tie that bound us, which led her into the trap of my melancholy; with no chance of the relationship ever taking a legitimate form, she could not bear being, as she once described herself, "an animal." What was certain was that her hatred of me would increase, because I was the one who'd made her like that.

"Why do people run from knowledge of themselves?"

"What do you mean? That I actually *am* an animal?"

So she asked, hoping for an answer, as though I were the one who'd decide her fate. In cases such as this, I was supposed to clutch her to my chest, denying the very idea until life resumed its course, but the desire to destroy her seemed more appealing. It might relieve the sense of humiliation I got from our relationship.

"We're all animals, sweetheart," I said.

She didn't get it.

The next step in her life was to get engaged to me. That was a given, otherwise she wouldn't have lost her virginity. That doesn't come free. You must pay for what you take, especially if it's the most precious thing a girl possesses. She would parrot things she'd been told and raised on without giving them a second thought, without the slightest effort to rephrase them. Which is why I never paid attention to what she said. Her conversation set my mind adrift and after a while I got hooked on her, like an old lady kept tied to life by her old sewing machine, placing her feet on the pedals to begin their familiar work: more clothes, for no one, and memories showering down with nothing to bind them, chattering incessantly, moving into a rhythm that holds steady no matter how tired she gets, and moaning, too, a changeless pulse, starting softly, then rising a notch or two, no more, and always and forever maintaining her steady pace, like a sleepwalker.

Huda never looked sexy to me, not once, despite my many attempts to find her so. She was careful to stress that she had only consented to keep me happy.

A 'harmonious' family, able to forget the tiny space in which their feet jostled as they sat across from one another in front of the television. Huda next to me, and Manal facing—when I leaned forward, she would almost fall into my arms. But she didn't lean away; she was determined to protect her own space.

Things had been divided up wrong from the beginning. Manal should have been mine: she was the more recent model. She could provoke me with her insistence on the correctness of her views. I was in awe of her extraordinary ability to believe in and accommodate fantasy. She played the most important role in transforming Lotfi from a normal man into a poet.

He and I had despaired of the whole thing. It was as though his mind refused to forget, though the famous Shubra poet had insisted that his transformation was conditional on him forgetting the thousand lines he'd learned.

He wanted the power to set words side by side, and make the faces of young women light up and songbirds sing. That is how he saw poetry, and to each their point of view. Maybe the poet had been drunk, as we most likely were, otherwise we would not have been so sure we'd found the way to turn Lotfi into a balladeer:

"Memorize a thousand lines, then forget them."

After the booze wore off, I forgot about it, but between battling the hangover and upset stomach that were my lot whenever I drank too much, I woke to find him hunting through the bookshelves for collections of poetry. I went back to sleep, trying to remember whether he'd just that moment come over or whether he'd stayed the night, his voice an inseparable part of my fevered dreams:

Wine that glows, as though charged with saffron,
When laced with waters hot.

I believe in no love that has not
The recklessness of revolutionaries.

I am the beginnings
And I am the endings.

And who made women less
than men; their only sure
way to a crust of bread
to whore?

The room was soon filled with poets—Mutanabbi, Qabbani, Darwish, Akhtal, Rilke, Rimbaud, al-Khansaa—and Lotfi's voice was a drumbeat in my head. I shouted at him to stop. And it went on like this for months. He would just turn up with a notebook in which he jotted the thousand lines, choosing a few new ones, then asking me to test him on what he'd committed to memory. This wasn't the way to make a modern poet, but I didn't dare tell him outright when he was so full of enthusiasm. And once we were done memorizing, how to put the second part of the plan into action?

Manal found the solution:

"To stop thinking is the quickest way to forget."

No sooner did she believe in an idea than her soul and mind filled to the brim, and she would act accordingly. But all the ways we tried to stop Lotfi thinking ended in failure. He was using his mind all the time. Of course, we were *all* thinking—that wasn't something exclusive to Lotfi, but that's how we thought of him, because he was in a broader sense so consumed by himself, only ever coming to us with some plan he wanted to put into action, projects that had nothing in common save their lunacy. Yet he believed that "There's no such thing as 'impossible.'"

No matter how many attempts were made, and failed, back he'd come with a different idea and an unyielding determination.

"Even when we're together he's thinking," said Manal, glancing toward their bedroom as though the words were in need of an explanation.

The leader and the intellectual. That's how we'd be, Manal and I. I'd tell her about Utopia, and she'd live it and take me with her into her ideal world. That might be the solution to the lack of space. Don't they say that happiness is a state of mind? If Manal would accept the swap, I'd take her as mine, and there'd be nothing more for us to do aside from a few formal procedures, sufficient repairs for each girl to see their hymens restored so that everyone could experience the pleasure of tearing them apart all over again. Why persevere in this error just because Lotfi and I mistakenly got the wrong hymen the first time around? Would any of them object on grounds of love? If so, I'd have no answer to that idiocy: we'd end up drowning in the swamp of vulgarity that humankind has thrown up time and time again over the course of its history.

Huda laughed at a comment Lotfi made about the film we were watching. Manal noticed, and a tigress's temper surfaced in her features. She leaned forward, resting her elbows on her knees, and I was swept with a feeling of insubstantiality confronted by the cleavage now laid dazzlingly bare before my eyes. It was a preparation for what was to come, and when didn't matter.

Our colleague, 'A,' failed to open the apartment's front door for the third time. We retraced our steps. Perhaps it was from being so long away from the job. He remained downcast, especially with the others criticizing him, and expressed a desire to leave, wishing us every success. The others put up no objection, but I refused. Sticking together, I said, was more important.

For two months, I helped him recover his lost skills. I went out with him to practice entering empty apartments. His spirits returned, and then we went back to work.

Mustafa Ismail
The Book of Safety

15

"WE ANTICIPATE A DAZZLING FUTURE for you. You are one of the individuals we hope to bring into our team."

In exchange for flattery, I gave my soul to the job. And the truth is I had no clear idea how I had failed, even when I heard quite different words five years later telling me that I was to be let go. Yet my inability to comprehend the reasons for this decision did not stop me making peace with it. There was no longer anything tempting me to stay; it was just that there are those whom, once you've gotten involved with them, you can't see how to get away from. You hope they'll make the first move, like you might wish the girlfriend you no longer want would leave you. This happens when the stories are no longer amusing or inspiring enough to distract you from your wretched existence. I'd reached the point where I longed to go back to things in the real world, even if they were of no great worth.

And who was I that Nabil al-Adl should request my consent to a deal between himself and Mustafa Ismail: the original copy of *The Book of Safety* in return for his freedom? No one would ask questions about what he'd stolen; his loot would be his, something the government would swear to before God and his believers should the testimony be required. That's if Mustafa cared about that kind of testimony in the first place. All he had to do was give his word that there were no other copies anywhere else, and likewise pledge not to reproduce it from memory in any format: no audio, no text, no interviews with other chroniclers. He must forget his book, as though it had never been. And perhaps they had requested, further, that the same apply to him: be as though he'd never been. And so he was. He vanished utterly. I always imagine that he's keeping out of sight, writing a new *Book of Safety* for some new enterprise, or that he's chosen the simple and logical resolution to his tale, becoming one of the hundreds of holy fools who seek shelter in the shrines of saints and mosques.

But when it was offered me, I had turned down the deal to release Mustafa, because it went against everything his project stood for. It didn't fit with his defiance. I did what needed to be done. It never occurred to me that this might have been his plan, that he had known from the outset that the case would never reach court, that the files would be burned or placed in some secret archive. The authorities would never risk placing them in the hands of the masses. Publishing the details wouldn't be wise. Better to claim these things had never happened—and that could certainly be arranged.

I left without saying goodbyes, as though I'd be back the following day. Just a few words from Nabil al-Adl informing me of the decision, hinting that I hadn't given what was expected of me, and underlining a previous warning:

"Everything you have seen and heard never existed, and the consequences should you dare to transgress will not be happy ones."

I rejoiced in my deliverance, but one thought would continue to plague me like a nightmare: what had I been doing? Where had I spent all those years? Everyone finds it easy to talk about what they do—doctor, engineer, pilot, journalist, policeman, baker, and so on to the end of the list. Fancy jobs and menial jobs, lawful and illicit. I was one of the few people in this world who couldn't carry an identity card. The only information I'd have been able to put on it would have been my name and phone number. I wasn't an investigator, or a cop, or a researcher, or a journalist, I was all these things and more; mine was the most cutting-edge profession of all, a blend of specializations that produced a job with no name, which is why I would dodge questions about what I did, like the timid man who prefers not to talk about the length of his penis. For the whole time I worked there, I had avoided social gatherings outside work simply so that we could never get to the question: "And what do you do, sir?"

Until he left his job, no one ever told this 'sir' what it was that he did. I'd get a decent salary—nothing over the top, but sufficient and encouraging—with many a hint that I could bring in double the amount with extra privileges if I would only shrug off the passivity that afflicted me. If I were to become a proactive member of the team, if I could look past the superficial limitations of my job title: a clerk who tran-scribes whatever is dictated to him.

But confronted by the question that no one would ever give me a clear answer to, I froze. "Just what is our job title, guys?"

Confidential report, with request for leniency:
Although Mr. Khaled Mamoun is possessed of abundant abilities and talents that might have qualified him for an important position, he lacks the conviction that would see his potential fulfilled. He stops on the brink of the question, and shies at any attempt to extract a response. More troubling still, he is reluctant to get involved, and that contravenes the first condition that all potential team members are required to fulfill.

After five years here, we have been unable to find any improvement in these passive traits of his, which were noted at the outset and which, it is now clear, we were wrong to regard as incidental. For this reason, we recommend that his services be dispensed with, and to pass over the procedures that are usually followed in cases such as this, since we are confident that he will not take advantage of the secrets to which he has been privy.

Like Ashraf al-Suweifi, I returned home furious at the years I'd lost; yet unlike him, I had no right to complain. I would find no sympathetic ear. "Good that you're coming to terms with yourself."

That self of mine was rent, and torn, and still didn't know what it wanted, and unlike my colleagues I hadn't come to terms with it. But I still had my place at home: I was yet to be cast out by a father of indulgent Eastern tendencies incapable of forcing his son (no longer a charming infant) to leave, in the hope that the boy would work out for himself where his duty lay, i.e.: leaving the poor man in peace and going off on his own quest. I emerged from the prison of my mysterious occupation into a featureless freedom. Once more, I found myself in a state of alienation, which led me to seriously consider the possibility that I was suffering from a real problem, one I must focus on to cure. I had lots of time, a lifetime perhaps. Achieving things wasn't the point. Isn't it the journey that counts, after all?

After leaving work, I spent a further two years trying to put the golden rule into practice: "Know thyself."

I would shut my eyes and listen to the sound of the world, trying to locate my position within it, hoping to reach the sound of my own self stripped of extraneous distraction. But I grasped nothing clear-cut: chimeras, deceptive thoughts, faked images. The only tangible thing was instinct. Impressed by its clarity, I would respond to its call without a fight. Is there anything inside us at all except for these instincts? Who was it that came up with those moronic lines about transcending and rising above the ephemeral?

Which is better, this or that?

I couldn't be like Ustaz Fakhri; I wasn't a true recluse. He never thought of what he'd left behind, didn't draw comparisons between himself and others, never stopped to wonder what was right and what was wrong, didn't concern himself with passing judgment on what others did and didn't do. This serenity of his, which I sought to embody, was ruined by hundreds of questions. Which is more honorable: to emerge, spent, from an experience in which you believed you'd found the way, or to grow frail and weak because you were never bothered to think of a 'way' in the first place?

"Sleep is brother to death."

Absorbed in myself, I hadn't noticed how serious were the changes that had started to overtake Lotfi. The above line, his commentary on my laziness, doubled my trepidation and nervousness. I was careful not to inquire after the source of the quote so as to avoid initiating a discussion on religion that I had no wish for.

"You're confusing what mustn't be confused."

As baldly as that did my only friend in the world deliver his opinion following the publication of *The Book of Safety*. He had said what Hasna was now saying—that I'd allowed myself to be tricked, and had then tried to trick others:

"The revolutionary can never be a thief. They're two paths that never meet."

In vain did I tell him that stepping outside the law took many forms, and that history was full of those who sought to burnish their image, concealing the true nature of their actions and tendencies. I invoked Egypt's most famous outlaw to make my case, the Robin Hood of the Nile:

"Take Adham al-Sharqawi," I argued. "He was a thief."

The debate over my book should never have led to the coldness that then crept into our friendship, and yet, in addition to this radical transformation of Lotfi's (which I was unable to accept), I feared the consequences that Nabil al-Adl had warned me of should I reveal what secrets I knew and

I was by no means confident that the sentence I'd put at the end of the book—*These characters and incidents bear no relationship to any in real life*—would be sufficient to assuage their anger. Would they treat me and my book as they had done Mustafa's, claiming that it had never happened, or would revenge pit them against me as a traitor?

What *had* happened, though, was that everybody found what they wanted in the book. The authorities turned me back into their loyal retainer, especially since I'd jettisoned anything that might in any way hint at their stupidity and ignorance; while those on the margins saw a story they liked about crushed dreams. And I didn't say a thing. I took refuge in the democracy of interpretation and the right of the text to have a life independent of its creator. But inside, there remained an uncontrollable anxiety over the schemes that were surely being drawn up for me.

Wrapped up against the unusually cold winter, Lotfi sat on the edge of the bed, his head bowed. There'd been a similar scene when I'd broken up with Huda, but unlike her he did not weep tears that poured unendingly like rain (I had thought of telling her about Alice, whose tears had formed a lake that almost drowned a town). He looked down at the books he'd placed on his firmly pressed-together thighs, just as Huda had done the first day she'd come as far as the bed—several books placed on her clamped thighs, taking refuge from surprise attack behind their authors, not perceiving that what they had written about love and seduction would flow into her blood and stir her desire to let it sully her.

What was the cause of this resemblance between the pair of them? Their virginal postures? Might desire find its way to him, too, and we would fuck? I laughed, concealing a nervousness that had lately been afflicting me each time we met. Ten minutes to nine. Eight to nine, to be precise. In this limp-wristed fashion our friendship was going to end. I'd been wondering what I could do to avoid the meeting, unaware he'd taken the same decision as I had—and that all we'd had to do to avoid cheap maneuvers was be open with each other.

"So I take it you've decided to kill yourself, then?" I said, in reference to the unexpected return of books I'd forgotten he had borrowed. His expression was unforgiving, one I'd never seen before.

"Render unto Caesar. . . ."

I'd never treated his displays with the requisite seriousness. Just another of his phases, I thought, and it would soon pass like all the others before it. From wanting to be a playwright to trying to emigrate, then attempting to build his body up into a mass of muscle, because—as he believed at the time—the regime was crumbling, and when it fell big bodies would be in demand. And then, when he'd realized that this physical strength would require him to lose some part of his mental capacity, he'd dropped it and started spouting theories about suicide, saying that it was the only act of will and protest available to us.

When they handed him the tools of revolution—a few Salafi tracts and a bike chain—I'd told him that this went way beyond 'discovering new ideas.' After every failed venture, he'd console himself by saying, "We met new people and got to know how they think."

He'd signed up to this latest venture after his failure with poetry and the resulting crisis with Manal.

She couldn't stand his depression over his inability to forget. Their relationship rested, in essence, on his repeated attempts to do so. When his fire had gone out, he had seemed ghostlike beside her unquenchable vivacity, but what was certain was that a large part of this vivacity derived from her interactions with his impossible dreams and ambitions—for as he grew still, so her behavior became characterized by falsity and exaggeration, and where before she'd been the motor that kept this household of four lovers running, she now wore a perpetual scowl. There's nothing more absurd than a grim-faced woman.

The previous autumn: love's crimson leaves fluttered down, and neither I nor Huda could come up with a solution. Quite the reverse—we were following what was happening between them with a degree of satisfaction. For the first time, our disputes were not the only subject under discussion. Lotfi and Manal had moved into that slot, while we made the attempts at reconciliation that they'd once made with us. And yet—with conscious malice, perhaps—we were helping make their quarrels worse. Huda did it to prolong the time it gave us to grow close, in the hope that our relationship would progress to the next level, while I was trying as hard as I could to wreck their relationship because my own with Huda would become unsustainable as a consequence and would come to an end of its own accord. She would never sacrifice Manal for my sake, especially since there was no future in what we had together.

"Can you explain to me why you haven't forgotten the poetry despite all the trouble we've gone to?" And before the poor guy could reply, she got in an even more important question: "Even though, O poet, you found it easy enough to forget the details of our life together."

The honorific wasn't mockery, though. She didn't care that his sole achievements in the field had been to learn one thousand lines of verse that had stuck in his brain and wouldn't leave, and to dedicate an execrable poem to her—she had thought of him as a poet ever since he had declared his wish to be one: "The moment we met, I told myself you were an artist."

Had he chosen another dream, she would have endorsed it in similar terms: "The moment we met, I told myself you were made for a life at sea."

And since Lotfi derived his right to be called a poet from Manal's assertion that he was one, it was only natural that his first poem should hymn her beauty and strength of character, the poem itself providing incontrovertible evidence of the legitimacy she'd bestowed on his talent—which meant that I was obliged to stop making fun of the pair of them. As she'd said, speaking frankly, "Art is a flower garden full of every hue and shade. Anyone and everyone can make art there, but jealousy is the start of a slippery slope."

I said nothing to her about her failing to spot his plagiarism from a considerable number of other poems, or that she'd no business talking about art when she'd noticed neither his outrageous metrical errors nor his complete absence of rhythm. But it wasn't like we were a circle of critics, and whatever makes your heart sing is poetry regardless of what others think of it—all Lotfi had to do once he'd written her that poem was spend two hours a day sitting at his desk covering the reams of colored paper she bought him with words and he would have himself a collection—proving to the world that here was a man with talent.

And her assistance and encouragement didn't stop there. She'd suggest titles and ideas for poems, like the one which spoke of our story, us four together, and about love's ability to transcend cramped spaces. She called it 'Days of Lilac,' suggesting that this also be the title for the collection as a whole. And when he had trouble setting the images that passed through his mind to paper, she'd said, "You have to combine reality and fantasy like Rimbaud did!"

"But Rimbaud's not some lifestyle you can imitate. The things he did came from his conviction in his chosen path—or better, his lack of faith in the conventional ways of doing things, and an attempt to create something different, however against the grain. He was bored with humanity at a gut level. For example, where are we going to find slaves to trade in?"

I went on about Rimbaud, trying to dissuade her from her idea. I made reference to his homosexual relationship with Verlaine, claiming that for both poets their time together had been their most creative period. "Could you accept Lotfi and me having a relationship like that for the sake of poetry?"

So I asked her, imagining that I was taking things to their extreme, but the game blew up in my face.

"If that's what you two wanted, I wouldn't stop you."

I turned to Lotfi to put a stop to her shamelessness, but he said nothing, as though it didn't concern him at all. Then I wanted to push the game further, imagining the four lovers fucking together to summon poetry's daemon. We might be able to trap the daemon in this apartment. We could drift around behind Lotfi as metonymy, metaphor, and meter rained down on him like revelation, me making love to his lover while he busied himself with the blank pages—a kiss from her the equal of a line of verse, an embrace a whole poem—and when she stripped naked, he would shout in fright as the poetry cascaded down over his head.

"How are you?" the waiter asked as he set our drinks down, taking extra care that nothing should spill onto the pages. This was also her idea.

"Your chess-playing friends have somewhere to go; the musicians have their own place. So do the writers, the actors, even the crooks. It's got to do with mutual spiritual inspiration, it's not just somewhere they meet. I mean, that's common knowledge."

Some inner conviction had prompted her to hand the waiter a sum of money once, following a short conversation in which she'd explained the situation, and he had assured her, "The ustaz will get the break he needs here, for sure."

This was a prelude, a state in which Lotfi was to lay bare his heart and soul, both of them mingling with the thousands of words and ideas once uttered in this place. Was there anywhere better than the Café Riche, with its rich history, to unpick a poet's block? Hunched motionless before the colored sheets, uncapped pen in hand, he waited for the spirits of the old masters to descend. He would mock her and her ideas, but he was drawn to her, most probably a compensation for the role his father had refused to play—the father whose function was to be unforgiving, allowing the son to uncover the extent of rebellion within himself.

But Manal, sharper than Huda, was not sharp enough to see that Lotfi being drawn to her in this way merely laid the ground for a mutiny against her, and that in pressuring him to become an artist, she was merely hastening his revolt. His admission that he hadn't forgotten the thousand lines was the first step toward the collapse of their relationship. If he'd still wanted her, he would have claimed that he'd forgotten them. It would have been no big deal—who was going to rummage through his memory looking for the remainder of those lines?

But he was letting her know that both she, and what she was doing in his life, were valueless.

Sometimes I think that I am the only person who believes in anything.

Mustafa Ismail
The Book of Safety

16

A GRAM OF KNOWLEDGE IS worth a ton of truth.

Though I might try to ignore this sentence, the letters of the original were still the last thing I saw at night and the first thing I opened my eyes on in the morning. There had been many other pictures, but this was the largest and most technically accomplished of them all, and for that reason the most effective. Its thirty-five letters were made up of a thousand images—so I was told, though I didn't get the chance to check; I never examined it long enough to count them, even though I received 'permission to inspect' in order to traverse the hard yards that lay between me and enlightenment.

"Start with the smallest and most obscure—the obvious-looking ones are booby-trapped."

This was my boss Nabil al-Adl's advice, on which basis I started out, inspecting the pictures enough to absorb their meaning, which was the fundamental precondition for membership of the organization. Two weeks I spent at it, wandering here and there, transfixed before picture after picture, text after text, as receptive as I could be but muddled by the words I saw before me, which always seemed somehow superficial. I once saw tears in the eyes of a colleague as he contemplated them. Neither I nor anyone else had the right to pass comment or question him. Curiosity should be directed at what merited it, otherwise you lacked seriousness. His tears were his business, and furthermore the reason for them was too obvious to have to ask: faith had dawned in his heart, and his tears had overwhelmed him. I felt a touch jealous, wished I wasn't like I was, that I possessed the innocence of ignorance, and that words might give me pleasure once again. I do not believe that had I gone on working in the Palace of Confessions I would have arrived at a faith like his, but at least I would have gotten myself a copy of the original picture. Employees got one as a mark of appreciation when they were promoted, or as a token of esteem when they made an honorable departure.

Every seven years, employee performance was reviewed, and those whose missions had turned into routine desk jobs, who had lost their faith and their spiritual connection to our creeds, were transferred to one or other institution of state at a higher salary and in an elevated position. There they would teach the no-hopers what they'd learned, and become a set of eyes and ears for their former employers at this new workplace—in which way the whole country was bound together in the sight of one all-seeing eye. The departing soul took nothing with him save his personal possessions and a copy of the picture, a thank you for his efforts, a little pledge that though he was leaving, more capable hands remained behind. He would keep the copy at home, sidestepping questions about where it came from or what it meant, taking refuge in the answer he'd been given himself and had off by heart: "Look and you shall see."

And he would raise his children according to its values, to lift them clear of the society which surrounded them and which venerated facts without considering, even for an instant, that they might be worthless. It would have been a nice little keepsake if I'd ever gotten it. I set aside an entire wall for it, and spent days peering at the images. I could only make a few out: a girl running in terror after the bombing of Nagasaki; beheadings in Saudi Arabia (a head flying through the air and blood fountaining from the neck); a man dangling from a noose, his last minutes on earth stretched out in a struggle against the pain of standing on broken-necked bottles. But the truly astonishing thing was that it contained the very picture Dmitri had sitting on his desk: two men and two women on camelback in front of the pyramids and Sphinx, and all of them, human and animal alike, staring out with a kind of defiance. I would have plenty of time to make certain it was the same picture, and to look for a link between Dmitri and the Palace of Confessions.

Scattered down the corridors were a number of other pictures, all resembling the original:

> Death is a dream.
> Failure is a choice.
> Today, we restore to you your sight.

The same idea: to create different ways of thinking. Al-Adl and I had more than once held discussions about cases that had ended with him referencing the picture over his head: "The right piece of information is worth a thousand truths."

It had taken me a while to get used to this kind of thinking, and for a time I'd believed that I might perhaps have become more like my colleagues, who lived their lives according to the pictures' precepts. From the beginning, I'd never had difficulty accepting that truths change over the course of history, and that personal whims and interests are factors of fundamental importance. What I was now doing with *The Book of Safety*'s second edition was the best example of this, and certainly I had no problem believing that what I thought true others would see as lies.

No, the essence of my dilemma lay in distinguishing knowledge from truth. For instance, there's no system of measurement that can tell you that this is a gram of knowledge and that's a ton of truth. And anyway, I thought the entire sentence was based on an outright error, undermined by a rhetorical grandeur that didn't sit well with its message, the interpretations and explanations it acquired no more than the product of wordplay:

"Knowledge is superior to truth because it is pure information, unprocessed by an ideological assembly line that might cut it with other substances to boost the size of the final product."

"Information is your existence. Truth is what you are."

Mustafa seemed like someone who understood the difference, which was why—in al-Adl's view—he sought to swamp us in truths rather than information, thereby turning the case (as Lotfi had hinted early on) into a philosophical issue—and in doing so, mocking the place and the principles it was built on. He was too clever to clam up, but at the same time effectively said nothing, especially when it came to those subjects he preferred not to speak about, which included his travels, his return, and the immediate aftermath (to wit: his relationship with his wife and her death).

His wife. Aliya had been an employee at the Center for Statistics and Census. She'd never had a medical issue, and the heart attack that descended out of the blue less than a year after Mustafa's return and which was recorded as cause of death by the doctor did not convince. Heart attacks are a cause of death in a general sense—but what had led to it? Had he disposed of her? Why? Had she gotten in the way of his grand scheme? Wasn't it possible that she had rejected him? That she shrank from him was one of the very few pieces of information we'd gleaned about their post-return relationship. Had she objected to the way he meant to raise their daughter?

Travel liberates you from ties. Things never go back to how they were, no matter how hard you try or how sincere your desire to bond.

That's what he told us, along with other hints insufficient to construct a picture of this period of his life. For this reason, it would be important to indicate that the chapter dealing with his travels and return was based on an interpretation of his statements, that it was an attempt to chart the changes that took place in his life while emphasizing that this attempt was bound to be inadequate, given that he had so successfully cloaked his actions—indeed, all his social contacts and relationships—in mystery.

He clearly had a plan for dealing with us. He gave us what we wanted, gave generously, a vast quantity of data that initially satisfied al-Adl, and the management, and those higher still. And then, with the natural sagacity of those in power, they realized that his continued presence among them, even though it might appear that they held his fate in their hands, in fact did nothing but sap their own strength and place him at the heart of the action. I was like a virus in the café, and he was like a virus in our Palace.

It would also be important to highlight the scale of Hasna's crucial intervention, in this chapter in particular. What confused me here was whether I had to apologize to the readers of the first edition or those of the second. Or was I not obliged to say sorry to either, on the grounds that "truths are always changing"?

Or they had never existed at all; that it was us who'd invented them and labeled them as we did? The first edition of *The Book of Safety* presented Mustafa as a stud; lovers of erotica would, I believe, enjoy perusing one chapter in particular, which contained details of his relations with his wife and his adventures with a girl from an unspecified foreign country where women "still knew their place." And though Hasna had been able to make me see how unpleasant I'd been to have so flagrantly violated the privacy of their home—to the extent that I couldn't stand the sight of the book, wanted it gone as though it had never been—I still found myself compelled to import some of the first edition's content about Mustafa's pre-departure relationship with his wife:

*

After Hasna fell asleep, her mother was alone with herself. She was so fortunate he'd chosen her, *the humble government employee. She had finished her schooling and laid down her books for good, even as he forged a career as a university professor. To her, it seemed that he knew everything. She spent a long time mulling it over: why had he chosen her of all people? She wasn't beautiful enough to gloss over the gulf in their education. Her family wasn't well-off enough to support her aunt's theory that he had been after financial support to help him see out two years while he completed his doctorate. Stranger still, he envied her her job. She didn't believe him. Assumed he was being smooth. What was so interesting about totting up citizens? Why would a university professor crave a job in statistics and census? She found it difficult to accept that "seeing how people live is a treasure."*

She had no idea how to respond to his request and tell him about what she had seen in the homes she visited. She didn't have his skill. She could tell him about herself, about her longing that he open for her his bolted doors, but how to talk about people whose connection with her would never extend further than a single, never to be repeated, visit—and if repeated, then unremembered? The homes, like their inhabitants, were all alike: numbers and names in her ledger.

In return for his choosing her, all she could do was love him as no woman had loved a man before, without conditions or questions, but his absence gave her time to consider what his presence had prevented her from turning over in her mind. And she had known the answer; it was just that being swept off her feet by lust had blinded her. Some god of sex had been toying with her. She had no experience of sexual complexes, but she was a woman, and where his touch had once numbed her brain she was now all alone, a body thirsting, wanting, needing to be made complete, and no one there to help. And necessity, before being the mother of invention, is the mistress of the mind's authentic truth.

At first, she had been unable to shake a sense that they were doing something forbidden. Her information about sex was hazy (as was the case with most of the girls she knew)—a veiled jest that was set aside before they could plumb the depths. Sex, she believed, was the levy women paid in exchange for the dream of family: each man forcing what he saw as fair on his woman. She had got herself ready, prepared from the outset to pay her particular due. She'd pictured it a number of different ways, but had never dreamed that it would be like this. Her nakedness before him wasn't just a matter of nudity: he controlled her body as though he were its creator. He had acquainted himself with it in no time at all, like he had memorized its topography or drawn a map that her soul obediently followed. He would say, as he teased her, as she lost control, that he was toying with the world and its future, that their tomorrow would be better than their today—as though the unspoken point was that she mustn't forbid him anything; that their future depended on the lengths she went to in bed.

He habituated her to foreplay, even when he didn't go all the way. The curtailed climax, he instructed her, leaves its echoes in body and soul for longer—reaching the peak didn't just kill delight, it left both of them unable to communicate for a day or two afterward. At the last moment, they would hold off the discharge of all that energy until, finally, they came to the point of no return, when she would sense that things were not going to quietly peter out, and with a violent surge would quit the cramped sleeve of her body, her soul soaring free.

But the pleasure she experienced with him did not prevent the slow accumulation of resentment. She was practically his slave, the bed the only space in which she was able to approach him. Other than that, he read or wrote, a different person entirely: polite, noncommittal, complimentary in a way that sat oddly with the things he got up to with her at night. Her instinct guided her to a bridge that might connect them—that she, like him, could be a creator; she the doer, he the done. She persevered in her discovery of him but, confronted with his impenetrability, gave in, bewildered by his limitless capacity to launch her body into flight. And with time she guessed the secret: that his body would accept her only when she stopped treating the thing as a debt to be repaid. She learned to desire him. Yet even as she embarked on this new game, he made up his mind to leave.

And when at last he returned, he discovered that he no longer belonged anywhere. His wife had chosen death rather than adjusting to his changes, body and soul rejecting him from the moment she'd opened the front door. His daughter needed to be reequipped so she could reach an understanding of what it meant to be in this world. She was a girl who longed to live like

the animals, unaware that their destiny was dust: how to make her under-
stand that renunciation was the way to possession, that love was a road
paved with hatred, that pain was the only way for people to feel happiness?

The first thing his wife said when she broke her silence: "Why did
you come back?"

Neither a reproach nor a demand for an apology for what had hap-
pened, for the unilateral decision he'd laid on her, for leaving without
giving her a chance, for being out of contact all that time save for a scant
few phone calls to let her know he was still alive and that he'd moved on
again. Behind the question was a hatred she made no effort to hide.

How could he explain to her that he had been driven off and had returned
the same way, that a force greater than him had taken possession of his self
and soul, and when it gave orders he had to do what he was told. She would
say she didn't want him any more: not him and not the 'force' that controlled
him. She wanted reasons from the real world, and he was no good at coming
up with these. He'd really tried, though, and had asked for time. Had made
her promises in the name of what they'd had between them, unaware that this
was precisely what was driving them apart, what led her to hide inside the
loose clothes, nothing showing, and then (deciding, faced with his gaze, that
this wasn't enough) pressing her legs tightly together whenever his male reek
came over her. Yet she was content. A part of her that she had no control over
wanted him, and wanted a different kind of relationship, just on condition
that he not come near her. He could stay in the apartment if he wanted, and
witness what time did to her. A game which he accepted, without being hurt.

It is not important how you play. What matters is that you win.

They would speak as friends. He would tell her and his daughter what
he'd been through.

Stories are the shortcut to people's hearts.

He was awaiting forgiveness, and he would never get it.

After years of waiting, her body had closed in on itself and her fears
had returned: a marriage contract can't justify prostitution. He'd turned

her into a whore and left her. After that, she'd decided, he would never touch her again. He returned, and she let him be: maybe he'd wake up and understand. But he just sat there, a lord brought low, a king who missed the thrill of his servants' groveling. She couldn't stand his brokenness too long, and a warning voice told her that this might mean her end.

But now, after months spent praying that he would return to his bed, beside her, like a child rediscovering his favorite game and playing a knight in love, she hoped he would have grown up and realized that the powers he was so proud of no longer meant anything to her.

It was nothing at all like before. When he'd leaned in to her, whispering that five years hadn't changed them, that yesterday was no different from today, she had wanted to say, "You're the stupidest university professor in the world."

But she couldn't speak. Yesterday wasn't today, and no matter the effort she made to believe it the feeling of humiliation was stronger, like she couldn't get enough air into her lungs. It wasn't arousal, like he'd assumed. Her pulse was gradually slowing, a car left to drift to a halt. A great cold gripped her, and her body shook.

"I'm dying, Mustafa."

He kissed her on her cheeks and lips, sampled her tears, whose taste he'd not forgotten during all his years of travel. It never occurred to him that she quite literally meant what she said. It was his body, stretched out over hers, that told him something had gone wrong.

She had gone out beneath him.

He lifted his face up from where it lay on the pillow, beside her head, smelling her hair, and poured the old praise of her body into her ears. She didn't give her usual shy chuckle. She was suspiciously quiet and still. It occurred to him, but he pushed the thought away, pleading in his heart that she hadn't really done it, that she could not be punishing him this way.

There's nothing like a woman's face transported by sex. Nothing like being the man who etched those expressions on her face.

He lay beside her, and his stiff prick made him mad at her. Briefly, he contemplated fucking her. The idea seemed degrading, inhuman; instead of feeling sorrow, all he sought was to douse his lust.

But, as always, he recovered himself, turned it over in his mind, and came up with a powerful justification for having retained his erection.

That it wasn't appropriate was the principal dilemma. The excuse? That it was a new experience.

Hasna and I had debated the entire contents of the book, and she had written out the emendations she viewed as necessary (this after farcical arguments whose only aim was to get me to pretend that I'd pay her a reasonable proportion of the money I made), yet we had never once looked at this chapter. And long may this state of affairs continue, I prayed. Hopefully she'd be prevented by shyness, say. . . .

"I hate the way the relationship between husband and wife is depicted. That's a properly sick imagination!"

"I respect your right to be angry, but what I've written can in no way be described as 'sick.' There's no such thing, anyway, and you aren't any therapist to be issuing diagnoses like that. The way I conceive of the relationship is an attempt to present a picture of Mustafa that renders his actions comprehensible. He shan't be obstructed by the taboos that others create for themselves. He alone will find the reasons to convince himself to undertake an action or forbear from it. And only experience shall guide him, nothing else. Not law, or custom, or tradition, or any other label of that sort."

"Well, if that's so, then after he'd experienced burglary and necrophilia, he should have killed himself, because it's the only thing he hadn't tried!"

"Of course, if it weren't for the fact that suicide's a one-way street," I pointed out. Did you know that Achilles slept with Penthesilea after he killed her? Of course you did."

"Oh yeah?" she retorted. "And who am *I* supposed to be then? Helen? Which would make you who? Homer? You have to get rid of these overworked and sick sex scenes. Remember, you're talking about real people here, not characters in a novel. I'm prepared to give you a story about Mustafa and I suggest you use it to revise this chapter first."

"If it's convincing," I said.

"Well, your story's unconvincing and it's untrue. At least mine's real."

"Truth is relative."

"There's no need to be annoying. That's the sort of thing failures say to mask their inability to come up with answers. And even if I were to agree with you, motivations are certainly not relative. My story contains a justification for what Mustafa did, and this is one of the glaring weak points in your writing: you never explain the reason for this transformation to the reader."

"Perhaps that was intentional," I argued. "I left it up to each person to find their own motives."

"They'd never realize—they'd just assume it's inability or incompetence, believe me."

"All right, well, why don't I hear it first, then make my mind up?"

And Hasna began her tale.

"Did Mustafa regret the decision to travel? He had lost nothing save the sensation of familiarity that had once been his companion on his evening wanderings. Since returning, he had lost the ability to leave the apartment after ten. He had come to fear the night, the surprises it would throw up. People had changed. They had become harder-edged, more hostile. Before, when there had been no one abroad but him and a few soldiers guarding important positions, the night had been his friend and confidante. He would swap greetings with the conscripts. They knew him by name. He would stand at their posts and corners, and lighten time's burden for them. They opened their hearts to him. Hundreds of stories of longing for family and far-off territories. They came from distant villages to stand rigid in their allotted posts for years, delighting at the sight of a different way of life, but one they were not part of. No one paid them any mind. In their wretched uniforms, they all looked the same. They only ever heard their names called out at roll call. Other than that, they were 'private' and 'soldier.'

"One night, before his disappearance, there was nothing abroad except for the street cats, who had begun to gather for a prearranged meeting with the woman who drove around in her car to feed them. He had tracked her until he knew the route she took: from Zamalek onto July 26th Street, where she stopped twice—once just after the bridge by a famous liver joint that served its customers till sunup, the staff emerging and asking her to move on, if only a short distance. She neither turned to them nor heard them, saw nothing but the cats. Finally, the staff let her be, muttering curses against madness and the rich folk who took pity on animals in a country stuffed with the starving. In Downtown, she made three stops that never altered—hidden side streets, perfectly still, where she could be at ease with her pusses, emptying the food from her trunk and departing with a happiness that would last her till the next day. He walked to Abbasiya, peering hard all the way at the things he'd seen before.

"Her shade kept him company through his years of exile. What was her story? How did she spend her day? Sleeping all day and getting up in the evening to prepare the cat food? Was that her relationship with the world? *She* was his reason for coming home. She had managed to stay in his memory, even though he'd moved so much that he had almost forgotten his native land. The faces and customs he'd seen swirled inside him till he couldn't tell exactly where it was he stood in relation to them all.

"He had traveled for so long that he could only visualize himself speeding down highways or suspended amid clouds that held him fast. He had gone to countries that no one had thought of going to. He'd seen all he had dreamed of and more—mountains with water pouring down from their heights and cutting its way through the rocks, water that had been flowing for thousands of years, in winter freezing inside its caves, then running again come summer, never wasting itself, completing the circle to fall once more. It had its own way of thinking. They had taken him up the hillside to spend the night there. He had a little water, a handful, no more. These people held the mountain water sacred, and allowed only the chosen to approach it. A handful of water to guide him, to course through his body and purge him of doubt. He had earned it, they said, and why not? He was almost one of them. By now he'd almost forgotten that he had been sent to guide them to the true path, a member of an organization funded by rich backers. If they agreed to the idea, he told himself, he would simply give them the money set aside to help them, and leave them be.

"He learned how a man must be unshakable at those heights, cold as the air that circled him, quick and decisive as the horses he rode here for the first time. He discovered other ways of being a man quite unlike the meek and mild types fashioned in the Nile's evening breeze."

"Okay," I said. "A lovely story. What's the motive for the change, though?"

A warning look. "Don't joke with me."

I fell silent, combing the story for what I couldn't see.

"I really don't get it. It might be my fault and not the story's, but that's the truth."

"Come on! And you call yourself a writer? Honestly, I don't think you're suited to the work at all. Plus the motivation's completely obvious."

I mastered my temper as best I could. "So would you be so kind as to explain? You know, without being rude."

"The cats," Hasna replied.

"Excuse me?"

"The cats! It's as clear as day."

"You're saying that he turned from a respectable university professor into a thief because of the cats?"

"Exactly."

"Exactly?"

"Think about it."

Why had Mustafa left? Where had he gone? How had he spent those seven years? As a line of inquiry, it mattered to us to be able to comprehend the changes he'd gone through. What kind of place was it that people could go to and come back so dangerous? In the future, we'd be able to welcome such returnees with a ready-made diagnosis: "They have lost their sense of guilt at breaking the law, which gives them the ability to toy with the law's enforcers using strategies and tricks undreamed of."

To gain paradise, you must pass through hell. We are fated to go through this by all that is earthbound and base. There are things you only understand once you are removed from the familiar. It is not just that you have sufficient time to contemplate—to contend with homesickness and the desire for comfort is to take possession of a contentment that will never fade.

Tolstoy has a story about a wager between a group of drunkards. One of them declares that he is capable of spending twenty years on his own. They are drunk enough to put the bet into practice. The next day, they place him in a hut situated in the garden of his main house, and lock him in. After a week has gone by, they come to him and say, "Enough, that'll do," as though there had never been a bet at all. He refuses. Maybe they try again later. It's a terrible thing to contemplate, of course, but he refuses and insists on sticking to the agreement. At first, they can hear his screams and laughter as he talks to himself. Then he asks for distractions and entertainment, and after that for books in all the disciplines and sciences. Then his voice begins to grow faint, and he rants and raves no more. At the end of the period set out in the bet, they come to the room carrying the money, but no sooner have they opened the door than he dashes out, fleeing into a nearby wood and leaving all his possessions behind him.

In Tolstoy's day, all books had the same purpose: to teach us a set of moral principles that must be adhered to. The story's most obvious meaning, and perhaps its only one, was that knowledge does not sit comfortably with life—a message that was common currency during my own youth: one must renounce; ownership is a sin. Of course, this idea was shown to be false, not only because those who pushed it were liars, but more importantly because you can't excise what is an inherent part of people: greed,

204

pride, and selfishness, qualities that have just as much right to exist as abstention, modesty, and altruism.

What can be gleaned from the struggle between the two—knowledge and life—is down to each individual. The point is that I may not deny you your right to sin. And despite my subsequent conviction that much of what I had read was wrong, idealism can only be plucked out with great difficulty. That is why I wished to go away, to smash what was left of those dishonest moral values. It was the way to reclaim my humanity.

Mustafa went back to teach at the university without any great expectations, but he hadn't anticipated that he would be side-lined completely:

This is a characteristic of our age: when you are talented and not a follower, you are shunted aside. Your place is on the margins. They leave you until you rot from the frustration and despair, from the doubts in your self-belief. Are you really as you picture yourself to be? Isn't it likely that it's all a fantasy? You're like anyone else. Your dreams and ambitions are not so very special that you can complain of injustice. When you manage to see things straight, you will understand that you are just one of millions who have suffered. Some of them got the point quickly enough, and others—like you—went on stubbornly resisting, and wasted time they might better have spent enjoying.

They can get you so you can't tell any more whether life comes first, or death.

Misdirection is our method and our way. Our working hours are not fixed, and are basically determined by when the security services are busy with a bigger case—a presidential guard of honor; a visit by another head of state; a critical football match.

Events such as these mean that we will be able to work without being bothered, and even if we are *discovered the getaway will be that much easier.*

Mustafa Ismail
The Book of Safety

17

WEDNESDAY, JANUARY 15, 1991. ON this day in history:

Hasna rid her father's library of all references to Mustafa Ismail, leaving just a few covers with his gold-printed name scratched off. Perhaps if he hadn't been so self-centered and had been able to keep books without appending his name to those of the authors, then she wouldn't have acted this way, but history tells us that behind all great works lie rage and the burning desire for vengeance. He himself couldn't have dreamed up a better approach had he chosen to lead a normal way of life. As the dawn of the second millennium drew nearer, she managed to take her first steps into a work she assumed would not immediately meet with much interest, though she was equally convinced that it would become a twenty-first-century classic in time.

She was content, but the contentment was not enough to mask a problem that was taking shape in response. With the last carton delivered by the doorman—sighing in relief at setting down his burden (no appreciation of his historic role)—she was now in possession of a city-sized jigsaw, the assembly of which would require not just effort and dedication, but more importantly that she penetrate to the puzzle's center, from where she could set out in all its other directions. The thousands of pages—now fortune had smiled on them and they'd made it through the preliminary selection procedure as the best pages of the books to which they belonged—waited to have their pages picked for the final work.

From the outset, she'd known that it would be difficult, but she had never imagined it like this. Now she saw it as an impossibility. She would leaf through the pages and, like the great authors, her feelings ranged from a sense of her own irrelevance to megalomania. Overwork left the words running together, indistinguishable, and their meanings grew clouded before her eyes.

A sentence is any clause two or more words long and complete in itself, and is known in Arabic as the *jumla mufida*.

After all this reading, she found that she needed to go back to her primary-school notes to brush up on the basics, because the completeness of the *jumla mufida*, the 'complete sentence,' was relative. What, after all, have we been completely informed of by 'The sun is shining' or 'The boy arose to perform his duties'?

The sun had shone for thousands of millions of years. Another problem! When exactly had the sun begun to shine? The basic stuff escaped her. Every sentence contained a trap into which she'd fall and find herself held up. Relativism reached out its hand. . . .

"The sun left its burrow a long time ago, and the boy rose with it to perform his duties. In the Arabic textbook, they call them 'complete sentences,' but I see them as terrifyingly deficient. What about when the boy grows up? He marries, has kids, and dies, but in the textbook he's still rising, without regard for change. A language of lies!"

Metaphors. One can see why, of course: she turned to them to palm her dilemma off on the Arabic language, on books and their authors. She was the boy, and the sun was her freedom. Hasna had obtained her freedom. Hasna had been unable to enjoy her freedom. Hasna was lost without the father from whom she'd longed to be delivered. Hasna was sad after her mother's death, though she had expected her passing. Were these sentences sufficient to sum up her condition? Were they 'complete'?

She had spent a whole year of her life doing nothing but liberating books, and very late in the game she woke up to the consequences: the sentences scattered over her bedroom floor had robbed her of the ability for rational thought. The job of covers doesn't stop at protecting books—they are gates, equipped with locks which prevent the books' worlds mixing with the real. Which is why they used to burn them in the old days when they wanted to get rid of them, to prevent the ideas and similes slipping out.

She reread the pages with a trembling heart. Though sure that the selection had been made with sufficient care and attention for her to be able to swear that she'd assembled the best of every book—her taste was sound, neither overly romantic, nor coldly rational, nor in hock to any school of thought, but based on humanistic criteria, an attempt to bring different methodologies together—her conscience pricked her: somebody had come up with this idea before.

There had been many compilers, true, but she awarded herself the prize for most comprehensive of all. Those who'd trodden this path before her had confined themselves to a single topic. Writing about love was the undisputed leader, with women and life runners-up; death rarely; then nothing you'd expect thereafter. This restored her confidence. The compilations of yesteryear were motivated by lust, and however much the authors might have claimed to be pursuing knowledge (in the absolute sense), their work bore witness to a shameful selectivity. What hypothetical value could be contained in a volume of sayings about women or love? What was the reader meant to learn from it—how to be a skilled hunter of hearts? The man who spends his whole life searching for someone to love dooms himself to dissatisfaction. And why didn't women compile *bon mots* about men? Was it because they regarded it as beneath them, or because they realized that there were more valuable things than sex and love?

Once more she'd found a reason to thank God that she was a woman of sound mind. She wouldn't have been able to set her desires aside otherwise; wouldn't have been able to forgo revenge against her father or avoid joining that ever-lengthening line of women who scolded the world in increasingly crude and more dramatic terms. She had chosen a more difficult path. Her revenge was a personal matter, and her book's purpose more distant still. Which was why it had no one subject, espoused no particular branch of knowledge. Its subject was the truth, and its means of dealing with this topic was to take on anyone who had ever penned a single word of any worth in the course of all human civilization on geography, history, poetry, the novel, astrology, magic, mathematics—the lot.

Nor was assembling the pages quite as simple as she'd imagined. To choose just one page from every book was more than usually troublesome, and she frequently found herself looking at several pages, bewildered: which was best? Some she liked for their rich sentiment, others for the plotting, yet others for their undeniably well-crafted language. After long consideration, she concluded that she must have a benchmark, completely uncontroversial, against which to manage the selection process.

When she was done with her project, someone was bound to ask her about it. She imagined the fame that would be hers, and this, false modesty aside, was nothing to be ashamed of. She took it as read that her work would draw attention, that the debate over it—its objectives and its worth—would be considerable, and that no sooner released than it would be included in the ranks of must-read books for those after a summary of human history. Of course, she would come across a few errors—that she'd forgotten to include some authors, or a whole literary period, even; or that there was an imbalance in what she presented from each culture—yet when it came to the idea itself, there was no disputing its value, its necessity, and its newness.

It had been a long road to her current feelings (despite doubts) of greatness and of being different from those who had gone before. As with most books, the idea had begun with a single subject, a single discipline no less—and one might claim that where she'd finished up had been the result of nothing less than a failure. The original concept could be summed up as an attempt to assemble various fictional characters within a single work of fiction: all the dreamers, crooks, and revolutionaries; the whores, struggling women, and drabs; warriors and noblemen, thieves and pimps, saints and lunatics—any character that had had any kind of presence in the world of fiction since man had first embarked on that art. Using them, she wanted to set up a life parallel to the one we lived. But dreams, however complex and ambitious, were easy. In her head, the idea had seemed dazzling, splendid, but no sooner was it put into practice than the problems began.

It wasn't just that the characters all had different destinies, and that the events and incidents couldn't be fitted together. The real difficulty was the vision that lies behind each novel. How could hundreds of characters be assembled without contradiction, without her intervention? She wanted the book to flow as smoothly and as easily as life itself, without its prime mover, its engine, ever showing up onstage.

Successfully combining two paragraphs by two different writers, she had danced around her apartment, transported by her own genius, her sheer ability. Hoping that the road would run smoothly now, she resumed work, but the crises kept on coming. Perspectives and styles clashed—the third scene didn't go with the second, or the first. Bringing the rest of the familiar faces into the book provided some kind of solution to this disharmony, and it became easy to imagine that they meant something.
From *Don Quixote*:

Liberty, Sancho, is one of the most valuable gifts heaven
has bestowed upon man; the treasures which the earth

encloses, or the sea covers, are not to be compared with it. Life may, and ought to, be risked for liberty, as well as for honor; and, on the contrary, slavery is the greatest evil that can befall us. I tell you this, Sancho, because you have observed the civil treatment and plenty we enjoyed in the castle we have left. In the midst of those seasoned banquets, those icy draughts, I fancied myself starving, because I did not enjoy them with the same freedom I should have done had they been my own. For the obligations of returning benefits and favors received are ties that obstruct the free agency of the mind. Happy the man to whom heaven has given a morsel of bread, without laying him under the obligation of thanking any other for it than heaven itself!

After this little passage, she chose Madame Roland denouncing the Jacobins as her head rolled away from the guillotine:

O liberty! The crimes committed in thy name!

Liberty was a supreme principle. No, liberty was something we strove for and never reached. The method she followed was never to privilege one principle over another. All would be laid out side by side, with no rhyme or reason, and—like magic— anyone who read her work would see the riddle that they had puzzled over solved before their eyes. By her reckoning, then, she managed to make ten pages out of every thousand, in addition to an introduction in which she recorded her hopes and dreams. Because she continued to suspect that the idea wasn't hers alone, and that she was building on previous work, she opened with a passage from François Mauriac's *Génitrix*:

Every so often he would pause from clipping the maxims from a popular edition of *Epicetus* with his mother's scissors. This former Centrale schoolboy had decided that a book supposed to contain the summation of all wisdom uttered since man first trod the earth must, by a process of mathematical inevitability, reveal to him the secret of life and death. To this end he set about assembling aphorisms from every possible source and the distraction of cutting things out, as he'd done as a child, was the only thing that made him feel secure.

This novel and this son astonished her. It had been a small book, packed in between massive tomes. Because of its size, she'd thought less of it, and hadn't expected it to cause her all this trouble. She herself had been searching for the secret to life and death within her work, but this son had made her feel hugely worried and a little humiliated—not because the secret was no longer worth anything, or because the two ideas were so alike, but because what she understood from Mauriac was that his protagonist had a limited awareness. People fascinated with what lies behind or beyond this world we categorize as 'touched.' While sure that this charge was unmerited, and that it was an attempt to prevent the wave of awareness broadening and spreading, she had nevertheless decided to keep her sympathy for the lunatics in search of the great secrets within reasonable limits.

In her introduction, she wrote:

> I am not like Mauriac's protagonist, searching for the secret of life and death. There is something more general and more important still. Life and death are just a game, and when it's done another will begin. Mauriac's 'son' and many others, such as children, collapse weeping when their playthings break, because they imagine that they only have the one. I have not thought to portray 'The Truth,' but I do believe that my book has the ability to guide each individual to a truth they seek.

The victim shall be my dear friend until the operation has reached its successful conclusion and we have all gone our separate ways. On my desk is a file containing his life: his age, his hobbies, his relationship with wife and children, the times he leaves home and returns, what he or any of those who take his side might be concealing. And most importantly, which of these secrets are we able to document without much additional effort. We can then assess our ability to possess these secrets without that becoming a reason to kill us.

Mustafa Ismail
The Book of Safety

18

Who said that there must be laws for us to abide by if we are to have principles?

The opening sentence of the first edition of my book, a condensed rendering of Mustafa's ideas. The possibility that it might not be true never occurred to me, taken as I was with his capacity to strike a balance between rebellion and obedience.

I was always of the view that as long as words grab you, there can be no doubting that they're right. Our capacity to control them is limited. All we have is our readiness to accept them. They emerge from their cave, roaming around in search of someone to take them up—and they would always return, having been adopted by someone or other, better able to stand the darkness than their neglected sisters. So far, I hadn't been able to shake the romanticism of the idea, but I'd added to it the understanding that the female nature of words lent them the capacity for deception; it was important not to rush in, but to consider what they were after, because they (hypothesizing with the best of intentions) were like women: they didn't consider the consequences of what they said. I would dream that this awareness gave me the right to visit the cave and make what alterations I saw fit to dramatic convention (so long-established and admitting of no intervention until it had become a mere game of narrative and technique). I might devise something new, something other than tragedy, comedy, and farce.

This was what drew me to the art in this story, regardless of what anyone else might think of it. In and of themselves, actions are pure, but as soon as people perform them they are sullied. If I were able to separate Mustafa's actions from their human context, and their social and political significations, I would have achieved self-sufficient art, with no need for outside definitions or for a private language—a story told not about *us*, but about our shadows, about that other existence that we are unable to apprehend (and so, chasing after it, we wander into exile, fantasizing that it is our selves fragmented before the light). In such a state, I would not search for reasons and excuses.

It is not 'art' that the thief be an honorable man, nor that the whore who sells her body be a virgin. How did I not see that this cliché's time had been and gone, and that we need to admit that we are turning our fears into dishonest formulae that are entrenched until they become like truth? How did I not realize that I was proceeding as the minds of many others were expecting me to proceed?

I made a hero out of a man who might not have been one at all. In the second edition, I'd write Hasna's story, and with it the absolute truth. I would confess and beg forgiveness.

I was a fool. I made a thief into a national hero. Granted him a heroism not his by rights. I was looking for a way of registering objection, of breaking the silence in which I found myself imprisoned, and which we were all obliged to maintain due to lack of space.

The apartment's tiny—it can't take shouting.

This last line repeated before the young child, the boy I was, hearing until he learned to swallow his own voice; and by the time his parents passed away it was too late to reclaim it.

Move softly lest the walls fall in on us.

Who is responsible for selecting the lives we lead with such precision? The silence of my companions at the café placed the seal on what my family had begun—as though there was no escaping what we're born to. Checkmate's nothing to crow over. Anyone who does so is a fool because, poor soul, he doesn't understand that none of what happened . . . happened. He hasn't worked out that humility is the path we must tread to reach insight.

Now, though, I wanted nothing more than to be that fool. I saw why, for the final operation that brought him down, Mustafa departed from his own *Book of Safety* and went robbing unprepared and unplanned. He wanted to feel alive, even if that meant destroying his legend.

A moment. Allow me to repeat my apology. I believe I was on the verge of falling into the same trap again—of going back to the old, remembered rules of the drama, of forging a fresh legend, this time of the holy fool.

Why not admit the simple truth? Mustafa was a thief like any other. It was just that he wanted to be more professional, more precise, and more skilled. Perfection is forbidden us. Picking its moment, fate intervenes to prevent the best from rising higher. He never abandoned hope that he might be the exception.

Though it be a crime, you must be committed. Seriousness is one of the prerequisites of our existence.

An old lady was begging at the rank, moving from microbus to microbus, leaning on the doorframe, her face inside the vehicle and body out. A driver asked her to move on.

"We're working here."

"And so am I."

The passengers hooted, but she was serious. This was her work. It didn't matter how we might see it, or how it might be reckoned up in the final analysis; what mattered was that she was working. Was she following Mustafa's instructions?

Most likely I'm going to end up being treated in a mental institution, ranting about his career and describing things from his point of view.

*

The worst nightmare is to live in the shadow of a man whose mind has been destroyed by books. He believes that he is the best, and tries to make you a prisoner of his consciousness, whatever form that consciousness might take. He does not permit you to leave the sphere of his control; your rebellion is a threat to his existence. He has no other way to be, like black holes that swallow up their surroundings—a negative energy that grows greater with each erasure. And no one is prepared to face this frightening truth. My father was not so different. It was simply that he broke the rule to which the majority adhere. While they move from rebellion to a conventional, upright life delineated by the common consensus, he—because the thing he hated most of all was to be like everyone else—went the opposite way, from obedience to liberty (as he conceived it). There is, you'll notice, a common denominator here. And it doesn't matter why the change occurred, or when, or how, because you discover that it is all one thing: an unbroken ring.

I did with Hasna what I'd done with her father: I wrote her up. What was happening between us I chose to think of as confession. I would carry out her wish and confess that I had deceived people. It would be a public confession, to rewrite Mustafa's story in the form she thought correct, but this time she would be a fundamental part of the story.

Mustafa said, "I wasn't so young that I didn't know stealing was wrong, but my mother's miserliness had taught me to pay attention to what God gave others, which is why I think she's played a fundamental part in my crimes. And seeing as you're so keen on reasons, I advise you to seek her out and ask her about her son—that's if you find her. The last time I saw her was when I was eighteen. She'd kept to the apartment for years, so much so that I couldn't remember her ever going out. Until, that is, that birthday of mine when she vanished without saying goodbye."

"What does your mother have to do with anything?" al-Adl asked. "You're a man in your forties, so why are you talking as

218

though you're a little boy? Unless you're referring to that psychobabble about the impact of one's upbringing? Didn't you know that psychology moved on from that years ago?"

Al-Adl seemed impatient and had interrupted Mustafa, breaking one of our cardinal rules: "Let them say what they want. This is how you'll understand."

The moments I loved best during the confessions were those when the confessor became detached from their surroundings, from me and from Nabil, when they reached an accommodation with the mystery that enveloped them, forgot their surprise, and communed with themselves. Our technique involved reassuring the fearful and giving them a feeling of being at home. After that, suggesting the same question over and over in all possible forms and formulations worked like mesmerism.

"Have you heard of Enigma?"

Al-Adl answered with a nod, and I did likewise.

"My mother was just like that machine. The way she acted and spoke made her seem as though she belonged to another people—an undiscovered civilization, even. Maybe she was even more advanced than the machine, because she used a logic so complex that it took her behavior out of the arena of the rational and into madness."

He fell silent for a moment, thinking of a way to explain what he had said.

"Her miserliness, for instance. That was strange. It wasn't tightfistedness so much as a childlike love of money. Beautiful notes, she thought, not to be squandered. She used to give me lots of them to play with in the evenings, on the condition that I didn't lose them. We'd spread them out on the bedroom floor and challenge one another to various games. It was a wonderful ritual, but the brightly colored book in the bookshop next door was more wonderful still. For a long time, I could think of nothing else, particularly since she refused to buy it; as she saw it, it wasn't worth us handing our gorgeous notes to the bookseller. And what's more, she had her own stories, much better than any in that book."

"You stole it?"

"My dear man. What I've been trying to explain to you since we began these little sessions is that you can't steal what is yours, or what should be. Fine, then, let's not quibble. Yes, I stole it. Or tried to. The bookseller caught me. Back then, I didn't have a plan."

A few moments of silence, then he added with a smile:

"Maybe the story I've just told is an illusion. Maybe we're in one of my mother's dreams. I never understood how her mind worked. I always used to think that she was in contact with other beings—call them what you like: djinn, ghosts, aliens. It was from them that she took her way of life. And mine."

At critical moments, when some emergency threatens to blow the operation, time becomes the principal enemy. At that juncture, you must take a decision that cannot be revised or second-guessed. You must be swift and exact, not only in making your choice among the many available escape routes, but also in moving between more than one type of route: becoming light, so that the breeze can carry you like a feather; even if they see you, they are unable to catch you.

Mustafa Ismail
The Book of Safety

19

"WOMEN REALLY ARE A WORLD APART."

Al-Waraqi's words intercut with the clatter of the microbus over an unpaved stretch of the road to Tell al-Faraeen. The faces around us stared at him, and their as yet intangible objection to our presence (which, I'd gambled, would be ameliorated by acquaintance) began to grow, to slip from eyes to mouths:

"Now, that's not right, ya bey. . . . You don't talk about women on high days and holy days!" Thus the driver, roughly, having turned the tape deck down as low as it could go.

We were the beys, come from the big city in our fancy clothes to take a peek at their annual saint's festival. Amid the celebrations of a man who'd thought nothing of the world and had turned his back on it, al-Waraqi's sartorial elegance was hard to stomach.

"Of course, driver, forgive us. We're your guests here, and we've only just begun to follow your saint's way. We're still learning."

Al-Waraqi started sniping at me for backing down, but I kicked him so he'd shut up. The hostility lost its edge. After what I'd said, they would think that we couldn't be as ignorant as they had supposed—we were devotees of the saint and shouldn't be treated roughly—while al-Waraqi's words might be thought of as a line from one of the praise songs that drifted into earshot whenever we passed through a village. Perhaps their Sheikh al-Desouqi had chosen a stranger as his messenger, to bring them his lesser-known pronouncements on women. Better that than wondering if the only thing this fellow could think about amid such spiritual atmospheres was women. The passengers might even repeat what he said, attributing the line (after edits that enhanced its Sufic aspect) to their righteous saint.

I hoped he'd stay quiet till we got there. The messenger would be well advised to make do with delivering his message; he didn't have the skills to append explications, and any additional line would ruin the original. But al-Waraqi was determined to be noisy, to be the center of attention.

"Now we're on the subject, I've a deep knowledge of Sufism and have attained the stage of spiritual revelation, so I take full responsibility for what I'm saying. That sheikh of yours loved women, and there's nothing wrong with that. Verily, God is beautiful and He loveth beauty."

No, al-Waraqi wasn't quite this stupid, nor was he simply looking for a fight. What he was doing was taking revenge on behalf of Talia, his wife-to-be, for the privations she'd suffered in the name of 'abstention' (an attitude, it so happened, al-Waraqi himself found quite unjustifiable).

And because those who love are obliged to journey long and hard through sands and wastes, we dismounted—ejected—at the fourth village along our route, meaning that we had to journey down an unpaved track on foot to reach the beloved's village.

For the thousandth time, I blamed myself for getting involved with this man. For the thousandth time, I pledged to cut all ties with him. This man, who had preferred to experience every detail of his future spouse's life and had refused to hire a private car, saying, "Come down out of your ivory tower. Take a look at real life. Live it!"

At which we had been packed like livestock into a ramshackle bus full of local residents and the purchases they were bringing home for the festival: sweets, clothes, toys—all cheaply priced and rendered priceless by the sheikh's blessing.

We had come to Kafr al-Sheikh, and from there to Desouq, passing beneath the vast green sign that hung at the city's entrance for a full week:

Unfurl the banners of my glory once the day has risen;
Hoist my flags aloft.

We didn't pause, not even for a minute. He was in a rush and I, in any case, had no desire to join a huge mob swayed by claims of miracles that had no basis in science.

Talia hadn't asked anything particular of al-Waraqi in exchange for her hand. She made do with what he gave her out of the goodness of his heart. He had already proved that he was more adept at getting past a woman's defenses than Ashraf al-Suweifi. The contest had been decided in his favor thanks to the generosity he showed her. He'd opened a bank account for her containing a more than reasonable sum, security should she want to leave him, and rented an apartment by the airport in al-Nuzha so that she could watch the planes taking off.

The price of Talia's heart as she defined it: one wall clock, blue with bright red hands and three yellow birds that popped out on the hour. There would certainly be many versions of what she asked for, but the exact one she wanted was hanging on the wall of her family home in the village. It had some mark on it that only she could see—or rather the others were fakes; she wouldn't be happy with them, and she wouldn't forgive any attempt to trick her with a lookalike.

Al-Waraqi had come to ask me to accompany him on this difficult journey. He'd found himself tangled up in complications, having assumed that it would be an easy marriage, costing nothing more than money (a girl with no close family and few demands), yet this request of hers, though strange, might still lead to the usual course of events: engagement, then dowry, then nauseating wedding parties and the friends and family you had to schmooze.

"Idiotic rituals," he scoffed.

He had assumed that following his struggle against, and victory over, al-Suweifi he would simply step up and claim the crown, but Talia had added this new leg to the race, the shortest but the bumpiest. Even so, he never rethought his desire to be with her. The crazier her requests grew, it seemed, the harder he clung to her. And this wasn't difficult to explain. He was entirely obsessed with the quest for sexual variety. The last thing he wanted was some fleshy woman who'd grovel at his feet—and Talia, so different from the remainder of her sex in both body and mind, held the promise of distinctive pleasure. More importantly, she wouldn't look too closely at how he passed his time. Her desires went no further than a space which she might occupy, glowering and grave.

"Remember a story by Ihsan Abdel-Quddous called *Another Kind of Madness*?" he asked me once.

"No. I stopped reading Ihsan in primary school."

"More fool you. In my opinion, Ihsan is the finest Arab writer. He's got an extraordinary knowledge of the way people work."

"Maybe," I said.

"Definitely. Give the story a go. I can lend it to you. It's incredible."

It may seem like the acme of idiocy for a man to want to marry a woman because he likes some story. He'd talk about that story every time I asked after his relationship with Talia, yet without telling me what it was about or lending it to me as he'd promised. And I proved unable to track it down myself because Ihsan had written words as others breathed. But leaving aside the contents of the story, men get with women for all manner of reasons. What they call love is driven by different things, and better that a man marry a woman because of some story than, say, for the sake of money.

This attitude of al-Waraqi's was what left me unable to break off the ties which bound us and which he called friendship.

*

"I'm certain the pharaohs were beings from outer space."

He believed in supernatural phenomena, in ghouls, and ghosts, and spacemen, in the power of djinn to command our bodies. After much explaining on my part, he was eventually convinced that I had never authored any books on the supernatural—not for his publishing house and not for anyone else—but I was unable to persuade him that he mustn't rush out quite so many books on the subject if he wasn't to damage the credibility of his fledgling enterprise.

"I think you need to be very careful indeed in choosing your words, here in particular," I said.

"What does where we are have to do with it?"

"This place is home to the cult of the goddess Wadjet; it's the land where Horus was raised."

I pointed him toward what looked from afar to be a statue. He peered at it, then shrugged. Night was falling fast. We'd spent a not inconsiderable amount of time walking after being chucked off the bus. There was no one else nearby: just us, that statue, and the huge cordoned-off space which the Antiquities Department had set aside for ancient Buto, the northern capital of a pre-unification, prehistoric Egypt. Nor was there any way forward except to skirt around that space en route to our objective: a small cluster of houses slumbering beneath Wadjet's curse—the goddess furious at those who plundered the tombs of her dead—the inhabitants blissfully unaware that just one of those sacred stones could bring in enough money to provide a comfortable existence to an entire family.

This was where Talia had grown up, playing by the Hill of Idols, as the locals called it. Like the other children of her village, she'd heard the warnings not to approach the wall around the hill. There were strange stories about boys and girls who'd tried to penetrate these sanctums going missing, with no trace of them ever found. The police who'd been sent at intervals from Desouq had found no evidence that these disappearances were criminal, their investigations concluding that the hill was studded with deep wells that were difficult to access, and they warned residents to stay away.

Yet this didn't fit with the constant presence of archaeological expeditions, none of whose members had ever fallen foul of this particular danger. The residents didn't believe the police account, and the police for their part didn't believe the residents' stories about gangs using black magic to locate the great pharaonic hoard—which would only reveal itself once the blood of a child (no older than fourteen) had been spilt over it. Stories derived from an older legend: that the land roundabouts was home to a woman with a serpent's head—a sorceress, burned alive for failing to cure one of the king's sons, ever since which her spirit had hunted down children the age the prince had been. This was what the households of Talia's village and the rest of the surrounding villages believed, which may be why said villages had stayed so changeless, their population never growing, each newborn child a replacement for one slaughtered for and by the witch—one of the more unconventional means of preserving nature's equilibrium.

The residents could do nothing but sit back and wait for the final confrontation between this evil being and their sheikh, al-Desouqi. They had met before, but this time he would make sure he'd killed her. It had not been enough to strike her with his staff, sending her plummeting into the bottomless pit of her grave, assuming she was dead while all the while she lurked down below, setting the darkness at defiance, silently waiting as her wounds healed and nurturing her hatred of mankind.

The poor residents hoped the battle would come soon. Each of them had a blood vengeance against her, which gave them the strength they'd need to rend her body apart and burn it so that it could never heal again. But until that moment came, there was nothing for it but to keep going on the basis that these victims were being sacrificed in lieu of more important souls, be they tourists or expedition members.

They must learn to live with worry. It was only when their children reached the age that their blood became taboo to the snake-headed lady that they knew peace of mind.

Clumsily, al-Waraqi told the tale of Talia's childhood. When he was done, silence enveloped us and the road ahead seemed endless. According to the directions we had, we should find the village about halfway around the hill. It was taking us quite a while, since, by unspoken agreement, we had preferred to keep clear of the wall.

Sunset was fast approaching, and the sun was sunk in red and going down into the void of the earth. I had never seen it like this. The sun in Cairo shines fierce and sets pale. If al-Waraqi had consented to bringing Lotfi along as I'd requested, the sight would have shattered my friend's poetic block. The poor guy had no idea: the road ahead was longer than he could imagine. Even supposing that he found some way of teaching himself to write, the harder task—to be different from what had gone before—would remain: to be different from what had gone before.

"You're sure the village is here?" I asked as our surroundings grew less than comforting. The howling of dogs in the archaeological zone grew louder, as though mythic creatures had waited for night before emerging from their lairs: the snake woman's guard racing ahead of her, striking terror into the hearts of her quarry so it would put up no fight when she finally arrived.

"We're here."

His response spoken low, the houses suddenly materializing as though my inquiry had been the prearranged signal for them to reveal their presence. But the uneasy feeling wouldn't leave me. It wasn't simply trepidation at what we were about—invading the home of people we didn't know at this late hour to demand the hand of a daughter who'd fled the place years previously—nor was it concern prompted by thoughts of how we'd get back along this very road. It was something harder to grasp.

Out of the blue, I thought of the Lotus House, the first house Mustafa had ever broken into. I thought of the glowing creatures. It was only at that instant, as I stood outside one of Horus's sanctums, that I saw what might have been the key to the entire riddle: the whole thing was more or less a question of rites. The water into which Mustafa fell was his path to transformation. And if I wasn't mistaken, Horus had been the god of change in pharaonic times; and the glowworms were the creatures that escorted the deceased on their second journey, when they turned from a normal person into an immortal.

Mustafa had been conducting a ritual inside that house that would equip him for what he was about to do. If that was the case, then the whole business was much more than a few burglaries with which a university professor sought to rebel against society's established values. There was something connecting the homes he burgled. Something he was looking for. With mounting terror, I suddenly realized that our investigation had failed to do any research into the university at which he'd taught. I'd asked al-Adl about it, and he'd said it wasn't necessary at that stage, but this state of affairs had then persisted until he'd been released. Why? Only now did I think of it, most likely when it was all too late.

I came back to reality again as al-Waraqi was knocking on the door, and a woman the exact same height and skinniness of Talia opened it, on her face no trace of surprise at these strange men who had sought her out so late in the day.

The target residence should never be on the upper floors of a building, to avoid the possibility of being trapped. Each floor must contain just two apartments, since the probability of two apartments standing empty at any one time is far greater than for three or four.

Mustafa Ismail
The Book of Safety

20

HASNA SHUT HER BOOK, PUSHING back at the shadow of regret that was stealing over her, trying to take control:

"You thought you'd come up with something no one had done before? That it? Pure nonsense, trash—a little girl playing cut and paste!"

She closed her eyes as she traced over the letters sunk into the cover, its title and her name—"Alif, Lam, Ha, Qaf, Ya, Qaf, Taa marbouta. . . ."—pronouncing each letter separately, breathing her spirit into them so they might grant the word they formed what it deserved. She concentrated. Maybe she'd find the secret that was eluding her.

"*Al-Haqiqa.*"

The Truth.

Seeing as it was the subject of the book, she had set aside a whole chapter for it. She'd simplified as far as possible, shunning the philosophical jargon that left the reader even more bewildered, and had done so with a clarity and self-confidence that, if the full title was any guide, appeared unshakable:

Al-Haqiqa al-Niha'iya.

The Final Truth.

If the title was meant to convey an undisputed truth, then it must be capable of persuasion the instant the eye fell on it, each reader crying, "This is what I've been looking for!"

Heidegger's words on truth were her example:

This word, so elevated, yet for all that worn and almost dulled, is what makes a true thing true.

A more than sufficient definition. Faith in the word is what's required to guide people to what they have missed. There was no call for Mr. Heidegger to complicate the matter further, for either himself or his audience, but like many others he wouldn't follow his gut. Doubts about his conclusion troubled him, and he went back to what he'd written, and reshaped, and buffed it in various ways until none of the original sense remained. This was the essence of what she had done: to rid words of the doubts in which their authors had swaddled them.

Yet for all her faith, she remained incapable of evaluating her work. Would people be able to deal with her title? Might the intellectuals who—thoughtlessly—took it as read that there were no absolute or final truths not mount objections, thereby exonerating themselves from the effort of having to provide answers? What was the point of them if they were just going to pose more questions in a world already built on questions?

She came to her name, and her finger slowed over the letters to restore her confidence. She came to the part that was her father's name, scratched it out, then moved on to her grandfather, about whom she knew nothing but his name. Her father: Mustafa. Her grandfather: Ismail. Two men to complete the label that accompanied her everywhere. She would not make do with Hasna, nor even Hasna Mustafa. Like that it was incomplete. Though the conversation that followed the declaration of her full name always ran the same:

"Hasna Mustafa Ismail."

"Er . . . , you mean, like Sheikh Mustafa Ismail?"

"It's a coincidence."

But it was no ordinary coincidence. Her name had always had an aura about it. She grew used to it, and only later did she understand why. She wasn't the celebrated Quran reader's daughter, but people showed her the deference that the man's name commanded. It was only when she listened closely to the reader's voice and compared it to others that the reason for this love became clear: the sweetest voice of them all, reading with his heart and soul, and lending each verse the sensibility that fit it. It became a habit: turning to the sheikh whenever her fear grew too great.

Her book must be good enough to bear the sheikh's name, then. People's minds would turn to him. They wouldn't assume the name came from the thief and not the sheikh, and in any case the thief business had been a flash in the pan, diverting the public for days, then over. The incongruity had appealed to them—how could a university professor be a thief?—and there the matter had come to an end, while *The Book of Safety*, which had attempted to elevate him into legend, had come and gone without leaving a trace. She'd read a review in a low-circulation paper, and had made sure to walk past the pavement booksellers who had it in stock, keeping an eye on availability. She'd bought a few copies and torn them up—would have bought every copy she'd come across if she hadn't realized that this would give it an artificially inflated circulation and might lead to another print run.

She sat in the living room, spacious enough now that it was free of the books that had once cluttered it up. She put the book down and lazily rose to her feet, searching for something to relieve her frustration, and stood facing the huge mirror she'd recently purchased. Her father had gotten rid of every mirror in the apartment, apart from a small square of glass over the bathroom sink which he used every other day to shave, and in which she was unable to see her whole face. He gave her no room to object. She'd come back from university to be ambushed by the changes he'd made, changes that extended even to her bedroom: everything thrown out— the toys she'd kept since childhood, the romances, the cheap thrillers, cassettes by foreign singers. The only possessions of hers he'd left untouched were two books that in his judgment deserved to survive—and which were the first two things she disposed of when he went to jail.

This had been the first move in his campaign to bring her under control. For the year that she'd stayed alive following his return, her mother had distracted him. There had been a few observations about how Hasna chose to lead her life, remarks that gave her no clue to his intentions. After all, she was, as those who knew her could testify, self-disciplined—everything in moderation—not like the other girls who'd figured out how to stay up late adventuring. She preferred to spend most of her time at home with her mother, eating together, watching TV: the series and the films, one after the other, taking refuge there from the sterility of their lives. When alone, she would read light romances of love and adventure, finishing a book, then, with herself as hero, drift back through the plot, rearranging events to suit her whim, the men relegated to the supporting roles they deserved. She became expert at devising melodramatic ends for these men, while the women reveled in the happiness they'd earned as the more elevated sex and as a consequence of the courageous sacrifices they'd made.

Once again, she went back over her life with him, despite her multiple attempts to stay clear of that vicious circle, despite being certain that if she was to start a new life she must come to terms with what was done and forget it. But she couldn't. Talk's easy, but the doing, well, you only know once you've tried. That aside, she reckoned her rage gave her positive impetus. The idea for her book had come at just such a moment.

Her father: "Most people are just . . . ordinary. Very few rise above. I'm sorry if I've caused you trouble—I forget that ordinary people have limited capabilities."

Had he been trying to provoke her into playing along as he wanted her to do? Perhaps, but she hadn't let him. She didn't like the way he was with her. She hadn't forgiven him for taking her beloved books away, nor for the strict regime he forced her to abide by, which consisted of reading two whole books a week. He started in with the classic novels so that she could get used to profound ideas. Russians first: Dostoyevsky, the architect of the modern novel, at the head of the list. And she wouldn't deny that at first she'd enjoyed it. A means, albeit strange, to communicate with this mysterious man about whom she had no clear idea of how she felt.

But the cultural program had been catastrophic for their relationship. He had met her evasions with rigor, and she had bridled, especially since it was a difficult and exhausting program. She would read, and then they would discuss, and she would learn the principles of analysis and how to penetrate to the depths of the text. Only in rare instances was she able to form a coherent view of what she was reading. *The Brothers Karamazov* was the toughest of all.

"Who is evil and who is good? If God didn't exist, would everything really be permitted—crime included—as Dmitri believes?"

She had no use for these complex questions. The stories alone appealed to her. The only response to his interrogations, and one she never found the courage to confront him with directly, was that men were the cause of every problem. They complicated matters until they'd proved their ability to solve them, and should they fail then they turned the whole thing into a philosophical question.

Hasna was unruly, like him—a wild mare he tried his best to tame, while she made herself a vow that this would never happen even if she ended up like her mother, laid out in bed, her spirit raised up out of her. She'd gone into battle against him—a man who thought himself God's anointed—and her a lone woman, and weak, without expertise or experience. But she believed in her cause, which was the cause of all women; her victory would mean a step forward in the historic war between the sexes.

She roamed the apartment, room after room, not the slightest bit reassured by his absence. Maybe this was one of his little games: he was watching her, his not being there a lie. Maybe he'd come back without her knowing. The first thing she'd done after he was detained was to change the lock on the door. When he returned, he'd have to knock. He wouldn't take her by surprise again. She'd do what her poor mother had been unable to do: she'd lay down a law that he must abide by if he wanted to remain by her side. This time *she* would choose the books that *he* must read, and *she* would question *him*. A mother giving her boy his first lessons. Who is the baddie and who is the goodie? The wolf is the baddie, and your job is to see through his disguise, not to make excuses for him. Dmitri, in other words, is the murderer, and anyone who takes his side is a wretch led astray, as you've been, by philosophy. And Dostoyevsky's a wretch as well—he can't tell a decent story, so he wraps it up in a lot of unconvincing macho melodrama!

I learned to listen to homes. There are those that don't want me inside them, and sound as though they are warning me, and others that receive me joyfully as though they have been waiting for me forever. This is a sense I trust in, gained from experience. Those who turn a blind eye to the signs lose their way.

Mustafa Ismail
The Book of Safety

21

ONE WHOLE HOUR IN WHICH the vehicle moved just meters. To avoid a breakdown of my own, I busied my mind with counting, one of the yogic exercises with which you maintain self-control so that you do not lose yourself in loss of focus:

"One, two, three, four. . . ."

Five before one hundred, I stopped—wasn't the rule that you counted backward?

"One hundred, ninety-nine, ninety-eight, ninety-seven, ninety-six, ninety-five. . . ."

Would a hundred count be enough to soothe my nerves? What was the number you needed for it to work? Five hundred? I struggled to recall the fundamental principles of yoga amid a rising sense of panic—corroborated by a series of incidents in recent years—that such basic information was being erased from my head, the most important of it the books I'd read.

It had begun with discomfort at my name: it wasn't Khaled; it shouldn't be; it never had been. As a child, I believed that names changed to suit you as you grew, and now it appeared that what I'd laughed at as a teenager had returned with an added nightmarish sense of loss. I would wake at midnight with an oppressive sense of disorientation, as though some unquiet spirit had taken possession of my body. What gave people the ability to come to terms with their bodies, and faces, and thoughts?

We were stationary, somewhere down the whip-like length of Shubra Street. There was no obvious reason for the terrible congestion, but after a while a clearer picture began to emerge: scattered words exchanged between drivers and passengers about an accident; a bomb detonated on a bus; no serious injuries but some painful wounds from the nails with which the primitive device was packed, tearing through bodies, little gifts for the flesh. The bombing campaigns of the Nineties at their height.

There was no point staying in the bus. I got out near where I'd gone to high school, my memory stubbornly refusing to yield up its secrets: what was its name? Before I could catch sight of the sign, I stopped, determined to dredge it up from memory, even at the price of reliving events I was so ashamed of I'd put them out of my mind.

He was somehow more like a girl. The way he talked. Walked. His diffidence. His hobbies, all founded on his love of music. Like everyone else, I envied him, particularly for the way girls loved him and trusted him.

The plan was that we would lure him to Tusun Pasha's old shut-up palace, in one part of whose grounds the school had been built. My deal with the masterminds was that we'd do no more than scare him.

"You have to man up. We're doing it for his own good."

Thus the boy whose bravery and insubordination set him over us, our leader. His tone lacked sincerity, his words unable to rid me of my hesitation. It was time, as he was well aware, to claim the debt I owed for my affiliation, and my part would be no more than to persuade him we'd found an old phonograph and records, and wanted to work out how much they were worth.

I was closest to him. He spent most of his free time in the library, reading or helping the librarian sort books, and I would go there from time to time myself. We would often exchange words about some book or other. But I wasn't as devoted to reading as him. I was scattered between two worlds, the real and the bookish. After what transpired, though, I would choose the world of books—until I met Mustafa, and he would restore to me my wonder at what happened in the real.

We would get into the palace through an opening in the cellar, to investigate or to steal what little brass was left, with the idea it might be worth something, though with anything of any value we'd been beaten to it by past generations of pupils. The palace was so enormous we spent the entire first year exploring. Break time was the time to do it, that was if we could outmaneuver the guard that the principal had posted at the palace entrance, or otherwise collect enough cash to tempt him to turn a blind eye as we slipped by.

For years afterward I would avoid walking past the school. Incredible what the mind can do: with practice, I got so I could walk past the building and not see it.

He screamed at me to help him, but I was incapable of movement. I just looked on, captivated. It was like a scene from a film more than anything else. On the palace steps, one of them was holding a knife to his neck and the originator of the whole idea and the one who hated him most was rubbing his nose in it, making filthy jokes as he fondled the smooth skin of his face, his buttocks, telling him he was really a girl and no man at all. They were reflected in a great antique mirror whose glass had shattered, their bodies parceled between the remaining fragments, illuminated by a pale daylight that filtered through dusty panes while I stood in a patch of darkness. Was I even capable of spoiling such a skillfully painted scene? Didn't its perfection mean it was fated to run to some conclusion? Yet I was also unduly provoked by the boy's passivity; his terror at the others' touches lent him an aggravating femininity. Maybe if he'd show a bit of backbone, I'd protest, but not when he was quite this spineless. Plain facts stripped of emotion and the right of the other to be as they please are not strong enough to survive the human proclivity for enmity. He had never understood, intuited even, the importance of making images of ourselves that others are able to deal with.

The very next day, his father had put in a request to remove him from the school. We watched them from the second-floor balcony beside the library. The crudest of us said, "The woman's collected her girl and gone," and I had laughed along with the others—yet I regretted what had happened, and the traitor's part I'd played, and the perfect punishment for me was that I remain the passive victim of my confusion and indecision, set against his sincerity and determination to be as he chose.

It was a punishment that would grow more profound. He would incarnate himself before me, would wear the guise of different characters—Mustafa, Fakhri, Hasna, Lotfi—their contentment with themselves unclouded by a single doubt. Would my salvation be to hunt him out and beg his forgiveness for what happened, telling him the remainder of my days would be spent waiting for his pardon? Would he understand? Had his life, too, been founded on that scene?

Something was definitely out of balance.

I lengthened my stride, trying to dispel the fear that I was aging at a faster than normal rate: why else would I be trying to relive ancient events? Yesterday morning, I'd woken up terrified of a school test I was due to take that day. Are such things signs of senility?

It would take fifteen minutes to get to my place if I kept this pace up. Our date had slipped my mind. I was practically mowing down the good people of Shubra. Why did they suddenly all seem to look like Ustaz Fakhri? Had they all visited the Soviet Union and brought back clothes that would last forever? Soon Hasna would be passing by. She would get out of the taxi five minutes away from my apartment—a custom she kept up unwaveringly and for no clear reason—outside Shubra Paradise, where girls, and boys, and families clustered to lap ice cream, everyone with their best outfits on and come from home especially for the big gathering.

*

The customers swapped jokes and easy stories summoned by the sweet taste of the product that the shop owner purveyed with such skillful variety. Hasna would never for an instant consider joining them. Her face would never betray a single one of the mocking feelings that surged within her. She would never give this scene, capable of seducing Chagall himself, so much as a glance.

Inside this shop was where Talia had stood before she married, patiently combining the flavors for each customer's order:

"Mango and strawberry."

"Peach and pineapple."

"Banana and chocolate."

She would come to the café to share her observations with us. People don't choose flavors, they choose colors, and are practiced enough in selecting combinations that they come out with something that sets them apart from the others. Then, in minutes, the colors are gone and they're back in.

Should Hasna and Talia ever chance to meet, they'd find much to agree on: their love of Medinat Nasr, of the barracks of happy government employees out in the desert. In Talia, Hasna would find a pupil to whom she might pass on her vision: "History and stories are worthless."

How to win the heart of a woman who believes that stories are a stupid thing to write and the obsession of people in crisis?

I didn't tell her that the chair she'd chosen had been my mother's. She would think it was a terribly obvious gambit. Mother's soul might be slipping inside her and transforming her as she sat there. I was sitting facing her. She was my mother, and I was my father. And now the child (the younger me) should come running from the linking passage and stand for a few moments at one end, spying on them, waiting for when they were distracted so as to take them unawares.

"Well and good, but are you convinced by my point of view? Or does the other perspective appeal to you artistically?"

Hasna had the right to ask, right? I had given her the right. I wasn't the author. If I had been, pride would have prevented me changing a single letter that I wrote. The price of knowledge is the suppression of desires. Why didn't I tell her straight that I desired her, and that I was prepared to alter any fact she wanted for that alone? I would stand in the courtyard outside the church door and declare that the earth was fixed in place if she would just undress for me. *Do you think those clothes conceal you from my gaze? You're naked, sweetheart. Do you have a single thought that's hidden from me? What now, after all this ducking and diving?*

A rap on the apartment door spared me from my mounting lust. Ustaz Ali stood there, flustered. It had been more than three months since Lotfi had gone missing, and the man had begun to lose faith in the importance of this ritual. We would meet nearly daily, and he would tell me about the results of his search, the places he had been and asked after him. People had given him to understand that his son had been detained under the emergency laws and wouldn't be released until the investigations had run their course, and then he'd heard himself being blamed for leaving the boy to take 'that path.'

"What path do they mean?" he'd asked me, without waiting for an answer. He was addressing himself, as he always did when distracted by some math problem that he'd brought with him on his wanderings. "Lotfi's a very peaceable guy. Do they want people to stop thinking?"

Ustaz Ali was a professor of mathematics and a one-off. His whole existence embodied European values, and Lotfi was the prime beneficiary. As teenagers, we had to come up with tricks and schemes to obtain our petty pleasures, but Lotfi could stroll out of his apartment like an American teen, at liberty to act as adolescence required. When he'd first decided to smoke, he and his father had sat out on the balcony together sipping tea and talking, the smoke from their two cigarettes a challenge to every moral code that Abul-Wafa Street and Shubra held dear. For which reason, perhaps, Ustaz Ali was not much loved by his neighbors. They saw him as the antithesis of all they did and believed in. No one had time for the classical music that came from his apartment during Friday prayers, nor for the fact that his son had a girlfriend that he brought home. The world-famous Azerbaijani (turned Iranian for the sake of convenience) had driven Ustaz Ali to madness with his theorems, they said. The fellow's 'fuzzy thinking' had led Ustaz Ali astray, and he could no longer tell right from wrong.

Interestingly, though Lotfi reaped the benefits of this freedom, he himself held much the same views as the neighbors, and was the main source of the rumors about his father's insanity. It was Lotfi who, through friends, had acquainted locals with the 'Iranian' his father venerated and with his theorem, whose equations decorated the walls of their home. The spite he evinced toward his father astonished us, given the advantages he had, but his arbitrary ways, coupled with his more general rejection of his father's personality, meant we didn't look too hard for reasons. But I, the closest to him, knew that it was all to do with the name his father had given him. Lotfi Zadeh, that was the full version. And though no one cared or remembered that Lotfi had this strange non-Egyptian appendage to his name, the mere presence of this Zadeh on official documents was enough to prompt a grudge against his father.

"So he's an idiot in love with some math genius—why drag me into it?"

I would discover that Ustaz Ali was not how his son portrayed him. Would it be appropriate to warn the man? It might be a way of snapping him out of the daze he was in; if the sentimental tie that bound him could be cut, he might be able to think more clearly.

"Feelings go against thought, and morals have no place on the field of battle."

Which was what made Ustaz Fakhri a Shubra chess legend, the district's brightest son. The only problem was that Ali's madness rendered the theory instantly null.

Now he collapsed on the closest chair and stretched his legs out, taking up a huge swathe of what little space there was. Hasna was looking at him with interest, but he was completely lost in his problem and she took care not to draw attention to herself. I was standing by the front door, leaning against the little chest whose drawers held some of the handicrafts my mother would make with obsessive focus before tossing them carelessly into the chest, never to touch them again. Since she'd died, I hadn't set eyes on the things, though I had kept them exactly where she'd put them. I wished Ali would go away so I could spend the remainder of the day looking though them all with Hasna—might make a fine new foundation on which to break the ice she'd laid over our relationship.

In the kitchen, I made tea. Ali talked to us about his work, about his theorems, about the trip he wanted to make in order to put his ideas into practice. Mathematics. Nothingness. The desert. Stars. The center of the universe. Scattered words which reached me from the other room.

When I emerged, Hasna said eagerly, "You heard of fuzzy logic, Khaled?"

Holding the tray with its cups of tea, I froze. I must have looked like an idiot. I knew that I had lost her. In him, she'd find the kind of father she was looking for: a man who had wisdom, and knowledge, and cared nothing for either.

Ustaz Ali delighted in outdoing his son in manliness. He didn't hide his pleasure at scoring a victory on the eternal proving ground of men.

Human existence is just a collection of arbitrary rules that will never change.

The only difference between us and those who work in security is that they have made a uniform for themselves.

Mustafa Ismail
The Book of Safety

22

LIFE NEVER GETS TIRED OF acting like a screenwriter enamored of tacky melodrama.

In his wheelchair, Lotfi sat facing the miserable trees that his father had planted outside their building after he'd gone to prison; an attempt to give Lufti hope once he came home. But they had defied him and, other than a few leaves, grew bare.

It was a life prematurely cut short, and setting this right would be Lotfi's principal concern in the second half of his span, one he would spend almost totally paralyzed—unless someone confessed to responsibility for what had happened and took on the exorbitant costs of his treatment. His hand sprouted a little pot that his mother and siblings ensured never ran out of water. An image easily retained in memory. I would watch him from a distance and lack the strength to confront him. Everyone avoided him and his family for fear of the curse. The trail of their movements had become uncoupled from their surroundings, as though they were invisible.

He came back, him and three other guys from Shubra who'd disappeared at the same time. They all kept to his apartment; whether following orders or a voluntary confinement, it made no difference. My desire to put him back together again was beyond my control. We both needed it: him so he could walk on his own two feet, and me so I could conquer the void that surrounded me. He who has experienced movement can never be still.

But we weren't up to the confrontation. We were bashful. He hadn't yet come to terms with his disability, and I was having trouble dealing with accusations that I worked for the authorities.

Of course, the tacky script had to play out to the end: he'd come to us at the Palace of Confessions to tell the story of how he had turned to violence in order to forget the poetry that, misled, he'd memorized. He'd revealed the betrayal of his dearest friend, who had drawn close to him out of desire for his girlfriend. I had transcribed his confession. Knowing his thoughts, my pen had outraced his words. I condemn myself by saying this, yet I feel no shame. Maybe I exaggerate when I set myself alongside him as a victim, but it's a feeling I can't shake.

To Beethoven's *Ode to Joy* from Ustaz Ali's balcony, I walked along, avoiding the sight of my crippled friend. Music like that once kept me happy for hours, swirling inside me and giving me thrills, but now it was discord in a nightmare world. People had changed along with Lotfi, broken as he was: they walked with no awareness of their surroundings or their actions. All they lacked were pots to water the trees that didn't grow.

At the corner of the street loomed a pile of garbage, and with it the hum of flies and the stench of rot. A resident had come up with the idea. An argument with a street cleaner had led her to dispense with his services, and others followed suit, preferring to keep their garbage where they could see it. And who knew, maybe the next step would be keeping it at home, rummaging through it in search of anything valuable, forgetting that it was their own waste.

Meters on from the mound, I almost bumped into a figure whose face I didn't fully register in the instant that he turned toward me. A common face, though; a local face. But no, our connection went deeper than being neighbors. At some point, some relationship had bound me to him, lasting no longer than a few scattered meetings, and yet I didn't have his name, and the circumstances of our acquaintance escaped me. It popped into my head that he worked as an accountant. He was standing facing a wall with his ass turned to the passersby, pissing in broad daylight, the liquid creeping between his feet and into the road. I filled my lungs with air so that I might hold my breath long enough to get clear of him, estimating that I'd need a little over two minutes if the stink wasn't to reach me, but some of it crept through and got trapped inside me. That's how I would spend the rest of my day: with the stink of trapped piss.

The Shubra Tramway, a just knife dividing the street equally between its inhabitants. I used to ride it the length of the line to escape the ennui of life at home, craving more of the sights it would brand on my eye, creeping along like a lizard, the racket it made out of keeping with its slow speed. Now it took an age to slide out of my way.

I crossed over to Sappho. It had been months since I'd visited Dmitri. I hoped he would have a bit of peace and quiet for me—one of his equations might manage to save me. His vast trunk stood in the dead center of the bookshop, occupying the entirety of the space he set aside for customers. What tremendous happening had taken him away from his chair behind the counter?

His expression did not bode well; it signaled to me a warning, but about what? I couldn't tell. Ignoring the absurd faces he was pulling, I opened the door, expecting the sound of panpipes, every cell in my body needing the music to feel at ease. But it came out distorted. From the machine, nudged by the door, silvery columns fell to the floor, and with them fell the melody.

"Well, I warned you," Dmitri said.

How was I supposed to guess he'd wanted me outside? And what, had he intended to spend the rest of his days standing there, looking panic-stricken and keeping visitors out?

Ustaz Fakhri believed that human history was a great hill of lies and exaggeration. He challenged anyone to tell him of a marriage, or a story of love, of friendship, of sacrifice that they had experienced themselves (or otherwise knew one of the parties involved), that did not come from the history books, or the media, or the stage, and that was lasting and true. We tried, but he'd found a blind spot that proved his point of view—this one, say, was about money, and that one power; elsewhere it was habit and timidity. It was a theory corroborated: man is an assemblage of diverse and momentary excitements, any one of which can deceive him into thinking it a permanent state, entangling him in relationships he later realizes were wrong.

Then, in his wise owl tones:

"Love means love thyself, and friendship is the same. The best marriage is hitching yourself to what you want to achieve."

Till this day, till Dmitri's tune at last gave out after lasting more than fifty years, I had been confident that Fakhri's beliefs only applied to himself—an extremist position that obliged him to live a life of unbending rigor. The 'women' in his life comprised one woman and the half a day per week he spent in her company. She was a domestic worker of about his age. He had known her since boyhood. They had grown up together and learned from one another the secrets of adolescence.

When his mother died, she continued to look after the house as she'd always done, and without asking anything in return, but Fakhri, past master of long-term strategies that opponents would only divine once the checkmate had hit them, saw a trap ahead. An obvious one. It took just minutes to draw up a plan to counter it, which he then implemented without breaking sweat: he would go on using her while maintaining the distance between them—him, a born and bred Shubra boy, an ambitious young man who lived in one of the few blocks given leave to be built alongside Tusun Pasha's palace, and then her, descendant of the slaves who'd dwelt in the miserable shacks set aside for those who labored on the pasha's lands.

Credit for moving their relationship forward went to her. He had managed to place a brake on his rabid lust long enough to put a few rules in place, supplementing her monthly salary with a fixed sum in exchange for every fuck. At first, she'd protested angrily.

"I'm not a prostitute!"

"Of course not!" In his hands, she had become a woman, but he sought to smother the ambitions circling in her mind. "It's additional labor and you should be paid for it."

Fakhri hadn't set out to humiliate her. That was just a straight description of their situation. Before long, he'd be a confidant of the king whose forefathers had invaded the country and carried off its women. It was no fault of hers that she was one of them—his sweet brown bounty, precious as his ivory pieces. He would lose himself in the minutiae of her taut body, no surplus flesh anywhere to be found. And it wasn't the beauty that caught in his heart as she stripped, a process she began lazily as soon as she came in and completed in the bed; his greater passion was for a perfection that seemed indifferent to itself, as though it were something quite ordinary. This he wanted to explore at his leisure. Yet he wouldn't allow her to stay longer than her allotted time. Like her, he was self-sufficient and superior for recognizing it, and he would not place the blessing fate had given him in jeopardy—absolute isolation.

Nervelessly he'd severed ties with anyone who had tried to snare him. The girls presented on silver platters by relatives he saw infrequently at family functions, dreaming of the well-to-do and obligation-free young man and clustering around to lend succor in his trial and loneliness: a father and mother, and the daughter he would, things going to plan, be getting engaged to. The father plotting his future for him, the mother taking care of his diet, while the girl's job was to hand out endless smiles. And then, like a pair of pimps bringing the curtain down on their careers with a noble gesture, the parents would abandon her to his company for the evening. Together they would read, would listen to classical music, and the poor girl would make her brain hurt trying to prove her worth at chess. Charming opportunities, in the course of which he took full pleasure in the carnal topographies of three female relatives, none of whom, spurred on by their parents, objected to his behavior, believing that said bodies were certain to become his property. Fakhri would rush headfirst into the game, knowing just how he would bring it to an end: cutting them dead. Off they would go, reassured by his (unspoken) word of honor, and yet, or rather because the word 'honor' is capricious, the anticipated next visit would not occur and ties would be severed forever.

Alone of them all, his servant had survived. She didn't demand—didn't desire—anything except love, and soon the ceiling of her expectations dropped to appreciation. But she never had the courage to refuse his humiliating her with cash.

"Take it, Neama."

She would go on satisfying him, and the customary farewell would go on taking place. She would throw up her hands, and he'd stuff the money inside her robe, brushing her breast—something to remember him by till next time.

And when, at his prompting, she got married and started bringing her daughter (stricken with infant paralysis) to work, he changed his habit and handed the money to the little girl, showing concern for her condition, wishing her recovery from what could not be cured, and peering into her face with a suspicion (which never left him) that she might be his. They kept up with the weekly copulation, feeling—though neither expressed this—that it was the only means still at their disposal to return them to a time when they might dream of better things. Neama would strip, and suddenly she'd smell the fragrance of a journey that had brought her all the way from the shacks to his apartment, the whole way lined with fruit trees and flowers, a single pace between two trees a pleasure trip through all the scents and colors that accompanied her to his soft bed.

The era that followed held nothing for her but fine words, which were cast down next to the trunks of those same trees, since cut down out of spite that the shacks might merge with palaces. It was a declaration that dreams were all at an end now that the justice of uniformity had been enacted.

Neama and Fakhri did it for the first time on the very day that the miracle had come true, when he had gone to the royal palace as a guest at the high table, the youngest and most brilliant of those present.

The king came to his palace in Shubra once a month to walk its gardens with the princesses who gladdened his heart as they chased butterflies—their cocoons imported from Europe because their bright colors matched the tiles. The royal day's schedule included the attendance of the most skilled games players from among the general populace, including chess masters, who came to prove their talents against the court's professionals. They played to catch the eye of the king, who followed the matches from a thicket of courtiers' heads that swayed at his brilliance whenever he whispered—as though to himself—the moves that one or other player should have made.

Fakhri had inscribed his name in the Shubra Palace register and waited for an invitation. It was no simple matter. Skill alone wouldn't guarantee you got there. There were other qualities—that you held rank, owned land, or donated to the king's charitable enterprises. And his name was no fit answer to "Who are you?" He had been no more than a chess player with a talent laid claim to but not yet put to the test. Month after month, coming to inquire, and the response always a courteous reception and a "goodbye." The rejection in the functionary's eyes had been unconcealed, and yet he'd been powerless to act, for this was not his board. Finally, when cold incomprehension had provoked him sufficiently, he had been moved to anger and, quite deliberately forgetting himself, snapped:

"Do you fear being defeated by a person who is not of your station? This is not chess, then—call it something else, for your behavior is out of keeping with the honor of the board!"

His words were grander than they should have been, inappropriately provocative, but he had been angry and this was the language of the times: when someone quarreled with you, you wouldn't curse his mother—you'd challenge him to a contest:

"Dawn tomorrow at the east village, and the choice of weapon is yours."

In those days, words had meant something, which is why they reached the ear of the king. The king had chuckled, then bawled out his men for preventing the young chess player from playing in the royal presence.

Fakhri received the invitation with joy and a sense of being caught in a dilemma. The rage that had secured him his wish had had a less positive consequence, and it vexed him. The phrase he'd let slip, 'not of your station,' had defined him. Out it had come, involuntarily, contravening one of his most treasured rules: "As you see yourself, so others see you." Setting this straight meant sticking by what he'd said, no matter how unpalatable the role: he was now the challenger from the barefoot back alleys—he and his like were required to be angry; had to be, given the injustice of their situation.

And so he struck down those brought before him without any pretense at civility, a raw display of skill and ill grace, and when no one was left he rose from his chair in accordance with the protocols they'd had drilled into them beforehand: to stand in place waiting for the ceremonial guards to step forward and escort him three paces, no more, toward the throne, where he would bow, and then to withdraw, making sure not to turn his back on the king. The standing went on for longer than he had anticipated, but he couldn't tell if that was actually the case or just his nerves. He distracted himself with the board, analyzing the last match, reliving what he'd done, the defeat he'd visited on his final opponent, who had been introduced to him as the son of one of the grand pashas. How shameful. Even worse, his rage had dissipated at the critical moment, leaving fear in its place.

Before thoughts of his fate could take him too far and he took to his heels, someone leaned in and whispered for him to stay put, to which he answered that he couldn't have moved if he'd wanted to. He hadn't the courage to put into words any of what was going on inside him, nor could he make out the reason for the noise all around him, the whispers, woven in with the female voices he had heard in the distance when he'd first entered the gardens. He tried hard not let the voices break his concentration as he pictured their owners in translucent gowns, thrilling to the touch of the plants' succulent leaves.

Now they were drawing closer, accompanied by young men. High society, he guessed, gathering for some great event. Were they going to cut off his head? Their entertainment to watch it rolling between their feet, punting it back and forth as they mocked the brilliance that had brought his head to the sword?

The officials in charge of protocol had made no provision for this, and no one told him what to do. He was completely on his own in an encounter whose possibility he hadn't even considered when the invitation first came. The king offered him white, a message that he was the stronger, or should be: that Fakhri must curb his desire to win. But how? When he played, he forgot the rules of human interaction and in their place saw only checks of black and white. Would he let the king win? And if he managed to, wouldn't the indignity have been doubled? Wouldn't there be claims he'd treated the king like a kid?

With the monarch's first moves, Fakhri divined the nature of his opponent. He could beat him easily—the king played like a spoiled child with nothing to force him through the mill of orchestration and duplicity. By his fourth turn, he'd come up with the best possible solution. He must drag the game out for as long as was possible without making it seem forced, and give the king's moves additional worth by the moves he made in response. Neither of them would look foolish. He used his skill to achieve parity in a match that did justice to them both, an achievement he wanted to immortalize in chess books and the chronicles of kings, to be analyzed by experts who could appreciate the effort he'd put in.

At home, she was waiting for him. A child, delighted with what he'd done, he leapt in the air, he spun and danced, and she joined in his joy, granting him his first visit to her fortress so that he felt his heart might almost stop. Caught between two types of pleasure, and both of ebony: her body and the king's own chess set, which the monarch had given to him in honor of his skill, with the command that he be added to the list of his men in the district.

"A proud lad, but charming, and devoted to us. The Shubra Palace is open to you."

It was only natural therefore that the king's chess set should take on an additional value, should make physical the ideas of luxury and lust. Whenever he touched it, a blend of the two would thrill through his body. Erect before the king, receiving his salute. Erect before her, receiving her payment in kind. At which Fakhri resolved that only those who understood would ever touch it, those who were worthy of even a small part of the honor he'd received. And he resolved, too, that no one should ever defeat him on it, and the day that happened would mark his final match.

It seemed, then, that happiness had chosen to take Fakhri in its arms—but even if we were to grant that happiness had done so, other factors also sought to intervene in Fakhri's story, and herein lies the source of all his tragedy.

If you are one of those who place their faith in horoscopes, then the best advice for you is to stay away. Stay away from the chessboard. Believing in mysteries won't stop you being a good player, but you'll never rise to the top ranks. However much effort you make, it won't be enough if you continue to anticipate the intervention of some random element in proceedings. This will be a barrier to your understanding the essence of the game—and I believe there's no need for fancy words to make it plain that 'game' here references many things beyond the immediate subject of our discussion.

The first rule of chess stipulates that:

> The final result is built on a series of successive moves, and is furthermore the product of talent, personal preparedness, the desire to learn, and lack of pride, which last is especially important, as it enhances the player's capacity to see the game. Dedication holds the key to being able to see the pieces move before they are touched.

There are those so dedicated that they are able to see the end result three or four moves in. There are those able to play with their eyes closed. All of which goes against the laws of chance, if there be such laws. Fakhri, like any player of genius, moved according to the rules. Which was why his experience was so difficult for him: a believer who is confronted by something that shakes his faith. Many curse bad luck when close examination of their complaints reveals them to be victims of error or idleness, but their weakness prevents them from admitting it.

Yet what Ustaz Fakhri went through truly deserves to be seen as the very acme of ill-fortune. What else to call it, for instance, when his face appeared for the first time ever in a newspaper—the ruler honoring him with the gift of his personal chessboard!—only for the revolution to come along the very next day and depose the king?

Had that been all, then he might have gotten on with his life and been able to see the whole business as a joke. But the kind of luck that was Fakhri's lot struck him like an earthquake, its subsequent shocks more destructive than the original convulsion.

The men whom the revolution brought to power were thirsty, hungry, and known for their love of three things: women, song, and chess—and for their loathing of three things: the king, his men, and liberty. Without delay, their personal preferences became policy. Umm Kulthoum was banned from singing, a ruling recorded by history, though the record fails to mention that it encompassed Ustaz Fakhri, too, for he was banned from playing chess in all chess clubs on Egyptian territory, and then banned from traveling abroad to represent the nascent republic—and in both cases, the king was the cause. For Umm Kulthoum had glorified him in song, while Ustaz Fakhri had conceded a shameful draw.

But the apogee of injustice was reached thereafter, when The Lady was permitted to return to the stage, while Fakhri—well, nobody paid any attention to the pleas he submitted to the revolutionaries' offices and, feeling humiliated, he took what was left of his dignity and kept to his apartment, making do with a single friend who came to him under cover of night to play a series of matches, at each visit begging him to keep their activities a secret; he couldn't face the wrath of their new masters. The experience, from which he was released only when the authorities were distracted by the events of the tripartite aggression, encouraged him to turn his back on the world and give his soul over to perpetual scrutiny.

I know that the fall is inevitable and close at hand. I no longer control the disputes that have spread like wildfire through the main group, nor the ambitions which have started to show their heads. And the cells are falling apart. Ordinary people do not have any long-term ability to control petty differences.

Among us now are those who conceal stolen goods from us, those who undertake independent operations, and those who are never sober.

The stories about me in the street all tell of threats to me. This chapter is nearly at an end. In my hands therefore, not theirs.

Mustafa Ismail
The Book of Safety

23

Prompted by a sentimentality only to be expected in a crowd come to watch Hindi movies, they made space for us to pass, to jump our place in the queue. Without such selflessness, it would have been days and nights before we reached the ticket counter. It didn't seem to me as though the reception came as any surprise to Lotfi. He took the greetings and the back slaps with the equability of a man accustomed to sympathy as I pushed the chair ahead, murmuring thanks and, when the wheels trundled over feet, apologies. Laborers, clerks, peasants, students, populating a canvas called Shubra.

Young men from the classier areas, wearing the fashions of the masses, collared shirts hanging open over colored T-shirts, and alongside them, the long robes whose owners strolled down the streets linking Rod al-Farag and Shubra to change things up for half a day. But the clear majority were men who worked with their hands, identifiable by grease spots which, leaving them no room to dissemble, became ineradicable physical markers, whose presence they accepted and boasted of—their badges. This blend of men, who would customarily not be found together, was united by a desire to obtain a ticket on this day in particular, clinging to optimism even though a simple calculation should have been enough to leave them downcast; ten whole cinemas couldn't cope with the queue we'd been pushing through for minutes now, and we were yet to reach halfway. The further we went, the more

I began to fear a sea change in their attitude toward us. Those at the far end of the queue had let us advance because they knew they'd nothing to lose, but those further forward had a greater chance of making it, and our unswerving advance meant that two of them must lose out on entry.

The queue snaked along the pavement, masking the entrances to buildings and to a line of shops specializing in electric goods, whose owners stood outside, their pleas for consideration disregarded. Their long history of commerce had begun with the foundation of Shubra itself and now, thanks to daily gridlock and its attendant quarrels, the last page in that history was being turned over. Customers preferred the stores in Ramses Street, for all that their products might lack the refined taste that the Shubra salesmen had inherited from forefathers whose wares had once illuminated the pashas' palaces. Losing hope, the owners retreated one by one inside their shops, where, amid what crystal chandeliers remained, they awaited the end with the dignity of warriors. Only one was vulgar enough to defy history; instead of embracing the end with his fellow traders, he'd converted his place into an outlet for fast food, cheap toys, and cigarettes, making profits that made the neighborhood's traditionalists seriously question the very point of principle.

There was nothing to prevent the queue slipping into the raging torrent of the main road except steel barricades and skinny, disheveled conscripts doing their utmost to stop the levee breaking. This was a common sight, but today expanded, the numbers multiplied tenfold, an audience of thousands, the barrier now two barriers lest the first collapse, conscripts by the hundred with officers in tow all screeching wildly, "Stand firm, soldier!"

But their frail builds left them incapable of carrying out the command. The first cordon was about to give way, and the concern of those in the second sharpened. They called out to those queuing, as though in entreaty, "Get back, captain, please!"

Not far off, major generals pressed walkie-talkies to their faces as they watched the arrival of Indian superstar Amitabh Bachchan, who had decided to dedicate an hour of his first-ever visit to Egypt to granting his devotees in Shubra an audience at the memory of which their hearts would thump for years.

"Hindi films are over the top, and Bachchan being there is going to turn the movie into a farce." During our journey from our street to the Shubra Palace cinema, I ventured one last time to dissuade Lotfi from his desire to see what he had described as "the most incredible Bollywood masterpiece: *The Final Truth*."

"A stupid title for a film that's sure to be superficial," I replied. "What does 'truth' mean, anyway? And a 'final' one, too? It beggars belief."

But my objections made him laugh and left him all the more determined. Even confronting him with the harsh reality of his poor health did no good, though it stopped him laughing. He went completely silent and, craning my head over the chair I was pushing, I saw his face pulled tight with displeasure. I hadn't realized that the terrible experiences which had left him chair-bound had also made him so emotional, so prepared to believe that reality would just go away if you ignored it.

I had a different Lotfi on my hands now. One who loved fake Hindi movies and who denied the facts. Who'd stay put here for the rest of his life.

"I'm trying to remember this poem you wrote," I said. "One of the lines goes, 'You, who see the world as ranked, and you on high, / Observe, look closely. "Fuck's sake!" you'll sigh.'"

In a faint, bored voice, he answered, "I've forgotten poetry."

"Great! Mission accomplished!"

He raised his head, trying to turn to face me and failing, but even so I caught a glimpse of the reproach in his eyes. Then the crowd's growing excitement at our progress distracted us.

"Hero!"

"On you go, tough guy! See you inside!"

Not one of them thought as I did, which only went to prove what Hasna had called my selfish nature. They proved her right by supporting our case when the ticket seller refused to let Lotfi in—on the grounds there was no space for a wheelchair and it would be too difficult to carry him up the stairs—and persuaded him to back down after accusing him of heartlessness. The ticket seller's awareness of the affecting nature of the scene obliged him to cleave to the wiser path, in order to ensure that the day passed peacefully. Someone came up to us, gripped the arm of the chair, and bellowed to the mob with a Shakespearian sense of melodrama, "It is our duty to assist him!" following which summons there was no room for me to move, hands that sought to lift Lotfi multiplying about me as tears welled in the eyes of the young women clustered by the ladies' entrance. What was prompting these tears, I couldn't say for sure: the unfolding drama or nerves as they approached the ticket booth? Most wouldn't get the chance to see their beloved star beyond the brief instant when he stepped out of his car. Could Talia be among them? Would she hear me amid this cacophony if I called her name?

"Aaaaand hup!"

He rose into the air and the throng took him forward, inside. He turned to me, smiling in contentment, a righteous saint at last getting the credit he was due.

An age ago, the cinema had been a shrine to Our Indian Master, a marabout who'd come by sea from lands where men ride elephants and, reaching Egypt, had let his boat sink slowly to the bottom. On this very spot he had scattered a handful of earth taken from his bag and formed an island, which those who came to live there with him had named, for good luck—after the thing he worshipped—Elephant Island.

His miracles multiplied, till the great Muhammad Ali himself heard of them and came to seek his blessing. But greed turned the ruler's head, and he took the man's island for his own, filling in with rubble all around it and laying out a thoroughfare, down which he and his noble companions might promenade, eradicating the last vestiges of the poor marabout by changing the name to Shubra.

I tightened my grip on my case of papers. The saint's chair was moving forward. They were carrying him, enthroned, up the red-carpeted steps. I walked behind, worried lest one might fall and the rest topple like dominoes—I would never find his body, which from the severity of the torture had become as pliant as a child's. There'd be nothing left but his good-natured grin plastered on the ground.

A burst of applause rang out from those observing the scene, and then his porters set him down close to the screen where he wouldn't get in anyone's way.

"It's a long film, sir. Will you be able to last till the end?"

Lotfi answered by handing over twenty-five piasters, at which the man, thoroughly satisfied and considering this a perfectly adequate response, gave Lotfi a sympathetic clap on the shoulder. The concern being shown him was enough to reassure me that all was well and I could leave, but he grabbed my hand.

"Sit with me till the film begins."

Swept away by emotion, I yielded.

"You have to see it. It might change your life," said an old man to me as I sat on the aisle steps next to the wheels of Lotfi's chair. I didn't tell him that I was far too weak to go through any life-changing experience, even a Hindi flick. The lights, which were doused that very instant, saved me.

"Okay, I'll be at the café," I whispered to Lotfi, and departed to the sounds of the opening scene, in which the female lead was raped while her lover stood roped to a pillar, howling in agony.

Compared to the ease with which I'd entered, leaving the cinema proved impossible. The officer in charge stated that our remaining inside was the only guarantee that we hadn't slipped a bomb in with us.

Phrases such as 'terrorism,' 'extremism,' and 'godless government' were perfectly familiar back then. They caused us no hesitation. He talked about a bomb as though it were just another item you weren't allowed to bring into the auditorium, like food and drink. For my part, the gravity of the charge and the thought of the procedures that had been followed in similar cases didn't bother me at all. I might even have been proud. This hypothetical bomb gave me a certain power in my confrontation with the authorities, except I wasn't looking for a fight. I just wanted to get out.

"And how would I have got it past all these security checks in the first place?" I asked him, trying to turn our encounter into a pleasant chat, but he closed his ears to reason, leavening his refusal with a certain wit:

"No, no, in you go, and enjoy the film, and get yourself a good look at Bachchan. What an opportunity! My friend, there are people weeping blood out there, and you're trying to leave?"

A priceless half hour was wasted pretty much begging. We argued in the lobby, the street and its din before us, the congestion growing worse and now the spectacle of whole families out on their balconies getting ready to watch the convoy depart. On the corner opposite, the café was still and quiet, cut off from its surroundings—my paradise and refuge, still a few paces out of reach. I might have turned to holy war if the officer had persisted in his refusal, but at last he released me, having made me sign a statement that I had left the cinema of my own accord and under pressing circumstances. I gave the document the benefit of my full name, *Khaled Ahmed Mamoun Abdel-Baset*, and my signature, my address, the number of my ID card, and all my phone numbers. If I hadn't been so persuasive, he might only have let me go once the document had been signed and sealed by two trusted government clerks, who would testify that I was not a terrorist and had no known tendency to declare others godless unbelievers.

✱

As I pushed open the wooden door, its glass long gone, Mustafa's voice burst in on me. Wood, especially if it's old, is bound to memories. Could he have come here to pursue me as I'd pursued him? To take possession of me completely, till I forgot to look closely at the change which had extended as far as what I, for years, had thought of as home?

"To forget shows lack of interest."

Not so, Hasna. We're fated to forget so we can continue doing what we do with passion. If it weren't for forgetting, boredom would have strung us up from the ceiling. Some day, when you realize this, you'll be back.

"And these tables, we take turns at them."

I awoke to the reality that no one and nothing is sacred. The table that no one could approach unless Ustaz Fakhri gave his say-so had been taken over by the common herd. It was sat at by strangers. If he had been there with me in that instant, he would have taken me by the hand and said, "King Farouq's palace itself was trampled flat. People create value, not the other way around."

"Can I help you, brother?"

I'd drifted for a few moments.

"No, don't worry, just . . . , you don't happen to know Ustaz Fakhri?"

"Sorry. Maybe the waiter can help you," one answered, while three others turned their heads away.

"No, you definitely don't know him," I said, "and I don't think he would have been too happy about you being here."

The heads swiveled back, alert to unprovoked insult.

From al-Suweifi's corner, Amm Sayyid swooped down, embracing me with an affection that took me by surprise. He laughed, and the anger of the four men was stoked by the sight of an intimacy which suggested that he would take my side.

They told him how I'd forced myself on their company and insulted them.

"Well, he's got a point."

271

Arguing wouldn't do them any good. They withdrew, one of them affirming, "I told you! A café of madmen!"

I sat at Fakhri's table, glowing with my little victory, and increasingly certain that I would see him that day.

What I'd come to bid farewell to was already gone. Al-Suweifi's grand museum was coated with dust, and spiders busily wove their webs across its carved surface. The man himself had dropped his habit of reading the papers, and just watched women instead. He didn't recognize me, and neither did I pick him out immediately. His features had grown loose and fleshy, and a bald spot had crept into his pride and joy. The old faces were gone, leaving just Amm Sayyid and his exaggerated decrepitude, awkwardly dragging his feet and having more or less lost his powers of hearing. Lucky him—he couldn't be hurt by the mocking words of the youngsters, the adolescents, who made a terrible racket playing backgammon and dominoes, and practiced smoking their packs of foreign cigarettes, puffing out smoke with a nervy agitation, eyes flicking to the road in anticipation of some passing female before whose frailty they could put their bravado on display, smacking their palms like gunshot, and faking the laughter with which they summoned up courage to face the fact that they had not yet earned their stripes. Rolling stones? Ten years ago, they wouldn't have had the balls to stroll past the door.

I expected no miracle. If I could be sure of only one thing, it was that there was no such thing as miracles. We were fools. Each one of us saw himself with astonishing self-regard, whispering to himself to expect something and then blaming everything else—the earth, the people, the heavens—when it did not come to pass.

Had I known this earlier, things would be different, but I've no regrets. Quite the opposite. I feel at ease. Only now can I shrug off the nagging doubt that I made some mistake, content to know that

All that was, had to be so.

The only sincere line of verse from the nauseating rubbish Lotfi wrote, and the reason, perhaps, why I'd never wavered in defending him before his persecutors.

I tried to master the shudder that swept through me. Just yesterday, I was the same age as these young men, at which rate I'd be seventy in three days' time—years and events compressed like one of Lotfi's Hindi films: long enough, but time admits no defeat, and you emerge from the darkness of the auditorium to be overwhelmed by the changes, the substitution.

The images followed one after the other in no clear order. I drew on all my experience to get them moving. I had three hours, after which a new era would begin. I was done with Hasna, and Mustafa, and al-Waraqi, and Fakhri, and al-Adl. I'd seen them off into a locked safe, and hurled it into a darkened corner of my mind. Even this café: this was my final visit. And then, perhaps, I'd go after Ustaz Ali, who'd taken Hasna off into the desert to help him put his research into nothingness into practice.

I opened my case and took out their file. *Fuzzy Logic.* I tried to take it in. Can a theory this complicated seduce a woman? Perhaps I'd travel to America to look for the original Lotfi A. Zadeh, the great mathematician himself. He could help me understand what I'd missed.

The theory as I understood it: the binary of right and wrong is not sufficient as an expression of all logical situations, and classical modes of understanding are deficient in their ability to categorize the stages between zero and one. What makes fuzzy logic distinctive is that it can provide a more comprehensive and general description of the relationship of the predicate, in so far as its state may be in an intermediary position between the two more conventional binary poles. Using this theory, one can move in gradations between these two positions.

Before she disappeared, Hasna told me the reason she was so dazzled by the theory was that it meant we could create scientific concepts for behaviors and desires that fall between the two stools of right and wrong, or good and evil.

"Just think. At last we'll be able to find a way to describe our relationship!"

I recalled her words, and the mischievous look in her eyes, and I was swept by longing for her, for what had been. Her disappearance had been the beginning of the breakdown. Contentment vanished, and everywhere the question: where now? The world was at odds—wars broke out all over it, the famines in Africa grew worse, and now, someplace, a nuclear bomb was about to go off and bring about the end of human history. Was Hasna powerful enough to prevent all that from happening?

Numbers and addresses:

███████████████

██████████

██████████████████

████████████

Mustafa Ismail
The Book of Safety

24

Had I made a mistake when I refused to witness Mustafa Ismail's release papers as al-Adl had requested? It strikes me now that his decision had been, in some sense, the correct one.

Order for release due to lack of threat:
... And on this basis, we advise the release of Mustafa Ismail, given that his ideas taken in sum represent no danger; not because they are not seriously held, but because they are largely fantastical in nature, and the majority of them would not persuade anyone.

If I hadn't refused, I would still be there enjoying more stories instead of these monotonous tales.

On the other side of the street, the audience began to emerge from the cinema, happy as children, chattering with clear enthusiasm about the film, its hero's adventures, and his historic appearance among them. I closed the documents before me on the table, file after file: the one on Mustafa, a copy of his confessions that I'd transcribed myself, a file on cryptology, another on fuzzy logic theory, a picture of Sawsan al-Kashef and her lover in a state of undress, a copy of the first edition of *The Book of Safety*, and a corrected proof of the second edition. I laid them one atop the other, and on a clean, white sheet of paper wrote: *To whoever wishes to know me.*

I tied them all together and took the bundle over to the museum display. On the top shelf, behind glass doors, sat the Samsonite case holding Fakhri's royal chess set, bequeathed me after a match in which he'd lost to an arrogant young man who'd marched into the café with the express purpose of beating him.

"I've heard of you. They say you refuse to be beaten with the king's set. I challenge you."

I'd never opened it, uneasy at the melodramatic move with which he'd toppled his king over onto the board, and the way he'd walked out. He hadn't answered the jibes of his opponent, who seemed to have been stunned by this collapse and had departed, dazed by the anger in the faces of the café's patrons. I had caught up with Fakhri and stopped him, and before I could open my mouth he'd laid his hand on my shoulder, saying:

"Save your words, it's over. The starlings are acting like eagles."

Whenever any friend would mention to me that he'd seen Fakhri aimlessly wandering the streets, I would answer confidently that he was capable of regaining control and making a comeback.

2, 5, 0

And the first lock opened.

7, 5, 2

July 25, 1952. The date of Fakhri's meeting with the king. Atop the container that housed his precious treasure, I placed my files, closed the case, and spun the dial so it would stay shut forever, or until someone came searching with intent, on the trail of what had been.

The audience was still exiting the cinema. I returned to my seat as Lotfi appeared in his wheelchair. People stood in the center of the road, forming a human chain that prevented the cars from passing, two parallel lines with a space between for him to roll. They let the chair down gently, one of them pushing it incredibly slowly, while those standing in the two lines bowed as he passed them by, reprising, so I guessed, a scene from the film. One of drivers who was being forced to wait lost patience at this farce and sounded his horn, at which the crowd threw him a look, ready to go, and he shriveled. It was their historic moment, and they would let no man ruin it.

Lotfi waved to me, ease and contentment written across his face. His escorts reached the other side amid thunderous applause, and two of them opened the door as they continued to bow and scrape. He waved them away with an economy befitting a great man. They brought the chair inside and left him, going back to the rest of the crowd that had formed itself into knots, all murmuring loudly—little herds, all full of energy, waiting for someone to direct them.

Lotfi's voice, running ahead of his trundling wheels:

"Your loss, I'm telling you," he said. "You need to see it."

Amm Sayyid stood looking on, unmoved.

I asked him to fetch us the board.